Turnaround at Sea

1, Volume 2

KAREN ROBERTSON

Published by BKR PUBLISHING, 2021.

Copyright © 2021 by Karen Robertson
All rights reserved. No part of this book may be reproduced or used in any manner without written permission of the copyright owner except for the use of quotations in a book review. For more information, address: karen@sayitwithhumor.com

FIRST EDITION

BKR Publishing

www.SayItWithHumor.com[1]

This is a work of fiction.

---

1. http://www.SayItWithHumor.com

This book is dedicated to all the readers of my first novel, *The Turnaround,* who encouraged me to write a sequel with some of the same interesting characters.

PROLOGUE

A LASKAN CRUISE PASSENGER LOST AT SEA

July 28, 1999 - A passenger has been reported missing from a ship headed for Alaska. The cruise ship Grand Iris left port from Seattle July 26. A thorough onboard search proved unsuccessful and has been expanded to the sea. Captain Manrova has given the order to turn the ship around and retrace their course in an effort to find the missing passenger. The Canadian Coast Guard is providing assistance according to the latest report.

CHAPTER 1

Grace struggled to speak through tears that threatened to overflow at any moment. "Honestly, Phil. You have no idea what Sadie did for me. She saved me from being beaten, took me to the hospital for stitches, and hid me in her apartment. I owe her my life."

The Partains seldom argued about anything during their twenty years of marriage. The last ten years, they hardly spoke. Phil spent his time seeking his fortune in the real estate business, while Grace taught school and played bridge with her friends. They were like two strangers living in the same house. A childless house.

From the outside, they looked like the perfect couple. Grace always had her blonde hair professionally coifed and wore beautiful St. John knit suits with stylish heels. She thought too many teachers came to school looking like they just rolled out of bed, and she wasn't about to be one of them. Grace kept gold tennis shoes under her desk at school and changed into them when she took the students out for physical education. Even then she looked prim, proper, and perfect. The children idolized her, whereas many of the teachers were either jealous or thought her ostentatious.

Phil dressed in expensive Armani suits with coordinated ties and looked like a Wall Street attorney. The Partains were the Barbie and Ken to the public in Highland, California, but at home, more like two ships passing in the night . . . until the Turnaround escapade.

"Why do you want Sadie to move in with us?" Phil sat down on the leather footstool with his knees against Grace's. He took her hands in his, obviously prepared to listen.

She could smell the mixture of his cologne and the leather sofa where she sat. His office, with a manly décor, had a dark wood desk, a floor-to-ceiling bookcase, and shelves full of his high school football trophies.

"Can't we just thank her and send her on her way?" he asked. "Maybe give her some money?"

Grace couldn't restrain her tears a moment longer. "She's pregnant! And because of me, she doesn't have a job or anyplace to go." Grace knew how loneliness felt. Just a week earlier, she took a turnaround bus to Las Vegas in an effort to escape a dormant marriage and clear her head. When the bus crashed and Grace was assumed missing, her adventure went from a lark to a disaster. She found herself telling one lie after another until she met Sadie McClarron.

Sadie, although much younger, befriended Grace, and together they narrowly escaped being shot for a crime they didn't commit. When Grace discovered her own pregnancy, they became a sisterhood of two.

Phil's words pulled her back to the present. "Can't she go home to her parents? I like my nice, quiet, undisturbed household."

"Ha! Have you forgotten, we're going to have a new baby to add to the mix? Our nice, quiet, undisturbed household will never be the same."

Phil seemingly ignored her comment as if he hadn't heard. "I repeat. Couldn't Sadie go back to her parents?"

Grace squelched her desire to scold him for negating her plea and forced herself to stay focused on the bigger issue at hand. "Honey, Sadie grew up in Utah in a huge family. Her Mom didn't have time for her. As a result, Sadie hung out with the wrong crowd, did drugs, and ended up pregnant. Her parents threw her out, and she has nowhere to go."

"So why did she take a job serving cocktails in a sleazy casino in Las Vegas?" Phil let her hands go and shifted on the footstool, eyebrows furrowed.

Grace inhaled slowly then pushed ahead. "She thumbed a ride to Las Vegas, and the casino offered her a job without a lengthy application process. She jumped at the chance to make some money in order to rent an apartment and get out of the hostel. Maybe you should ask me how I ended up there." Her words shifted the blame back to herself, and Grace hung her head in shame and sat back.

"Grace, when you took off on that bus trip to Las Vegas, I didn't give it a second thought. Closing a big real estate deal had my full and undivided attention, and nothing else mattered. But when you went missing, it shook me to the core. I was terrified I might have lost you, and I actually cried. I hadn't cried since my grandmother died."

Grace put her arms around him. "I wondered if you'd come after me or just let me go. When Madeline hit me across the head with the broom handle, I prayed for you to come. Then I feared you *would* come, and you'd find out what a mess I was in. When I look back on it, I can't even believe I did what I did. Conservative, perfectionist me, getting involved with criminals. My hormones had gone nuts, I guess. I thought menopause had overtaken me, but it was pregnancy that played havoc with my system. I was so confused and anxious."

Phil nodded, his eyes softening as tears formed at their edges. "When I found you alive behind that casino, bruised and battered, my heart nearly beat out of my chest. I felt happiness beyond what I could ever imagine." He cleared his throat. "Nothing else mattered; I just wanted to bring you home to safety. I never want to let you out of my sight again." Tears fell on his shirt and tie. He took a deep breath.

Grace sat quietly before choking out the words. "When you showed up to save me, I felt like Superman had arrived, or the posse or the cavalry. I'm surprised I didn't hear trumpets announcing your arrival. I couldn't wait to tell you I was pregnant and that I loved you. The rest of the story is too embarrassing to tell." She reached over and wiped his tears away. "You said Sadie could come home with us then. Remember? You actually said it before we even got to the car."

Phil paused before responding. "Yes, but I wasn't thinking clearly, and I didn't know it would be for any length of time. If you hadn't come into her life, what was she planning to do about her baby?" Phil folded his arms across his chest in what she knew was an attempt to look relaxed.

"A nice guy named Scott came into the casino to tell people about Jesus," she explained. "Of course, he got kicked out, but he left some reading material with his contact information. Sadie called him for help, and they became friends. She went to church with him, and their relationship grew. He came to love her so much, he said he'd gladly accept the responsibility of her baby, and they planned to marry."

"Well, that's a nice story, but where is he now, huh?" Phil shot her an accusing look and raised one eyebrow.

"One night Scott drove some kids home from youth group, and after he delivered them all, a carload of hoodlums chased him down and rammed his van." Grace choked on her sobs as she spoke. "When he got out to confront them, they shot and killed him."

Phil took her in his arms. "I'm so sorry I fought you on this. I can see now why you want to help her. Let me think about it."

Grateful, Grace nodded. "She helped me realize how my life had gotten off-track. She's a redheaded angel with fake eyelashes." Her mood lightened, she cocked her head and gave a big smile. "Who would have thunk it?" She chuckled and gave Phil a peck on the cheek. "Let me fix you a scrumptious lunch." She knew she'd won, and it was settled.

Phil took a deep breath. "Okay, then. She can move in for a while. If it makes you happy, we can give it a try."

"How long is a while?" Grace winked then headed for the kitchen to make Phil a delicious lunch to show her gratitude.

"We'll see," he called as she disappeared through the door. "But if there are any problems, she's out."

Grace knew they each had more to say on the subject, but it was settled for now, and the heaviness that had weighed on her heart was gone.

"You won't be sorry," she called back. "It'll be so much fun to have her here. You'll see. Two pregnant women will really change your life." She giggled as she made her way from the refrigerator to the counter. "I hope we can keep the hormones under control. Sadie will definitely add to the laughs. You'll see."

As Phil joined her in the kitchen, Grace was already thinking about how she couldn't wait to tell Sadie she'd be living with them . . . indefinitely. She pulled condiments from the refrigerator, put them on the counter, and intercepted Phil as he entered the room. Euphoric, she kissed him and squeezed him tightly.

"Trust me on this." With her arms still embracing him, she attempted to dance him around the kitchen, but he resisted stiffly.

AFTER LUNCH, PHIL SAT in bewilderment and pondered the drastic change this new housemate and two babies would bring. He never considered being a parent, because he didn't have a father figure in his life. His own parents were killed in a car accident when he was just a baby, and his grandmother raised him. She was loving and kind and supported Phil in every way.

Through high school, football dominated Phil's focus, and his grandmother never missed a game. He could hear her voice over the crowd, yelling at the top of her lungs, cheering him on. Two days after graduation, he found her dead in her bed. She must have slipped away during her afternoon nap. The peaceful look on her face made him believe she didn't suffer and was in a better place. She had wholeheartedly filled in as the only parent he ever knew, and he shed tears at her bedside before he called 911. When the tears were wiped away, he became an adult – alone.

When Grace disappeared in June, Phil desperately searched for several days. He enlisted the help of a private eye, law enforcement, a pastor, and his partner Sheldon Hargrave. When he found Grace alive and discovered her pregnancy, it super-charged his parental spirit, and he could hardly wait for the birth of their first child. He wanted to shower Grace with the joy and intimacy she had always deserved.

But two pregnant women in one house? Phil couldn't even imagine what to expect from the "expectants." He wondered if it would be an adventure or a frightening journey for which he had no preparation or roadmap.

CHAPTER 2

Summer in Southern California could be brutal, and the high temperatures forced the women to work on projects inside the air-conditioned house. Sadie and Grace busied themselves creating a beautiful nursery that would be perfect for two babies.

"I'm sure glad you thought of going yellow and green. It looks so fresh and bright." Sadie danced around as she dangled a colorful mobile over her head.

"Since we don't know the gender of these two babies, it makes sense. What if we had two boys and we'd painted the whole room pink?" They giggled.

"Like the Johnny Cash song, we might have *A Boy Named Sue*." Sadie laughed as she flopped down on the floor with the mobile pieces draped over her face like a fluttering hat. She was agile and childlike. At five foot two, she couldn't reach the light fixture to attach the mobile, but she got up from the floor and held the stepladder for Grace.

As Grace had promised, Sadie surrounded them with fun and brought a new energy to the Partain home. Her pregnancy blossomed, and in the evenings Grace and Phil sat on either side of her as they watched TV, with their hands on her belly so they could "oooh" and "aaah" every time they felt the slightest movement. The three of them were in this together now, and it warmed Grace's heart to see how Phil had joined them in their mutual adventure.

"It won't be long before we'll have one hand on Sadie's tummy and one hand on Grace's," Phil commented with a grin.

"Maybe we can put our bellies together and they can communicate." Sadie pulled herself up straighter. "Hey, in the Bible, Mary was pregnant and went to see her cousin Elizabeth who was also pregnant. When Elizabeth heard Mary's greeting, her baby leaped inside her. Wow! I wonder if our babies are trying to communicate from inside." She knocked softly on the top of her belly and said, "Hey, in there, is there something you want to tell us?" All three of them laughed out loud.

"Sadie, you're such a clown." Grace enjoyed every bit of Sadie's silliness. She laughed at everything she said and did. Phil often shook his head and left the room with a look of despair. Grace figured he didn't get it or was afraid he might lose his sophisticated composure. She imagined he went in the other room and laughed in secret.

Sadie thanked the Partains over and over for the offer to move in with them. "I want to be helpful and not a burden to anyone. I've always wanted to be part of a normal family."

"I don't know how normal we are with just Phil and me, but with you and two babies, we'll sure get a jump on it."

"Please let me do the laundry and housekeeping," Sadie begged and fluttered her fake eyelashes. "If I'm going to be part of the family, I want to do my share. I need to earn my keep. Please don't treat me like I'm a guest."

Grace smiled reassuringly. "We didn't invite you to stay with us to be our slave. But when school starts and I go back to work, I'll accept your offer to help out. Meanwhile we'll do household chores together. I'm kind of a perfectionist, so you can see how I like chores done. How's that?"

Sadie nodded. "That'll be great because I have a lot to learn. My mom didn't teach me anything. With eleven kids, we were lucky to get fed and off to school on time. I fell right in the middle, number five. I'm surprised they didn't name me that. 'Hey, Number Five, you'll be sharing a room with Number Three, Four and Six.'" They both laughed.

"I can't imagine eleven kids in one house on a regular basis." Grace chuckled. "Right now I'm just trying to wrap my head around *our* one plus *your* one."

"It's not that unusual in Utah . . . I'm just saying."

Grace struggled not to comment. A thought kept coming up, but she thought it best not to mention it . . . yet. She didn't want to hurt Sadie's feelings, but when she couldn't hold it back any longer, she took a deep breath and blurted it out. "As for the housework, it's up to you, but you probably don't need the fake eyelashes anymore. They may be a little overkill for washing pots and pans and scrubbing floors."

The two women burst into laughter again, and Sadie puckered up her lips pretending she might cry. Her blue eyes sparkled, and her curly red ponytail bounced rhythmically.

SOON SCHOOL WOULD START, and Grace would return to her fourth graders. She always thought of them as her children, but now she would finally have a child of her own. She was uncertain of the due date, but as close as she could figure, it would be around Christmas.

When Sadie moved in, she brought her collection of ceramic and glass angels, fairly extensive for someone who owned little else but a rocking chair. Finding a place for them was a challenge, which Phil undertook.

"What if I build a couple of shelves?" Phil hadn't built anything in years, but Grace was sure he could figure it out. "One could be for the angels with little waists, wispy wings, halos, and fly-away hair. The other shelf for the white clay cherubs or cupid-types with potbellies and wings that are not aerodynamically sound," Phil teased.

Sadie grinned. "That sounds great. You may not appreciate them, but you did a pretty good job of sorting them into two categories."

Grace studied the project then turned to Sadie. "Tell me more about your angel collection."

"When I first became a Christian and heard about angels who watch over me, I bought some of those cupid-looking ones. The little ceramic ones were pretty cheap. Then Scott gave me one of those pretty glass ones, and I've added others when I could afford them."

Grace hesitated. "Do you really believe in angels?"

"Yes, of course. They're all over in the Bible. But I've learned that when they actually appeared, they were men . . . big strong warriors." She wrinkled her nose. "Isn't that funny? We've made them into beautiful women with hourglass figures or little babies with fat bellies and pinchable rear ends!" Sadie shrugged, rolled her eyes, and laughed. Her laughter was contagious but Grace felt uncertain about laughing at angels and limited herself to a smile. Sadie had a tiny little-girl-like frame. Her curly red hair was usually pulled into a ponytail, and her lightly freckled skin appeared almost pink. Grace thought her clothes were colorful but terribly mismatched. Sadie's observation regarding angels puzzled Grace, and no doubt Phil too, as neither had much Bible knowledge.

"You're so funny, Sadie," Grace observed. "Even when you're being silly, I learn from you."

"What do you mean?" Sadie wrinkled her forehead in question.

Grace shrugged. "Well, I've never really thought much about angels, but obviously the Archangel Michael wouldn't be a woman or a baby with a . . . pinchable rear end." This time they both laughed.

GRACE LEFT TO BUY GROCERIES, and Phil had his first chance to talk to Sadie alone. He was getting used to having her around. "I hope you don't mind if Grace and I leave you here alone for a week in July," he said.

Sadie raised her eyebrows. "No problem. What's up?"

He smiled. "I want to take Grace on a trip before your due date and before she doesn't want to be seen in a swimsuit. It's actually our twentieth anniversary, and we never had a honeymoon. We were young, and I worked non-stop to make a buck, so it just didn't work out to have one."

A delighted smile spread across Sadie's face. "I think that's awesome. I can hold down the fort and take care of things. I'll water the plants, but I'm not sure I can sell any real estate."

"We're taking Sheldon and Marilyn Hargrave on the trip," Phil explained, surprised Sadie would even imagine she should be responsible for selling real estate in their absence. "Sheldon is my business partner and best friend. So the real estate business will just have to go on hold until we return."

"I was joking!" Sadie said emphatically with a grin.

Phil felt his cheeks redden slightly. Why hadn't he realized the girl was kidding? He often wondered if he and Grace had been too serious about work for too many years. Sadie brought an element of levity they hadn't experienced for a long time, and it was refreshing.

"Okay, I get it. You were kidding." Phil smiled and shook his head. He knew there were other agents in the office who would handle listings and sales while they were away, but he didn't feel the need to tell Sadie. He was still trying to recover from her joke about selling real estate.

Sadie took on a more serious topic. "Is Grace friends with your partner's wife?"

Phil thought carefully. "With Grace teaching school and Marilyn's work as a hairdresser, they didn't get together much unless we went to a Real Estate event where spouses were welcomed."

"So they don't have much in common."

"They both like to shop, but not for the same styles. Grace usually wears suits, and Marilyn likes jeans and T-shirts. Grace likes to play bridge with her girlfriends, and Marilyn is the catcher on a women's softball team called the Highland Whippers. I coaxed Grace into going to one of her games, but she spent the whole time grading papers until she almost got hit by a foul ball and came home."

Phil thought about the two women and how opposite they were in most ways. Grace, tall, blonde, and slim, worked out in her gym at home, while Marilyn, olive skinned, dark haired, stocky, and muscular went to ball practice every night.

"But you and Sheldon? Best buds, huh?"

Phil was surprised at Sadie's curiosity. "We played football all four years in high school. I was the quarterback and Sheldon the receiver. His parents didn't want him to play football and never came to the games, so he was glad to have my grandma cheering for him. We were like brothers, even though he and Marilyn were high school sweethearts and married the week after graduation."

"How did he end up in real estate with you?"

"He worked in construction, and Marilyn went to cosmetology school. They had two kids in the first two years and were struggling to make ends meet when I asked Sheldon to come into the real estate business. We've always been a great team until recently."

Sadie persisted. "Recently? What happened?"

"Sheldon's been edgy and out of sorts lately. He and Marilyn were having problems last summer, and she kicked him out for a short time. Sheldon and I had to draw out a large sum of money from the business when we thought Grace had been kidnapped, so that didn't help things. Sheldon and Marilyn's relationship suffered, and then the big real estate deal we'd worked on for months went sour, and things haven't been the same since."

Even as he explained the situation to Sadie, Phil wondered if this trip with the Hargraves was a good idea. He hoped getting away together was all they needed to reset their brotherly relationship.

PHIL PUT HIS CONCERNS aside, and when he and Grace were alone in the bedroom, he let her know what he was up to.

"Grace, I hope you're up for it because I want to take you on a beautiful cruise and lavish you with attention." Phil felt like a new person with new direction. His drive to make millions of dollars paled to his desire to show Grace how much he loved her. Soon there would be a baby to add to their circle of love, and he could hardly wait.

Grace threw her arms around Phil's neck. "Oh, thank you, sweetheart! The hot flashes and dizzy spells have passed, and I'm feeling great. A cruise sounds wonderful!"

"You aren't worried about getting seasick or anything, are you?" Phil tipped his head to the side.

She shook her head. "I don't think so. The only thing that worries me is . . . will they have enough food onboard? I feel like I could eat my way from stem to stern." They laughed together.

"I guess that's typical during pregnancy, though I wouldn't know." He grinned. "But I've heard that the food is the highlight of a cruise. Some people gain a pound a day."

Grace grimaced. "Oh, my goodness, you'd better rein me in or I'll be the size of a tugboat when it's time to come home."

"You're beginning to sound like Sadie," Phil said. "I have to admit, having her here is working out great. And while we're gone, she can watch over the house, take in the mail, and answer the phone. Maybe she can even look into taking some classes next semester."

Grace nodded. "That's a good idea. I'll mention it to her and maybe give her some help getting started. I think a catalogue from the community college came a few days ago and might still be in the den."

Phil was glad Grace liked his idea and was willing to propose it to Sadie. He felt more comfortable having Sadie around as long as they all stayed on the same page. "Are you okay with me inviting Sheldon and Marilyn to come along on the cruise?" He thought Sheldon and his wife deserved a luxurious vacation after all the years they'd been friends and partners. Sheldon had also committed to participate financially to get Grace home safely from Las Vegas, even when Marilyn objected.

"Yes, I'm sure we'll get along fine." Grace hesitated for a moment. "If it's okay with you, before we leave, could we make it clear that we don't expect for them to spend every minute with us? That way they'll feel free to do whatever they want, and we can too."

He nodded. "I'll try to put it to them in such a way so they'll know we're concerned about giving them their own space. I don't want them to think we want to get rid of them."

"Agreed. You're always the diplomatic one. I tend to avoid talking turkey." Grace swatted Phil playfully.

AT THE OFFICE, PHIL worried about telling Sheldon they should plan activities separately on the trip. The two of them had spent almost every day together since they were kids. He rehearsed over and over, trying to find the right words.

Phil waited until Sheldon asked, "Do I need to break out my tuxedo for the cruise?"

It was the perfect opening. "I'm just taking a suit, but it's up to you. By the way, if you and Marilyn want to do some side trips on your own, feel free."

"Are you saying, we're on our own when we board the ship?"

He shrugged. "Yeah, I guess so. We don't want you to feel like you're tied to us if you want to do other activities."

"I thought we were doing this vacation together."

Phil swallowed hard. "I'm just saying, with Grace pregnant, she may or may not feel like doing some things, so we don't want to hold you back from doing what you and Marilyn want to do." He felt a little guilty for throwing Grace under the bus, but it made sense at the moment.

"Okay, I get it. We'll still be eating meals and going to shows together, right?"

"Absolutely." Phil was relieved to have that out of the way.

PHIL KNEW GRACE'S TEACHER friend Janine would take pleasure in helping him select an Alaskan cruise. She owned a little travel agency franchise she worked in the summers, which allowed her and her husband to travel at a low cost. Phil saw it as a multi-level marketing scheme, but it didn't affect the price of the cruise for him.

"Let's make the reservation as soon as possible. I want Grace to enjoy this trip before her tummy expands, and she'll start back to school in mid-August."

"So will I," Janine added.

"Oh, yeah, of course." Phil and Janine put their heads together, and the reservations were soon made for late July. The Grand Iris Cruise Ship fit Phil's travel dates perfectly. Under normal circumstances, it would have been impossible, but last-minute cancelations opened up unexpected opportunities for both couples.

A WEEK BEFORE THE TRIP, Phil and Sheldon were still trying to close a deal with Frank Wilburn & Associates. Mr. Wilburn had been their biggest investor ever, but the sale stalled when Phil discovered Grace's disappearance in June and turned all his attention to finding her. Now that Grace was back home and safe, the deal with Wilburn rekindled and Phil and Sheldon hoped to close it before the cruise.

"Sheldon, could we keep the whole story of Grace's disappearance a secret?" Phil asked. "If anyone asks, simply say we found her safe and sound. There's no reason to unfold that wild episode for the whole world to know. Better left a mystery."

Sheldon nodded. "Of course. Not a problem."

The details were still a mystery to many of those involved, including the would-be kidnappers, the private investigator, and even Grace. *But all's well that ends well*, Phil thought.

Wilburn wanted to buy fifty acres of open land to subdivide and develop, but the sellers were determined to stick to their asking price. Ten million dollars seemed high, but the location was absolutely choice and the terrain ideal. Wilburn would go eight million and not a penny more.

Both Phil and Sheldon were stymied. "What will it take to get these guys to agree to a counter-offer of some kind?" Sheldon questioned.

Phil's voice was tinged with frustration. They had tried for months to make this come together, but to no avail. "The seller doesn't need the money, and the buyer has plenty of it, so neither is motivated to get off their price. We, on the other hand, won't receive a commission until we can bring them to an agreement." He put both hands in the air. "At the moment, it seems like we're the only ones motivated to close this deal."

"What would have to happen to get these guys off the dime?"

Phil shrugged. "I guess if Wilburn lost interest in the piece of property and made an offer on something else, the Fortures might think they were going to lose the sale and soften their price a little." It wasn't the first time Phil had tried to think out of the box and create a scenario that could get the ball rolling. He knew they had spent way too much time on this deal, but it would be worth it if they could close.

"What else is listed in this area that might be comparable?" Sheldon mused. "Maybe we can create a love triangle and get Wilburn to fall in love with another piece of property."

Phil started thumbing through their company listings, and Sheldon brought up the multiple listings on the computer.

"Here's an eighty-acre parcel for eight million dollars," he said, "but it would need a lot of work. It's on a slope, and a fourth of it's a rock pile."

Sheldon lifted his eyes from the company listings and smiled. "You just might be on to something. Keep looking."

CHAPTER 3

Marilyn could hardly believe she actually had reservations to board a luxury cruise ship to Alaska. She grew up in a poor neighborhood in San Bernardino. Her mother worked part time as a clerk in a Rite Aid Store, while her father drove bus for RTD until he lost his license because of a DUI. His love for alcohol caused his undoing every time he got a good job. Marilyn grew up hoping to meet a guy who could take her away from her family. When she and Sheldon started going steady, he talked about going into the military, and she thought they would travel the world. But when Phil invited him to go into real estate, Sheldon went arm-in-arm. They moved all the way to Highland, six miles from home. It certainly wasn't what she dreamed about. But Sheldon had provided her with a lovely home and never said no to her spending until it got totally out of hand, which happened a couple of times a year.

Marilyn needed to call Grace and talk about details.

"Hi, Grace. I thought maybe you could help me." Marilyn hated to ask Grace for help. Grace was always so much more put-together and fashion-wise, which intimidated Marilyn.

"Sure. What do you need?"

"I'm packing for the cruise. I thought maybe you could give me some hints about what to take. This is my first cruise, and I'm a little nervous about it."

"It's my first cruise, too. I know they expect us to dress up for dinner, but otherwise I think you can wear any of your regular clothes. We'll be out for a week. I think I'll take a couple of evening gowns . . . maybe one long and one cocktail dress for evenings. I don't think you need a different dress for every night."

"*Dress*? How about pants? Do you think I could get away with some nice black pants with heels and some fancy tops?" Marilyn could not see herself in an evening gown. A pair of jeans and low-cut blouses summed up her style. She already worried her wardrobe would be tacky compared to Grace's selections.

"That sounds perfect. Throw in a fancy jacket or two, and you'll have it made. They don't allow jeans anywhere on the ship."

"Are you kidding me? No jeans? Glad you told me, or I'd have really embarrassed myself."

"I actually heard about one woman who forgot her dress pants," Grace said, "so she wore her satin pajama bottoms with fancy tops every evening for the whole cruise. Nobody knew the difference. Necessity is the mother of improvisation."

"Really? That's hilarious! I didn't read the paperwork they sent us. Guess I'd better do that." Marilyn only read *People* and *Redbook* magazines. It hadn't occurred to her that she needed to read all the rules and regulations that came in the Welcome Aboard Packet. She never claimed that etiquette was her forte.

"There's a whole section on proper dress, seating times, etcetera." As Grace spoke, Marilyn imagined she could almost hear Grace laughing at her, reinforcing her sense of inferiority. "We signed up for late seating. I hope that's okay. That way we can sleep in and go late to breakfast. Is that okay with you?"

Marilyn thought it strange that nobody asked for her choice before choosing for her. But Phil took charge of planning, even though it was probably going to be paid for out of the business.

"That'll work, I guess. This is all new to me. I'll feel like a fish out of water." They both laughed at the idiom that fit the situation perfectly.

GETTING FROM HIGHLAND to LAX could be done in an hour and fifteen minutes in light traffic, but it could be jammed up and slow depending on accidents, construction, or law enforcement.

"Let someone else worry about the traffic. There are shuttles we can take, and they're actually quite reasonable," Grace suggested as she and Phil lingered at the dinner table. "They can drop us off and pick us up, and we won't have to worry about parking the car."

"Couldn't Sadie drive us?"

"With five of us in the car and all our luggage, I don't think that would work. Besides, she doesn't know her way around the metropolitan area. Please, let's get a shuttle." Grace had initiated the idea and would gladly make the arrangements.

"I just want everything to be perfect and stress free," Phil said, "so if you feel better about taking a shuttle, I'll rent a limousine."

Phil always went the extra mile, and though his suggestions might not always be the most practical, Grace appreciated his thoughtfulness. "Thank you, honey. It'll be so much easier and more comfortable. Taking a limo will make me feel like a queen." She smiled and so did Phil.

GRACE NEEDED TO PREPARE Sadie for their absence, so as they were folding clothes, she brought up the subject.

"So, Sadie, if you need anything or if there are any problems, I've left some numbers for you to call. If it isn't serious, you can call one of my teacher friends. In fact, Janine would be a good one since she arranged the cruise. If it's something serious, you can call Pastor John

Troude. We've become close friends with him and his wife, Nancy. If he can't help, he'll know someone in the congregation who can." Grace handed Sadie a list with Janine's number, Pastor Troude's, and a few others. "You already have the number for the obstetrician, but I'm sure you won't need that until we're home. We'll make an appointment to go together when we return."

Grace didn't want to treat Sadie like a child whose parents were going away, but she realized it sounded like it. Time to wrap up the instructions. "I can't think of anything else. You've got your car, a list of names, and a well-stocked fridge. I hate to leave you alone here, but I'm sure you'll be fine."

Sadie smiled and nodded. "Don't worry about me. I'm gonna try to get a little part-time job so I can pay for room and board, and I'll also look through the college catalog you gave me. Maybe there's a class I could take."

THE FLIGHT TO SEATTLE proved to be smooth and uneventful. A shuttle from the airport to the harbor got the foursome there with time to spare. Just a few blocks away, they walked through the Pike Place Market and back to the holding area.

Their luggage had been checked through from LAX to Seattle, and from the airport to the ship. Everything was carefully organized and efficient.

ABOARD SHIP, STEWARDS hustled to clean rooms and put them in pristine shape for the next guests. Lina found the job exhausting, but she loved to get acquainted with new guests as they arrived at their stateroom for the first time.

Her dark brown hair pulled tightly in a bun on top of her head made her look taller and thinner according to her friend Marta. She wore a white apron over her light blue uniform and carried a towel to wipe off and polish wherever she saw a smudge.

Born in France to French parents, Lina looked forward to seeing the world. As soon as she finished her *lyceé classique*, she applied for a job on the cruise lines and left home.

"Hey, Lina, are you about finished in here?" Her friend and cabin-mate, Marta, stood in the doorway swinging a wet towel.

"Almost."

As Lina made all the final touches, she wondered what guests would inhabit this room. It had to be perfect. Sheets tight enough to bounce a coin, military corners, ice in the bucket, towels folded perfectly, shampoo and other niceties in the bathroom, and the TV turned to the onboard channel with music. Lina looked back one more time to make sure she hadn't forgotten anything.

Everything looks shipshape. She smiled at the thought as she and Marta exited the cabin together.

CHAPTER 4

The walk to the fish market kept the Partains and Hargraves busy for a while, but now they waited with anticipation to be welcomed on to the ship. The holding area, with minimal artwork, displayed posters of various amenities on the Grand Iris and a big welcome sign.

"I'm so excited!" Grace checked her purse for her passport for the sixth time then silently scolded herself for being a worrywart. "I wasn't even sure how to dress. I knew it would be warm here but cool inside the ship. I've heard it can get cold and rainy as we go farther north. I must have changed clothes six times."

"I finally read all the papers they sent us and decided I'd better have a raincoat for sure," Marilyn responded.

Grace overheard their husbands, deep in conversation regarding the Wilburn negotiations. Sheldon leaned in. "This trip would've been a lot more fun if we could've closed that deal before we left."

"I agree," Phil said.

Grace knew they had tried to get Wilburn interested in another piece of property, but he rejected the idea of a rock pile that would require excavation and extensive earth moving.

A voice rang out over the loudspeaker. "Welcome, guests of the Grand Iris. You have been cleared for boarding. Please have your passports ready as you line up to be checked through."

Grace trembled with excitement as she drew the passport out of her purse and clutched it in her fist. A few months ago, she thought her marriage with Phil was over, and now here they were going off on a wonderful cruise. It didn't matter that Sheldon and Marilyn were along. Phil had promised to let them know they didn't plan to buddy up for the whole trip.

Phil and Grace moved through the check-in quickly and headed for their room on Concierge Deck. Lina waited by their stateroom door to greet them.

Lina straightened her apron and gave a little curtsy before speaking. "Welcome aboard, Mr. and Mrs. Partain. The Grand Iris is honored to have you as guests. I hope you'll be very comfortable. My name is Lina, and I am at your service."

"Well, thank you, Lina. It's a pleasure to meet you. I'm Phil and this is my wife, Grace. We've never been on a cruise before, so please let us know how to experience it to the fullest."

"Every day there will be a newspaper put out by the crew that will tell you about all the activities onboard, the times and the locations. There's also a channel on the TV that will update you, tell you about the emergency drill, show all the lectures and nightclub shows . . . in case you don't want to leave your room. You'll be amazed at the variety. You have the late seating, but you are always welcome at the buffet." Lina pointed out the ice bucket, the snacks, and the menu for room service. "And you can order room service at any time. I suggest you order breakfast before you go to bed, so it will arrive right at the time you request."

Grace's excitement level continued to rise. "Seriously, we can have room service for breakfast? Does it cost extra?"

Lina chuckled. "No, Ma'am. Nothing costs extra. You've already paid for your lovely cruise, and now we just want to serve you and give you a wonderful vacation."

"Wow! I feel like a queen." Grace noticed the bottle of Martinelli's and a large bowl of fruit. "Is the fruit provided by the cruise line?"

Phil stepped toward the table with the bowl. "No, Honey. I asked Janine to order that for us. It's only one of the surprises I have for you." Phil motioned for Grace to come closer.

Lina smiled. "Don't forget there'll be a drill in about an hour. You'll have to put your life vests on and report to your muster station. It only takes about fifteen minutes." Lina opened the closet to point out where the vests and the map of the evacuation route were stored.

"Would you like your slider opened or closed? It's very nice to go out on the balcony as we pull away from the dock." She pulled open the curtains, pointed to the view, and left the room.

Grace opened the slider and got busy unpacking her clothes and hanging them in the closet. Phil hung his own and put the suitcases out of the way. When the announcement came over the TV and the PA system to listen for the drill alarm, which came moments later, they put on their vests and followed directions to their muster station. Everyone seemed a bit confused, but Phil led the way and Grace followed happily as they moved with the flow down the stairs.

It took only a few minutes, and they were back in their cabin, where they immediately peeled off the cumbersome life vests. Grace's excitement about the cruise was only slightly dampened by the exercise they'd just endured. "I know it's a necessary drill," she commented, "but I wonder if a true emergency happened, would everyone be so calm and cooperative. Seemed like we were being herded like cows to and from the muster deck."

Phil gathered both life vests, wrapped the straps around them, and jammed them back in the closet. "Thank goodness that's over. I hope we have no reason to go through that again."

Grace laughed. "Did you see the guy who had his life vest on upside down with straps dangling out of reach?"

"Yes, two crewmembers were trailing him trying to help him get untangled as he walked along, but he was oblivious."

"I tried not to laugh at him because we all looked pretty silly, but at least we had ours on right-side-up . . . I hope." They laughed.

Grace picked up the Welcome newspaper on the bed and glanced over it. "Oh, look, Phil, there's a magician performing tomorrow night after dinner in the big theater. What fun! I want to do everything."

Grace wished yet again that Phil and Sheldon could have closed the Wilburn deal before they left. She could tell it was still on Phil's mind, and she didn't want anything to spoil their trip. She hoped he would quit obsessing about it and relax.

Grace sat on the end of the bed and let her body fall back easily. She had been so nervous about the trip, she didn't realize the toll stress had taken on her. When Phil announced he was going to sit out on the balcony and watch them push away from the dock, she nodded silently and closed her eyes, slipping into a quiet snooze almost immediately.

WHEN SHE AWOKE, IT was 7:30. She rubbed her eyes, patted her slightly expanded tummy, and looked toward the sliding door. "Phil?" No answer.

Grace sat up. She could see the ship was now moving along rapidly. The sliding glass door to the balcony stood open, but she wasn't able to see behind the half-pulled drape. She stood up quickly – too quickly, and her head spun. The roll of the ship caught her by surprise, and she staggered toward the balcony. Surveying the whole area made it obvious that Phil was not in the room or outside. The bathroom door swung slightly open but no Phil there either.

Grace picked up the phone and called the Hargrave stateroom number.

"Hello," Marilyn answered.

"Marilyn, have you seen Phil?"

"Yes, he and Shelly are out on our balcony talking."

"I fell asleep and just woke up. It's after seven-thirty, and our dinner seating is at eight. I'm going to have to rush to get ready. Could you please ask Phil to come and get ready also?"

"I'm almost ready myself, but the men seemed so intense I didn't want to bother them."

"Well, intense or not, we've got to get going or we'll be late for dinner. It always takes me longer than Phil, so I'll get started."

Grace hung up the phone and stripped down for a quick shower, then busily toweled off as Phil entered the stateroom and let the door slam shut behind him.

She stuck her head out of the bathroom. "I couldn't believe I fell asleep until seven-thirty. I guess I needed to de-stress."

"Yeah, well, I just had a conversation with Sheldon, and it certainly didn't help de-stress me." He frowned as he shed his clothes and threw them on the bed.

"I'll take my makeup and hair dryer to the dresser," she offered, "and you can have the bathroom. It'd be a little cozy for two of us in there." She flashed him a coy smile.

Grace loved her blonde hair cut short and simple. It took only a couple of minutes to blow it dry and fluff it up with a little hairspray. It made it easy to get ready for work—or, in this case— dinner. She grabbed her makeup bag and, wearing her towel like a sarong, moved to the combination dresser and desk.

"Hope nothing's wrong between you and Sheldon," she commented. "That would be a bummer."

Phil had just stepped into the small shower, so since she received no answer, she assumed he hadn't heard her.

AGAINST ALL ODDS, THEY were out of the room by 8:15 and headed toward the dining room.

When they were seated, Phil and Sheldon didn't have much to say, but the women chatted away, taking note of the variety of evening gowns.

"I can't believe what some people call 'formal attire,'" Grace commented. She was wearing a grape colored gown with a chiffon overlay to hide the fact that her waistline was expanding. She was relatively certain no one would guess she carried a four-month fetus. Pearl earrings and long multiple strands for a necklace gave her an elegant look she found comfortable.

Marilyn wore designer jeans decorated with rhinestones across the back pockets and a bright lime green oversized blouse with splashes of dark colors. Grace thought it looked somewhat like an artist's paint shirt. Her huge gold hoop earrings and matching necklace screamed, "Look at me! I've got it going on!"

"There's a magician performing after dinner tomorrow night," Grace said. "Sounds like fun. Tonight's kind of an introduction night. They'll introduce the dancers and singers and do a musical show. Do you want to go?" Grace fell into the usual leadership role of a teacher.

Sheldon chimed in. "I thought Phil said we weren't going to do things together."

"I didn't mean we *couldn't* do things together," Phil corrected. "I just wanted you and Marilyn to have the freedom to go and do whatever you wanted, and we could do whatever we wanted. We don't necessarily have to do the same things."

"Well, I want to see the show," Marilyn said, and Grace agreed.

"You don't have to sit with us if you don't want to," Sheldon smirked.

Grace began to wonder what they had words about earlier. "Hey, guys, let's order our dinners and enjoy the evening." Grace looked forward to the lobster dinner all day and hoped they could eat in peace . . . soon.

THE SHIP'S COMEDIAN performed a short bit to warm up the audience. His jokes were specifically aimed at older travelers and those from various countries and ethnicities. The young dancers and singers wore flashy costumes and entertained enthusiastically.

Grace wasn't a drinker and never had been, and being pregnant thankfully gave her an excuse to turn down every offer. Phil had a glass of wine, but Sheldon had a couple of drinks at dinner and followed it up with another during the show.

When the show was over, Phil took Grace's arm and steered her toward the door. "We're going to call it a day," he announced to Sheldon and Marilyn. "It's been a long time since we got up this morning and left Highland."

"Marilyn and I are going up to the late show for drinks, huh, Babe?" Sheldon turned Marilyn toward the elevators abruptly.

Marilyn hissed, loudly enough for Grace to hear, "No, Shelly. Let's call it a night. Please."

She tugged at his sleeve, but Sheldon grasped her arm harder and through gritted teeth said, "We're going to the late show."

Marilyn signaled a brief goodbye to the Partains as Sheldon pulled her away.

Back in the cabin, Grace put her arms around Phil as she pushed away the memory of Sheldon and Marilyn's brief disagreement. "Thank you so much for planning this cruise. We're going to have such a wonderful time. I loved the lobster. Yummy. And I love you. Thank you so much."

Phil kissed her softly. "You're welcome. I'm happy you're happy. I'm sorry Sheldon and I aren't seeing eye to eye. He isn't happy at all."

"Could we have breakfast with someone else besides the Hargraves? They're fine friends, but they're off to a bad start, and I'd like to give them a chance to stabilize . . . if that's possible on a rolling ship. We could meet some new people by eating at the buffet. Could we do that... please?"

Phil kissed Grace on the nose and gave her a gentle squeeze. "Sure, why not? Maybe I won't have to hear Sheldon ragging on me about screwing up the Wilburn deal again."

"I was responsible for that, I guess," Grace said. "If I hadn't taken off on the Turnaround bus to Las Vegas, none of that would have happened." Still feeling badly about the possible effects of her recent Vegas trip, she began to undress.

She felt Phil's eyes on her as he spoke. "But a lot of good came out of that escapade. You and I found out how much we loved each other, and we also discovered we were pregnant. What a bonus. Hang the Wilburn sale. It's not as important as our marriage."

Grace finished changing and looked around the cabin. She quickly discovered a bunny made out of a twisted towel, the bed turned down, and a chocolate mint on the pillow. "What service! Can I change the plans for tomorrow morning? It'll be fun to order breakfast in bed. We can always meet new friends at lunch. I've never had room service before, and it would be delightful. How about it?"

"Whatever your little heart desires. This vacation is all for you to make up for all the years I was too busy." He sounded lighthearted, but Grace was sure he was faking it while something still bothered him.

CHAPTER 5

Sadie felt like a queen with the Partain home all to herself. It wasn't a castle or a mansion, but in comparison to the houses she'd lived in, it seemed quite luxurious. She flopped into Phil's leather chair to watch TV. The wooden rocking chair she brought from Las Vegas resided in the nursery and needed a cushion, so until she purchased a cushion and had a baby to rock, Phil's chair was far more comfortable.

Her tiny waist had expanded so she looked like she had a concealed watermelon. She wondered what else she could do while Phil and Grace were away. There wasn't much to clean up, no pets to feed, no phone messages she could actually do much about. She wasn't used to having nothing to do. Grace had made everything "shipshape" before she left.

Sadie chuckled to herself. *They went on a cruise, but the house is shipshape.* She could cook macaroni and cheese out of a box, but it got tiresome in a hurry, and she loved Grace's cooking. *They're probably eating lobster and having breakfast in bed.*

She thought about Lianne, the friend she met when they worked together at the casino. Lianne graduated from the University of Nevada, Las Vegas, by working as a cocktail waitress. Sadie had some other friends she met in the church, but she didn't know their contact information.

This would be a great time to make a quick trip to Las Vegas and visit Lianne and some of the others. There's nothing going on here and nothing to stop me.

Sadie loved people, and the empty, quiet house made her fidgety. She needed to get out, and it wouldn't be long before the baby would come and she would be a fulltime Mom. Before the Partains left, she and Grace had filled all the drawers and shelves with the necessary items, and there simply wasn't anything left to do.

Grace wanted me to sign up for some courses or get a part-time job, but nobody would hire me once they see I'm over seven months pregnant. I don't want to sign up for classes until I see how I can schedule that along with a new baby. I may not get another chance to enjoy my freedom, so I'm going to Las Vegas. I'll be back by tomorrow. No big deal.

Sadie packed a small bag of essentials to stay overnight, called Lianne to let her know she was coming, and made a stop at the gas station. She thought about taking Grace's Lexus. Grace had given her permission to use it, but Sadie didn't want to take advantage of Grace when she didn't need to. Her old Honda Accord had always gotten her where she wanted to go, and they got along just fine. Except for having a problem squeezing her pregnant belly under the wheel, she'd be okay. She had pushed the seat back as far as it would go so that her feet barely reached the brake or the gas pedals.

Sadie rubbed her lower back as she felt everything shift inside her. The baby was outgrowing his or her cocoon. She cupped her hands around her mouth as if to call the troops to attention, "Hey, take it easy in there. I'm going to take you for a little trip."

Halfway to Baker, Sadie's little Honda started to heat up, but with no place to stop, she kept going. She slowed down, but that didn't seem to help. She turned off the air conditioner, but that didn't get results except to make her miserable as the brutal heat filled the car. Steam began coming from under the hood, and the engine seized. The pain in her back became more intense and worked its way down her legs.

Oh no. This is not good. Sweat rolled down her face. Some of her curly red hair had escaped her ponytail and now stuck to her cheeks in ringlets. The temperature soared to one hundred ten degrees outside, and it wasn't much better inside. She knew the approximate miles to Baker. Walking would be out of the question, but waving for help and standing outside unprotected would kill her. Her fair skin didn't lend itself to frying in the sun, and she imagined she would turn into one big skin cancer in minutes. But the pain in her lower abdomen wasn't like any she had felt before. Sadie didn't even want to think about what that pain meant. Surely it had to be Braxton Hicks, that early false labor she had read about.

Maybe I could just stand outside for a minute or two and see if someone will stop to help. Lord, please send help. Sadie started to open the door when she espied a tow truck rattling to a stop on the shoulder of the road behind her vehicle.

"Yes! Thank you, Jesus," Sadie said out loud as she struggled out from beneath the steering wheel and nearly fell out of the car.

GRACE AND PHIL DIDN'T hear from Sheldon and Marilyn the next morning. They enjoyed coffee and eggs benedict in their room. It promised to be a beautiful sunshiny day and they would soon be stopping at Ketchikan. They were able to have the sliding glass door open and hear the wake of the ship. Phil picked up the newspaper from the desk to check out the daily events.

"Why don't we get dressed and take a walk around the ship to familiarize ourselves with the location of everything?" he suggested. "When the ship docks we'll get off and take a walk. I wonder if we could still sign up for some tours. Maybe we can do that on our walk."

The day went quickly. They visited the concierge desk before leaving the ship to sign up for a kayak adventure and a train-ride later in the trip. Other guests filed down the hallways to disembark, and the Partains followed along.

A woman glanced at Grace and said, "I remember you from last night. You wore that beautiful grape colored gown. I loved that! Where are you headed?"

Grace hesitated. "Thank you. We didn't really have a plan. Just thought we'd have a little lunch in a local place."

"We were gonna do the same thing. Want to join us?" The lady came across a little too forward for Grace, but she had a smiling face and had admired Grace's dress, so they agreed to have lunch together. Grace and Phil had wanted to meet new friends, but Grace didn't expect it to happen so quickly.

"Where are you from?" the woman inquired.

Phil replied, "Highland, California. It's above San Bernardino. How about you folks?"

"We're from Branson, Missouri. I'm Calvin Conover and my wife is Clarise." Calvin wore a plaid shirt with khakis and a cap to cover his balding head. Tall and lanky, he could tuck Clarise right under his armpit. She had straight blonde hair and didn't wear makeup. Grace thought she looked plain, but her vivacious personality gave her a colorful aura.

"Phil Partain and my wife, Grace." When Phil introduced her, he lifted Grace's hand that he held in his. "I've always wanted to go to Branson."

"You wouldn't want to go there at this time of year. It's muggy, buggy, and humid." They all laughed. "Not to mention the town is full of tourists, and it's impossible to get from one place to another. It's crazy!"

"Well, you wouldn't want to be in Highland either because there's always traffic, it's about a hundred and ten degrees, and there are fires in the hills."

Lunch of fish and chips suited them all, and they enjoyed some lively conversation about being first-timers on a cruise. Calvin and Clarise didn't realize they could order room service for free. "No kiddin'," Calvin exclaimed. "How about the snacks?"

Grace smiled. "You don't have to pay for those either."

"It depends on how you look at it," Phil added. "You paid plenty for them when you booked the trip." They all chuckled.

Grace added, "So now we can pretend everything is free!"

Clarise piped up in her jolly voice, "I can't wait to order our breakfast and have room service. I'll feel like Mrs. Gotrocks, for sure."

THE CONOVERS AND PARTAINS spent two hours in the Discovery Center in Ketchikan before returning to the Grand Iris. Grace checked the phone for messages, but Marilyn and Sheldon hadn't called, left a message, or made an attempt to meet up with them. She was relieved.

In the late afternoon, Grace discovered the ship's high tea event was being served in the Vista Ballroom. She called the Hargraves and told Marilyn about it. Maybe they could make peace over sweets.

"High tea! Wow! That sounds great. We'll be right there," Marilyn said.

Grace hoped they would enjoy some yummy sweets together and be more amiable. She wasn't interested in tea, but she thought coffee would be available.

When the four sat together, Sheldon was sullen and had little to say. Marilyn poked around at her dessert plate full of goodies. Grace could feel the tension in the air and was glad when Marilyn finally broke the silence. "I spent most of the day sitting on the balcony. Sheldon talked on the phone the whole time."

"I'm not giving up on the Wilburn deal," Sheldon said sharply, directing his words at Phil. "We can't just take off on vacation and leave him hanging. We almost had the sale made in June, and you dumped the whole thing at a crucial time."

"For crying out loud, Sheldon. Grace's life meant more to me than the Wilburn deal." Phil raised his voice a bit, and Grace began to feel very uncomfortable. She put her hand on Phil's leg and squeezed gently.

"More important than a million-dollar commission?" Sheldon fired back. "Seems to me the whole threat turned out to be a hoax anyway. Grace left because she wanted attention, and you didn't give her any." Sheldon threw down his napkin and stood up. "Come on, Marilyn. Let's go."

"That does it, Sheldon," Phil said. "I'm sick to death of trying to work with you. We've had a thriving business for twenty years. Are you going to spoil our friendship, our partnership, and our trip on account of one deal we can't close? Maybe you need to go to your room and cool off."

People at other tables glanced over as the heated exchange continued.

"Don't talk to me like I'm a child or your underling!"

Marilyn rolled her eyes and cowered. She put her hand on Sheldon's arm as if to reel him in, but he shook her off. "Come on. Take the dessert with you. The only way this vacation is going to be a vacation is if I take a vacation from Phil." He practically drug Marilyn away from the table.

Grace sat quietly with her head bowed. "I'm so sorry about last summer. It's all my fault." A tear slid down her cheek.

He laid a hand on her arm. "No, it wasn't your fault. If I'd been the loving husband I should have been, you would never have taken that bus trip. Sheldon is obsessed about the million-dollar commission, but Grace, we've made many huge deals over the years. In fact, the whole time you were fixing up the nursery, I was thinking it was time to move to a bigger house." Phil abandoned his sweets and moved his chair closer so he could put his arm around Grace.

"You're everything to me. If I never made another dime, I'm happy. Sheldon should be also. With Marilyn working, I'm sure they have plenty of money to put aside for their retirement. Their kids are grown and on their own. With you teaching and us being too busy to even take a vacation, we've saved plenty to take care of us, the baby, and even help Sadie for a while."

"Sadie. I wonder how she's doing without us. It must be pretty quiet at home without us." Grace felt comforted by his words and glad to change the subject.

CHAPTER 6

Sadie realized she had forgotten to let Pastor Troude know she planned to leave town. Grace had asked her to keep him posted, just in case she had any problems. But she had decided to travel to Las Vegas on the spur of the moment, and she didn't give it a second thought.

She could still hear Grace's warning, speaking to her as if she were her mother. "At seven and a half months pregnant, I don't want you doing anything crazy." Sadie appreciated her concern, but didn't plan on doing anything "crazy" anyway. But with the car broken down in the middle of the desert, the heat, and the rising uneasiness in her gut, she began to think this might not have been such a great idea.

As Sadie gained her feet and looked around, her heart sank. The tow truck looked like a pile of junk that could fall apart at any minute. The driver squeaked his door open and pulled himself loose from the steering wheel with a grunt. He was round as a ball, wearing bib overalls without a shirt, and a cigarette hanging out of the side of his mouth. His partner got his heel caught in the rusted running board and flopped out face-first in the dirt, then scrambled up, swearing.

"Dang it, Pete! Are we ever gonna get a new truck?" His overalls hung on his skinny body and reminded Sadie of one of those rodeo clowns wearing a barrel with suspenders. Tobacco spit had run down his chin and was now covered with white sand, looking like a powdery goatee. Sadie thought for a moment of Abbott and Costello or Laurel and Hardy who entertained her on TV as a child.

"Hey, Ma'am, we're here to serve ya," the driver said as they came closer. "What's the problem?"

Sadie vacillated between maybe I'd better lock myself in the car and hope for a better rescuer and . . . any port in a storm. She opted for the latter and prayed they were not bad guys. "Thank you so much for stopping. I'm Sadie. My car overheated and just quit. I didn't know what to do. Maybe you could give me a tow into Baker? I thought I'd be stuck here forever."

"I'm Pete, and this here's my partner, LeRoy. We see this all the time. Let's take a look just to make sure. Pop the hood." His gaze landed on her distended belly as she waddled around to the front of her car with her hands supporting her lower back.

A quick look under the hood seemed to confirm what Sadie had told them, and they offered her a solution "We'll hook her up and get you outa here in a jiffy," Pete said.

Pete Jensen and LeRoy Ratcliff were regulars on the road between Barstow and Las Vegas. If they weren't going to the aid of stranded motorists, they were towing off abandoned cars before the owners returned to lay claim. A quick sale to a guy out in a remote area on the desert, who stripped the vehicles down and sold parts, kept their business going. It wasn't a regular practice because getting caught would be bad for business. They had both done jail time for petty theft and some minor infractions, so stealing cars might land them in prison. Of course, Sadie didn't know any of this.

"This don't look too promisin'." Pete turned away from Sadie and toward LeRoy, kicking the dirt as he spoke. Unfortunately for him, Sadie was still able to hear their conversation. "She don't look like nobody with any money. I hate to drive all the way to Baker and not get paid."

"We can't just leave her out here." Leroy spit a line of juice partially in the sand and partially down the front of his overalls.

"Yeh, I s'pose we'd better help her cuz she's pregnant and all."

The two men had been together for a long time. As children, they grew up living on the same unpaved street on the outskirts of Barstow. No sidewalks or gutters, just dust. Through elementary school, they played outside, stole bikes, rode bikes, made trails, and were dirty all the time. LeRoy, always small for his age, fell prey to the neighborhood bullies, and Pete found himself constantly defending him.

Pete's father worked in a garage and had a bunch of old broken-down cars parked forlornly on cinder blocks behind their house. He kept promising Pete's mom he'd fix them up and sell them, but he rarely got home before dark and never sober. His paycheck usually got spent on beer with nothing left over to buy parts to fix the cars or feed his family. Pete had two younger brothers, so his mother stayed home and took in ironing to pay for groceries.

LeRoy's parents were split up. He hadn't seen his father since he turned six, and his mother was a waitress in a truckers' café in Barstow. LeRoy had no siblings, and his mom wasn't home much, so he spent most of his time at Pete's house.

During high school, they both found jobs in gas stations and saved whatever money they could. When they got their driver's licenses, they fixed up one of the old junkers in Pete's backyard. Drag racing after school became their favorite pastime. Auto shop was the one class they attended regularly, and only so they could use the shop tools to tune up their own hotrod. If it hadn't been necessary to read parts manuals and figure out costs, they probably would never have learned to read, write, or do simple math.

On the side, they did mechanic work for other kids who couldn't do it themselves. When they saved enough money to make a down payment on the old tow truck, they quit school and hit the road.

They both still lived at home but considered themselves business owners even though they almost never made a profit or were lucky enough to break even.

Sadie stepped away from the car and abruptly grabbed her belly, and bent over. "Whoa, let me catch my breath. There's a bottle of water in my car. Could you get it for me, please?" LeRoy hurried to grab the bottle out of her cup holder and started back. Pete pulled the truck into position in front of Sadie's car to load up the Honda.

"So you're going to tow me to Baker. Oh, thank you so much. I'm not feeling well at all. My back is killing me." Sadie knew there would be a cost that she probably couldn't afford, but for the time being, she just wanted to lie down. "Could you help me get into your truck so I can sit down?"

Against her better judgment, Sadie reached out for Pete to give her a hand, but he stepped away. She could see he didn't want her grabbing at him, but she didn't care. She doubled over in pain again.

"Hey LeRoy, see if you can help her get up in the truck."

"Come on, lady, lemme help you up. When is that baby of yours comin'?" LeRoy took her arm and half-guided and half-pushed her toward the tow truck.

Sadie thought she had plenty of time, but these pains were almost more than she could bear. She wasn't due for at least a month, but now something inside her was telling her otherwise.

"Oh, oh, ooooh. I'm not due until September. This is too early." Sadie nearly snatched the water bottle from LeRoy, gulped between pains and poured some of it over her head. *Lord, please help me. Don't let me have heat stroke in the middle of the desert.*

"Oh, oh, ooooh! Please help me. What are we going to do? I can't make it . . . ohhhh." Sadie hung on to LeRoy's overall strap. He scooped her into his sweaty arms and sat her up in the truck. She screamed in pain and flopped down across the seat, panting and feeling like a beached whale.

Sadie knew this meant trouble. She took up the whole seat of the broken down old truck, which left no room for the driver or the passenger. *Okay God, what now?*

———⁂———

GRACE HUNG ON TO PHIL'S arm to steady herself as they exited the elevator and headed toward the grand dining room for dinner. "I'm glad we met some new people today. Calvin and Clarise were fun; maybe we can spend some more time with them later. They said they were going on the same kayak tour we signed up for." Grace paused. "I wonder if Marilyn and Sheldon will show up for dinner." She secretly hoped they wouldn't.

Phil nodded. "I'm glad I made it clear we want some time to ourselves. But if we meet up for dinner every night, that's fine. They know where we're seated if they want to join us."

"Inviting the Hargraves to join us on the cruise might have been a bad idea," Grace said. "I didn't realize so much friction existed between you two right now. After all, you've been great partners for twenty years."

Phil shook his head. "I don't get it, but maybe tonight we can smooth things out."

As Phil and Grace entered the grand dining room, Calvin and Clarise greeted them from their table.

"Would you mind if we joined you?" Calvin signaled to the server and asked if they could switch tables.

Phil spoke up first. "Sure, it's a table for six, and I'm sure the Hargraves won't mind. He's my business partner, and they came with us."

The four of them walked to Phil and Grace's table, but it was empty. Calvin pulled out a chair for Clarise and they settled in, chatting immediately about the fun they'd enjoyed together on shore.

Without warning, a loud voice sounded and brought everyone to attention. "Well, I see we've been replaced," Sheldon said as he approached the table. Marilyn stood behind him and looked away.

"Not at all," Grace chimed in. "We met Calvin and Clarise today at lunch and asked them to join us for dinner. There's plenty of room for all of us. Calvin and Clarise, meet Sheldon and his wife, Marilyn. Come on and join us."

Sheldon hesitated. He turned away and said something under his breath to Marilyn.

When he looked back he said, "You know what, I think we'll try getting into one of the specialty cafes tonight. Maybe tomorrow night." Marilyn looked like she wanted to say something, but Sheldon herded her away from the table without another word.

"I hope we didn't make a mess of things." Calvin frowned. "We didn't mean to butt in."

Phil shook his head. "No, there's been a bit of a riff for some reason, and it looks like it isn't getting any better. Sheldon and I have a real estate brokerage, and we recently lost a big client that would have made us a huge commission. Sheldon blames Grace and me."

"That's too bad," Clarise said, joining in. "I've always heard partnerships are tricky at best."

"Yes, but we've been partners for twenty years without a wrinkle," Phil responded. "Shoot, we went to high school together."

"They were the football heroes," Grace added with a grin.

"But why would he blame you and Grace for losing the deal?"

"Grace and I were in a rough spot in our marriage last year. She took off to Las Vegas and got herself into an adventure she never expected. In her absence, I realized I had let her down as a husband." He turned his gaze toward Grace.

"Yes, and without going into all the gory details . . . ," Grace interrupted. She didn't want him telling the whole story. "I realized how much I loved Phil. But he had to rescue me from the mess I'd gotten into. In doing so, he had to abandon Sheldon and the business deal that hung by a thread." Grace paused. "So Sheldon blames both of us."

"That's too bad," Clarise said, her face softening.

"I'm sure it'll work out," Phil said. "Sheldon still hopes to find another piece of property to interest our buyer and recoup the loss. But I'm worked out. Grace is pregnant, and this trip not only showed her my love but started a new chapter in our lives."

"That's beautiful. Maybe they're just in a different place in their lives." Clarise seemed sympathetic.

"Tomorrow I'm going to get together with Sheldon and see if we can clear the air," Phil said, then brightened. "But tonight we're going to the magic show. Want to go with us?"

As they ate, the two couples shared stories about their high school and college years. They enjoyed an instant friendship. After dessert, the foursome headed for the showroom in the other end of the ship.

"What a wonderful dinner," Grace exclaimed. "I'm glad they give us sensible portions, or I'd burst out at the seams. It must be this pregnancy because, I'm always feeling either hungry or sleepy . . . or both."

"Yep, I remember that," Clarise said, having already talked about their five kids.

The Partains and their new friends were early to the show and got seats in the front row. When the magician asked for a volunteer, Phil raised his hand. Grace couldn't believe it. "Phil's usually too dignified to take a chance on being fooled," she told their companions. The magician had Phil pour some water in a glass. Grace laughed out loud when the magician accidentally poured the water over Phil's head, but to everyone's surprise, nothing came out. Phil ducked, but the water had disappeared out of the glass. Each trick got more complicated, but Phil remained a good sport until the magician wanted him to climb into a box to be sawed in half.

"No, thanks. My wife needs me in one piece," he said as he laughingly left the stage to return to his seat. He gave Grace a peck on the lips, bowed to the crowd, and got a round of applause from the audience.

On their way back to the room, Grace could hardly keep her eyes open. "Too bad we couldn't have brought Sadie along. She would've loved all of this. I hope she's doing okay at home. She said she'd keep in touch with Pastor Troude if she needed anything."

CHAPTER 7

"This can't be happening." Sadie writhed as the pain became more intense. She panted as she spit out her words. "Please get me to a doctor . . . a nurse . . . an EMT . . . *anyone*. Flag down an ambulance. Call the fire department. Do something . . . *I need drugs*."

Pete had the car hitched up to tow, but there wasn't room for him in the driver's seat with Sadie's head there. Pete's belly would be jammed against the steering wheel, so he couldn't let Sadie rest her head on his lap. In fact, he didn't have a lap.

LeRoy stood on the rusty running board, but Sadie's legs were draped over the edge of the seat on his side. He was near tears. "I can't get in. What are we gonna do? Can you drive from the runnin' board?"

"No, *stupid*," Pete shouted. "How would I reach the gas or the brake?"

Sadie was terrified. "Please do something to get help. *I think this baby is coming.*"

"Oh, no, oh, no. This ain't happenin'." Pete stood on the running board and spoke over Sadie's head.

"We can't drive you nowhere, cuz I can't get in the truck! And we ain't deliverin' no baby. We don't have no clean towels or . . . heck, we don't even have clean hands." He looked down at his grease-stained hands and shook his head.

"Pete, I ain't never seen a baby be born," LeRoy said, his voice shaky. "Not a human baby. What do we do?"

"Doggard had puppies on the back porch," Pete said, "but they just kinda popped out. She licked 'em all over, and that was it."

"I ain't lickin' no baby." Leroy squinted his eyes and scratched his sweaty chest.

Sadie didn't want to sound ungrateful, but she was getting desperate. "Oh, my goodness. Quit talking and do something!" She could not imagine exposing herself to these two rubes. "Look around your truck for some towels or a blanket or something. Wait . . . bring the bag out of my car. I've got a clean robe that'll work. *Hurry*."

She pulled herself up as much as she could so she could peer out the window and see what the man named LeRoy was doing. She saw him jump up on the back of the flatbed to get her bag out of her car. Before he could accomplish that, a white Patrol cruiser slowed and pulled off the road behind them.

"Uh, oh, Pete," she heard LeRoy say, "We're in trouble now."

"I'm Officer Mike Purcell," the man said as he opened his door and stepped out of the vehicle. "What's going on here? I see vehicles broken down between Baker and Las Vegas all the time, but something doesn't look right about this."

Sadie was so relieved she screamed, "Help! Help! Somebody help me!"

Purcell pulled out his service revolver. "Put your hands up boys, and step away from the vehicle."

LeRoy, who was taking Sadie's bag out of her car, raised his hands and froze.

"Drop the bag and get down off there," Purcell commanded.

LeRoy dropped the bag to the ground.

"Now, jump down from there and . . ."

His words were interrupted when a wrenching pain pierced Sadie's back and abdomen. She screamed, then cried out, "Please, somebody help me!"

"What's going on here?" she heard the patrolman say.

"Honest, we ain't done nothin'," Pete said. "We're just trying to tow this here car for the lady, and she's trying' to have a baby in our truck."

After a brief pause, Purcell asked, "What's in the bag? Did you steal that?"

LeRoy spit a stream of tobacco juice and stuttered. "We . . . we . . . got dirty hands and dirty stuff. She told me to get her bag so we could use her clean clothes."

Officer Purcell had moved around the truck and peered into the cab. His eyes and Sadie's met. "Oh, my goodness!" he exclaimed, turning back to the two men. "You were serious. Get some clean clothes out of her bag, and let's see if we can deliver a baby here." Purcell holstered his gun and rolled up his sleeves. "I have a couple of kids of my own. Didn't deliver them, but I watched 'em be born."

GRACE FLOPPED HER ARM over to Phil's side of the bed, expecting to find him next to her. To her surprise that side of the bed had not been disturbed. She had slept late again and enjoyed every minute of it. Before the steward arrived with breakfast, she had combed her hair and donned a robe, but still no Phil. She opened the door to allow the server to place the food on the table. The coffee was steaming, and the aroma of bacon sneaked out from under the stainless steel dome covering the food.

"Thank you so much. Did you happen to see my husband?"

"No, I'm sorry, Ma'am. I didn't see anyone in the hallway." He shut the door behind him.

Grace picked up the phone and called Marilyn. "Hi, Marilyn. Have you seen Phil? Last night he mentioned he wanted to get together with Sheldon this morning."

Marilyn said, "We're getting ready to go to breakfast, and we haven't seen Phil this morning."

Grace frowned. "He kissed me goodnight, and I haven't seen him since. That's weird."

She hung up and decided to eat her breakfast while it was still hot. Surely Phil would return soon. He had helped her order breakfast, so she knew it was what he wanted. She chuckled because she was sure she could easily eat both breakfasts. It smelled delicious, and her stomach growled approval.

A tap on the door caused Grace to jump. As she hurried to answer, she thought, *He must have forgotten his key and didn't want to wake me.*

It was Lina checking in to see if Grace needed anything.

"Thank you, Lina, but I'm fine. Have you seen Mr. Partain this morning?"

"No, Ma'am, but there are a lot of places onboard to get coffee or breakfast. Maybe he is at one of those."

"Yes, but we decided last night we were going to have breakfast delivered by room service. He'd better show up pretty soon because I'm hungry, and I'm going to start eating while it's hot. If you see him, tell him to hurry."

"Yes, Ma'am. I'll take a look in the Concierge room. You are on the Concierge Deck, so you can find snacks, coffee, TV, and other amenities there twenty-four hours a day. Maybe he's there."

"Thank you, Lina. I didn't realize that. How nice."

After breakfast Grace's concern grew more acute. Phil had kissed her goodnight, but she didn't know when he slipped out. Maybe she snored, and he sneaked down to the concierge salon for early coffee. But his side of the bed didn't even look like he'd been there. She called the concierge on her deck in case Lina had forgotten, but he hadn't seen Phil.

Grace got dressed and thought maybe Phil had gone to the buffet. It wasn't like him to just take off. She looked around the stateroom for a note or clue that would tell her where he might have gone. Putting on her makeup, she noticed her hands were trembling, and she felt anxious. The delicious breakfast was turning sour in her stomach, and she rushed to put on a minimum amount of makeup. Shaking, she gave up on her brows and threw the pencil down beside the sink.

Wait a minute. There must be an explanation. Why am I getting so worked up? Calm down. Phil will probably be having coffee with Calvin or someone, just letting me sleep undisturbed. He might have needed to make a business call, although he promised not to.

She took three deep breaths and let her shoulders relax. She put her room keycard in her pocket, locked her purse in the safe, and exited the room.

Wait a minute. She unlocked the door and reentered. Using the eyebrow pencil, she wrote on the mirror in large letters. SEE YOU FOR LUNCH AT THE POOLSIDE CAFÉ @ 12 O'CLOCK.

As Grace stepped out into the hallway, she realized lots of people were exiting their rooms, headed for the lower deck where they could disembark. She was hoping Phil would take her ashore again to look at the shops and whatever Wrangell had to offer. Few cruise ships stopped there, so it might not be as commercialized as some of the other places they would go ashore. She had read something about garnets being sold there by the children and wanted to buy one in memory of her dad's January birthday.

Where to look first? Grace had to remind herself that Phil wasn't a child, but a grown man . . . not one of her students. He didn't need a mother or a teacher to tell him when he could come and go. In the past years, with both of them working, they seldom crossed paths. Phil often left for work while Grace pulled herself from the bed. He rarely got home in time for a sit-down dinner together. She gave up waiting for him years ago and would keep his plate in the microwave so he could just warm it up when he got home. It made it easier on her nerves not to expect him to be there. She often left messages on his bathroom mirror, knowing he'd see them before he left for work.

But after the summer escapade, they had committed to try harder to mend their relationship. They called it "the episode or the escapade" because it was a dark time and painful to talk about. Grace didn't want to talk about it, and nobody involved knew all the facts. This cruise promised to be the grand re-welding of their marriage vows; a new beginning. And with the baby coming, they would be a real family. But something was wrong.

Lord, help me find Phil. He couldn't just disappear.

Grace headed for the buffet located at the back of the ship. The sun shone through the scattered white clouds as she stepped out onto the veranda. She fully expected to find Phil seated with some new friends, munching away on some tantalizing breakfast goodies. Nothing but disappointment and rising fear greeted her.

She circled it twice just to make sure, but there was no sight of Phil in the buffet or on the veranda. She rushed through the hallways, taking the stairs without as much as a pause to say "good morning" or even to give anyone a friendly nod.

How does anyone find a spouse on this thing? She realized preplanning was imperative or you could wander around all day without finding your mate. While she searched in the buffet, he could be headed for the stateroom. If she went to the stateroom, he could be headed for the poolside café.

She picked up a phone near the buffet and called the room. No answer. She called the concierge again. "Is there any chance Phil Partain has left the ship to use a pay phone on land?" Her mind tried every possibility, even if it seemed farfetched or ridiculous. The concierge called down to the area where guests disembark, and they had an instant record of who had left the ship.

"No, Mrs. Partain. He has not left the ship."

"Thank you. At least I know he's still here." She called the Hargraves' room again, but nobody picked up. She went to the registration counter to get the room number for the Conovers, then called them from the desk.

"Hello, Clarise. I know this is weird, but have you seen Phil this morning?" Grace's heart pounded raucously.

"No, Grace, but when you find him, we'd like you to join us for lunch onboard before taking a walk. No sense to buy a meal in town when we get free meals onboard. Huh?"

"Yes, that's true." Grace hesitated to share her concern with Clarise. "I left Phil a note to meet me for lunch at the poolside café. Would that work?" They agreed. A solid lunch date made her feel confident Phil would show up. After all, he must have gone back to the room and read her message by now.

For two hours Grace walked through the bars, the showrooms, the salon, gym, cardroom, library, movie theater, restaurants, casino, and infirmary. Most of the places were closed while in port, but she looked anyway. She circled back to the room a couple of times, but except for Lina's skillful hand putting everything back in perfect shape, there was no sign of Phil. Her note was still on the bathroom mirror. At each men's restroom she passed, she asked those who were exiting to take a look back and see if Phil might be in there. *He could have gotten sick and be on the commode somewhere.*

At noon Grace found Clarise and Calvin waiting at the poolside café. "Okay," Clarise asked as she joined them, "where did you find that wayward sailor?"

"I didn't." Grace slumped down in the chair, completely distraught, and began to cry.

CHAPTER 8

Sadie looked up to see the officer's face.

"Can you tell me your name, miss?" His kind eyes and friendly voice helped soften her fear, if not her pain.

"I'm Sadie McClarron. I didn't expect this to happen so soon."

"Looks like it's happening. That's why they call it expecting, I guess." He smiled. "When you least expect it . . . well, never mind. I'm Officer Purcell, and I'm going to help you. We can do this together."

Sadie clenched her teeth in pain and started panting again. "Have you done this before?" she asked.

"No, but I've seen it done a couple of times. I've got two kids of my own." He seemed confident. "Okay, Sadie, hang in there. I'm going to run to my car and see if there's an ambulance in the area. If not, maybe we can get you to Baker. There's a medical center there. I have a first-aid kit that might come in handy, too. I'll be right back."

Sadie had a firm grip on the steering wheel, and when the pain was intense, she thought she would surely tear it off.

Oh, Lord, please help me get through this. Sadie never dreamed she would be delivered by a highway patrolman and two greasy tow truck drivers in the desert by the side of the freeway. When she tried to get in the right position, her knee hit the glove compartment and papers fell out onto the compartment's open door. One of them looked like a driver's license. Sadie saw it, but excruciating pain consumed her, and anything she saw appeared as a blur. She threw her head back and cried out as Purcell returned with the first-aid kit.

LeRoy delivered her pink terrycloth robe to Purcell and stepped back. "Thanks," the officer said. "Just stay out of the way, and I'll take care of this."

Another vehicle slowed to a stop behind the highway patrol cruiser.

"Ah, maybe this is help coming," Purcell said as he peeked back over his shoulder. "Hmm, it's my friend, the sheriff."

"Officer Childers," he greeted someone, and Sadie could hear the footsteps nearing.

Oh, great, that's all we need . . . more spectators.

"We should get some help now," Purcell said. He folded his jacket to put under Sadie's head. She appreciated his effort to make her more comfortable, but not for long as another searing pain gripped her. She let out an ear-shattering scream.

When the contraction passed, Sadie heard the new voice say, "Well, if it's not my favorite car thieves. What are you up to this time? I thought you were still in jail from when I arrested you a couple of months ago."

Sadie heard nervousness in Pete's voice as he answered from the back of the truck. "We ain't doing nothin' wrong this time, for sure. Just tryin' to help this here girl to have a baby."

Sheriff Childers moved toward Purcell. "What's up? Someone having a baby, are they?" The two law enforcement officers greeted each other with a handshake as Sadie looked on.

"It seems these guys stopped to help Miss Sadie when her car overheated and broke down," Purcell explained. "Then she overheated, and it looks like her baby decided to be born on the desert in a tow truck. As you can see, she's laying across the seat, and if you can help out, I'd appreciate it because it looks like we'll have to deliver this baby any minute now."

The older officer nodded. "Actually, I've done this once before on this same stretch of freeway. It's kind of scary, but we can do it. Do we have anything clean?" Childers moved toward Sadie's feet. "Hi Sadie, I'm Officer Tom Childers, Sheriff, and I'm here to help." He glanced toward the glove compartment with the driver's license resting on the open door, but said nothing.

Purcell handed Childers the pink robe and a few knit shirts as Sadie felt the need to push. She grunted and groaned and screamed, but it didn't seem to rattle Childers. He calmly encouraged her in between her gasps. Sweat and tears flowed freely until the finale when out came a small but active screaming baby girl.

"We did it!" LeRoy yelled.

Pete answered, "What do you mean *we* did it? We ain't even seen the thing yet."

Sadie looked up and saw LeRoy's head peek over the officer's shoulder. His face turned white, he grabbed on to the squeaky door, and just hung there with what Sadie imagined were rubber knees.

"It's a girl!" Childers said as he cut the cord with the scissors from Purcell's first-aid kit, and placed the screaming infant in the pink robe on Sadie's chest. "She's kind of messy, but I've got some water and gauze. We'll clean her as well as we can, and then we'll put you in my backseat and transport you both to the Baker Medical Center. They can check you out, and from there you can call someone to come and get you. How's that?"

Sadie could do nothing more than nod her grateful answer. Tears of joy flowed down her temples and into her curly, sweaty red hair. *Thank you, God. Thank you, God.* "Thank you, officer. I can't imagine what I would have done if you hadn't come along."

"My pleasure," Officer Childers answered. "It's pretty exciting to be a part of a new birth. It certainly isn't an everyday occurrence."

"She's so beautiful," Sadie cooed, looking down at the tiny angel lying on her chest. "I'm going to name her Angel. I can't name her Tom or Childers, but you were my angel today."

"Ahhh, that's nice." Childers gave Sadie a drink of water and suggested she lie still and rest for a few minutes. She relaxed, more than happy to do just that, as she admired the Angel in her arms.

STILL SITTING WITH the Conovers at the poolside café, Grace couldn't even think of eating. Her stomach was in knots.

"Would Phil have gone to the gym?" Calvin asked.

"I looked there at least three times."

"Maybe he took a walk up on the deck where the walking track is," Clarise suggested.

"I was up there several times also and asked every walker and jogger if they'd seen him. Why wouldn't he have let me know where he was going? It's been over four hours since I started looking. Something's wrong. He wouldn't do this." Grace pounded her fist on the table in frustration.

"Maybe he got off the ship and they missed checking him out," Calvin suggested.

Grace looked up as if to try to see how that could have happened. "I suppose it wouldn't be impossible. I'm going down there and see what they say. I know they must be very careful because they have to keep track of everyone who gets off so they can check them back in when they get back aboard."

She got up and started to leave. "Hey, thanks for caring."

Calvin and Clarise got up too. "We're leaving the ship for the day anyway, so we'll go down there with you."

Lord, show me a clue. Help me find Phil. Please.

On the Lido Deck, people jammed the area waiting to disembark. As the elevator opened, even more guests flooded into the already crowded area.

"Folks, please be patient," a crewmember called. "Have your room keycard ready. We'll get you off momentarily when the gangplank is cleared for your safe debarkation."

Other crewmembers were struggling to roll a large container off the ship, and it caused a pile-up of those waiting to get off. Guests were anxious to get off and meet up with their assigned tour guides.

"I wish they'd hurry up." Grace could feel her fears rising. *Trust in the Lord with all your heart,* she prayed silently, trying to believe this strange situation would have a happy ending and an entertaining story to tell upon Phil's return.

When the men were clear, guests began to file off. Grace and the Conovers patiently worked their way to the front of the line.

"Ma'am, do you have your room keycard?"

"Yes, but I'm not getting off the ship right now. I'm looking for my husband, Philip Partain. I've looked everywhere for him. Did he leave the ship today?"

"Let me check. . . ." After looking at the lengthy list on the podium, he shook his head. "No, I don't see that he checked out."

"Is it possible he left the ship, and you might have missed him?"

"To my knowledge, that has never happened. That's why there are three of us monitoring this area. The only way he could leave the ship without us knowing would be to jump overboard." He laughed, but Grace did not. In fact, it was something she had not considered . . . until now.

The Conovers didn't want to leave Grace, but she insisted. "Go and enjoy your day. I'm going to talk to the purser and find out how to report a missing person. What else can I do?"

"Okay, then," Clarise said. "I'll bring back a garnet for you. I hear the children will be selling them at tables on the street. You probably didn't even get to read about it. A lady left an island where there are garnets to the Boy Scouts with the understanding that only children could sell them. We'll see."

Grace remembered the story, but her mind was occupied elsewhere. She wanted to believe this silly mix-up had a perfectly logical answer. Bewildered she went from deck to deck again, wandering aimlessly from one end of the ship to the other, putting off asking the purser how to file a missing person's report. *I wish I had a photo of Phil so I could show it to people when I ask if they've seen him.* She decided Sheldon and Marilyn must have left the ship because they did not answer her knocks at their door or the numerous calls she made to their room. Everyone began to look suspicious to her, but for no good reason. She probably looked suspicious to them, rushing up and down the halls, peeking in every nook and cranny. Exhaustion and fear drained her.

At 4:00 in the afternoon, Grace decided to turn in a Missing Person's report. She had no other option; it had become absolutely necessary. She even thought about asking the purser if she could call home from the ship. After some thought, she realized it made no sense to upset Sadie, who was probably living the life of Riley with the whole house to herself. By now she might be seeking out college classes, looking for a job, or adding angels to her collection.

Grace approached the door marked "Security." A crewman looked up from the paperback book he was reading and nodded curtly as she walked in. "I'm Clyde Garrison, and I'm Head of Security. And you are...?"

Grace introduced herself, but she was anxious to tell him about Phil's disappearance. The man motioned for her to sit down.

Bound by law to take reports of missing persons seriously, he listened to her story. But the disinterested way he regarded Grace, made it obvious he wanted her to know she had interrupted his reading with her mere presence.

"My husband is Philip Partain. He kissed me goodnight last night, and when I woke up this morning, he was gone, and I haven't seen him since. I've looked everywhere."

"Mrs. Partain, before I can do anything, do you mind if I ask you some questions?"

"Of course."

"Could it be possible that your husband knows someone else onboard that he might have gone to visit?"

"Visit? For eight hours?" She shook her head emphatically. "No. We came with another couple. Business partners. But I've talked to them, and they haven't seen him since last night at dinner." She sensed his annoyance when he had to get out a form and start filling in some details, repeating her name and Phil's as he wrote.

"We only met one other couple," she offered. "I saw them for lunch, and they hadn't seen him either. I don't know what else to do."

"I hate to ask, but has Mr. Partain ever . . . have you ever known him to . . . ." He tapped the desk nervously with his pen and then continued. "He couldn't have taken up with another woman, could he? You'd be surprised how many times a wayward husband has spent some unscheduled time with alternate female guests or staff members."

She gasped. "Another woman? Are you crazy? No!" Her temper flared.

"I'm sorry, ma'am, but it happens. We recently had to let one of our own employees go because they . . . well, *she* . . .uh . . . had been intimate with a married guest during a cruise."

Grace felt the emotion explode from deep inside as she erupted in huge, wailing sobs. "How could this happen? I'm pregnant, and this cruise should have been a new beginning for us. Almost like a honeymoon before the baby comes." She blurted out the story of how she had run away to Las Vegas and got tangled up with crooks and kidnappers. She imagined none of it made any sense to the man taking notes, but she couldn't stop herself.

"You must think I'm crazy, but my husband kissed me goodnight last night, and I haven't seen him since. *That's a fact! Where is he?*" She was screaming now, but she couldn't seem to stop. She slapped both hands on the metal table in front of her with every word. Again she repeated, "*Where is he?*"

The security officer backed his chair away from the desk. He calmly offered her a box of tissues and a small bottle of water.

"I'm so sorry, Mrs. Partain. Please relax and try to calm down. We'll do everything possible to locate Mr. Partian. Everything. When everyone's back on board, we'll do a complete search with every employee participating. We won't leave an inch of the ship unturned. Even the guests will get involved. I promise."

His words helped enough for her to dare to voice the unthinkable. "Could he . . . could he have fallen overboard somehow? Does that ever happen?"

"Well . . . yes, but the railings are designed high enough to make it almost impossible. It's very rare and usually has something to do with intoxication or foul play. Does either of those seem possible in your husband's case?"

"He has a drink once in a while, but he ordered Martinelli's Sparkling Cider for us on this trip because of my pregnancy. I think he had a glass of wine at dinner, but nothing during the show that followed."

"What about foul play? Was your husband getting along with his business partner?"

Grace was embarrassed to think about Sheldon's refusal to eat dinner with them the night before, and she was hesitant to share that information with a stranger. "His business partner's been his best friend since high school. They played football together."

"Well, were they getting along?"

Grace hesitated. She knew Sheldon could get out of sorts at times, but he and Phil had always worked through it just fine. Finally she decided to tell Garrison about it. After all, if she wanted above all else to have her husband found, she couldn't hold anything back.

"They had a little uncomfortable moment last night at dinner, but it really wasn't anything. Sheldon thought we'd made new friends and cut him and Marilyn out. Just silly jealousy. Nothing serious. He and Marilyn chose to eat elsewhere, but I'm sure he was just blowing off steam. I talked to Marilyn this morning, and she seemed just fine."

"Why would he blow off steam over a little thing like that?"

She sighed. Might as well tell him the rest. "Some months ago they had a huge sale that fell through. Sheldon blames Phil . . . and me."

"Why would he blame you?"

Just thinking about last summer brought on another crying jag. "Last summer, when I ran away, Phil kind of left Sheldon holding the bag on a big real estate deal. He focused on finding me, and in doing so, he let the business slide. Phil asked Sheldon to help him get ransom money together . . . and it was a big mess. Meanwhile the buyer lost confidence in them and pulled out."

"If it's just the same to you, Mrs. Partain, we're definitely going to want to question your husband's partner if we don't find your husband in our onboard search. What are their names?"

"They'll be so embarrassed." Grace wiped away the tears and cupped her jaw in her hands. She gave their names and cabin number.

"As soon as everyone is onboard, we'll conduct a thorough search of the ship. If we don't find him, we'll turn around and retrace our exact route in case Mr. Partain did fall overboard."

That did it. Grace burst forth with another flood of tears. "Have you ever turned the ship around before?"

"Yes, but it's very rare. The only thing harder than falling off a cruise ship is surviving the fall. But it does happen. We'll be contacting other cruise ships in the area and also the Canadian Coast Guard. We'll find him."

"Please keep looking."

"Searching for someone who's fallen from a ship isn't easy, and speed is essential. We have a fast rescue boat that can move quickly ahead of us, but everything will depend on slowing down and yet getting there in time. Sitting here in port is cutting down on our chances of finding him alive, I'm afraid, if indeed he's in the water. But we'll get under way soon."

It did not seem a bit hopeful to Grace, but she did believe in miracles, and perhaps they would find him clinging to a life preserver or picked up by another cruise ship.

"I don't want to be alone in my cabin," she confessed. "I just don't know what to do with myself."

"I'll send a doctor and a nurse to see you. Perhaps they can give you a sedative or something to help you relax. One of the stewards can escort you back to your stateroom. Have you eaten today?"

"I had a good breakfast but skipped lunch."

"I'll have a nice tray of food sent to your room. Please stay there until you hear something from me. Okay? I want to be able to contact you immediately if we find Mr. Partain . . . I mean, *when* we find Mr. Partian."

"Okay. Thank you." A steward soon arrived to escort her back to her room. She dreaded being alone. Lina came and went now and then, but she tended to business, gave Grace a sweet smile, and exited quickly. It didn't seem appropriate to ask her over and over if she'd seen Phil, or to share her fears. Maybe Marilyn would come and sit with her for a while.

CHAPTER 9

Pastor John Troude paced the floor nervously. "I haven't heard a word from Sadie since Phil and Grace left. I hope she's getting along okay. I know she wouldn't want me breathing down her neck, but I might check in on her," John mumbled to himself. He knew his wife, Nancy, had likely overheard, as she was sitting just a few feet away. But she didn't speak up, as she no doubt knew he had already made up his mind and would follow through.

John went to the phone and punched in the numbers. No answer, just Phil's message. "Hmmm. I really thought I'd hear something from Sadie, but she probably wouldn't call unless she needed help with something. Maybe I'll drop by tomorrow. I'm sure she wouldn't leave town without letting us know."

Pastor Troude had married Phil and Grace, but through the years, the Partains had fallen away from the church and lost contact. When Grace went missing in June, Phil called John in desperation. They renewed their acquaintance and became close friends. When the whole episode ended, John counseled the Partains and helped them transition into a much more dedicated life to each other and to the Lord. He even helped them adjust to Sadie being a temporary part of their family. Now he felt responsible for her while the Partains were away.

IT WASN'T EASY, BUT Childers and Purcell managed to move Sadie from the tow truck to the back seat of Childers' vehicle. He gladly transported her and Angel, even though he had other business with Pete and LeRoy. The two men had to bring Sadie's car to Baker, so they would end up right where he wanted them. He wouldn't have to track them down this time.

Childers helped Sadie check into the medical center. The women at the desk eagerly welcomed the premature baby and mother. It wasn't a regular occurrence.

"Would it be possible for me to call my pastor in Highland to come and get me?" Sadie felt weak and tired, but she was thrilled to be where there were other women.

"Of course. We don't have hospital beds here, but I'm sure we can find a quiet place for you to be comfortable while you wait."

Sadie couldn't figure out how she could get her car fixed and back to Highland. She hadn't intended to be any problem to Pastor Troude, but she had no choice. Thankfully Childers had been careful about collecting her belongings from the car, and she dug around for the phone number in her purse. She found it and punched in the number.

"Hello, Mrs. Troude. It's Sadie. I'm so sorry to bother you, but it seems I need help."

The older woman responded with a soothing voice that indicated she was ready to listen. "Well, sure, honey. What can I do for you?"

In rapid fire Sadie replied, "I was going to visit some friends in Las Vegas, and along the way my car overheated and quit, so some tow truck guys came, and I went into labor. Then a highway patrolman showed up, and a sheriff thought the tow truck drivers were stealing my car, so he delivered the baby on the seat of the tow truck, and it was so hot, and it's a girl. . . . I mean *she's* a girl. I named her Angel, and she's beautiful and healthy." She took a big breath.

"The cop – I mean, the sheriff – brought me to the Baker Medical Center, and the tow truck guys brought my dead car, and I need Pastor Troude or someone to come and get me. I don't know what to do about the car."

When Sadie took another breath, Nancy asked her to slow down and start over. "Honey, my husband just came into the room. I know he'll want to hear what you have to say, so you're talking to both of us now."

Sadie immediately launched into a retelling of her story. When she finished, she waited for their response.

"We'll be there as fast as we can get there," the pastor said. "Don't worry about the car. We'll figure that out. Have them drop it off at a garage. We'll see about it when we get there."

Sadie began to cry. "I'm so sorry to be so much trouble."

"Hey, it's okay," Nancy added. "It's wonderful news about the baby. Sounds like a unique delivery you'll talk about forever. We're coming as fast as we can."

The nurses were very accommodating and did everything they could to make Sadie comfortable. They sponged off the baby, and one of them even rushed out and brought back some tiny diapers, a little preemie-sized onesie, and a receiving blanket.

THE TROUDES STOPPED by the church to pick up some things from the nursery that would be helpful. Nancy knew exactly what to get: diapers, blankets, wipes, bottle, and cap. It would take a couple of hours to get to Baker.

"I hope they take good care of Sadie and the baby," Nancy said, her grandmother instincts kicking in. "I wish we could get there faster. Won't it be fun to have a new baby in the midst of us again? Grace will be so surprised when she gets home." It had been a long time since the Troude kids had been babies.

John opened the car door for Nancy and put the provisions in the backseat. "You take care of Sadie and the baby . . . Angel, and I'll figure out what to do about the car. We could leave it and go back for it later, or if it runs and we can put it in working order, I could drive it back today. We'll see."

Nancy nodded and smiled. Her husband was a good man, always ready to go the extra mile.

CHILDERS FELT ECSTATIC about successfully delivering a baby by the side of the freeway. It wasn't an everyday occurrence but far more satisfying than giving speeding tickets to belligerent motorists or DUI's to people who had too many watered-down free drinks in the casinos. Sadie was so appreciative when he left her inside the medical center he hated to leave. He was smiling, but it was time to go back to work, and since he was parked right behind Pete's rattletrap tow truck, he'd start there.

"Okay, Pete, let's talk business."

"Oh, come on, Officer, we helped that lady. If we hadn't stopped, no tellin' what she'd done," Pete pleaded. "We did our time in jail."

"Yeah, well, when you're driving a stolen car, it's pretty hard to overlook it," Childers said, referring to their past.

"We wasn't stealin' it. We was just borrowin' it cuz our truck ran out of gas. I told that to the judge," Pete explained.

"You do understand that running out of gas doesn't give you the right to steal someone else's car, right?" Childers had a hard time keeping a straight face.

"We was *borrowin'* it," Pete loudly corrected.

"Okay, what about your expired plates?"

"I can explain that. I got 'em at home. I'll put 'em on tonight. Honest." Pete promised.

Childers nodded, far from convinced. "Now the real question is . . . what are you doing with Grace Partain's driver's license in your glove compartment?"

LeRoy waved his hand in the air and jumped in to the conversation. "See, Pete, I told ya that driver's license was gonna be worth somethin' down the road. How much is she willin' to pay us for it?"

"Shut up, LeRoy. We don't want any trouble over that thing. I just found it. That's all." He threw his stub of a cigarette down in the sand and stomped it out.

LeRoy waved his hand again and relieved himself of a big spit of tobacco. "*He did not find it! I found it*," he shouted. "Pete was the one who thought of the kidnapping idea. I was the one who got the idea to borrow the car."

Childers took off his hat and ran his hand through his thick hair. "So you were the kidnappers who called Mr. Partain when Mrs. Partain went missing? Aha, now I get it."

"Yeah, but we never did really kidnap her. We never even seen her until that night behind the casino."

"Well, why don't you boys just drop the new mama's car at the garage, give me the keys to your truck, and jump in the backseat of my car for a little ride back to jail. Let's see what the DA has to say about calling for ransom money and pretending to be kidnappers. I'm not sure what that's called, but you're guilty of it. Let's go."

CHAPTER 10

Grace called the Hargraves and told them Phil had disappeared and couldn't be found. She had experienced denial, worry, anger, and fear. But she was not ready to accept loss.

"I'm going to lie down for a while, but the captain said he was sending a tray of food. If you don't have dinner plans, would you join me for a while?"

"Of course," Sheldon said. "When would you like us to come?"

Grace hoped for a quick nap. "I'll call you when the food comes."

Sheldon quickly agreed and hung up. Grace wanted to get into her gown and robe but didn't feel comfortable about greeting Hargraves in a nightgown. The ship's doctor had delivered a sedative, but she resisted taking it in case the captain called with news. She couldn't stop the thoughts whirling around in her head.

Phil didn't leave the ship, so he must be held hostage somewhere onboard. That's ridiculous. Or he fell off the ship. That's ridiculous, too. The railings are high. You couldn't accidentally fall over one. Phil wasn't apt to be drinking or drunk, so that doesn't seem possible. If someone pushed him, they'd have a fight on their hands. And besides, who would push him? Why would anyone push him? Maybe he couldn't sleep and got up to take a walk. Sometimes when he has a lot on his mind, he'll take a sleeping pill. Could he have taken a pill and gotten disoriented and fallen overboard? The covers weren't even disturbed on his side, so . . .

Every thought seemed worse than the one before. At the beginning of the summer, when their marriage was falling apart, she had taken a turnaround bus to Las Vegas. When it crashed and she was unaccounted for, they reported her missing. What they did not know was that Grace never got on the return bus because she stopped to help an elderly woman who faked a heart attack. When assumed missing, Grace decided to stay missing and never go back. *Could Phil be paying me back by hiding somewhere? But he wouldn't risk breaking his neck in the fall by jumping off a ship. How else could he disappear? And why would he do that now when we're supposed to be honeymooning and preparing for our new baby? It doesn't make any sense.*

The announcement came over the ship's PA system directing every employee and guest to search his or her area for a missing person named Philip Partain. They were to cover every stateroom, storage area, under every bed, balcony, bar, or bathroom. Up and down the halls staff members searched and checked off stateroom numbers. Grace could hear people hustling up and down the hall.

An hour later, as the ship was moving away from the dock, another announcement came over the ship's closed TV channel and the loud speakers outside.

"This is Captain Manrova speaking. In regards to the disappearance of Philip Partain, one of our cruise guests, I have given the order to turn the ship around and retrace the path we sailed since dinner last night. If anyone has information regarding the whereabouts of Mr. Partain, they are to come to the bridge and report to me or Security Officer Clyde Garrison. The Canadian Coast Guard will be joining us in the search on the water. This will not affect the onboard meals or entertainment schedule. Please allow us to do our job and don't be tempted to hang over the railings as the search takes place on the water. Thank you."

Grace thought about going out on deck in the front of the ship to watch, but it terrified her. What if they didn't find him, but what if they did? *Can he still be alive, floating in the ocean?* She had no idea when he disappeared. She just knew the last time she saw him he kissed her good night, and almost twenty hours had passed since then. She was exhausted mentally and physically.

Grace had given up on sleeping when someone knocked on the door. Hoping it was good news she dragged herself up off the bed and across the room. She opened the door and the server swooped in and put the tray on the small table. "Will that be all, madam?"

She nodded, but couldn't think of anything to say except a weak "Thank you."

Grace took a peek at the food and called Sheldon again.

"They sent me a whole tray of food, and it looks wonderful. Please come over and eat it while it's hot. There's plenty for all three of us because I don't feel like eating."

What a relief to open the door to Sheldon and Marilyn. Grace fell into their arms and wept again. She usually appeared so put together and proper – her clothes, her hair, her makeup, her emotions – now disheveled, broken, and completely vulnerable.

"We can't imagine what could have happened to Phil. This is just terrible." Sheldon hugged her again and sat down on the sofa by the table. "We can stay as long as you like."

"I can even stay the night if you need me to," Marilyn offered. "We may not be able to do much but listen and eat your food. Do you mind?"

"No, please help yourselves. It smells great, but I just can't."

Sheldon lifted the domed covers, Marilyn pulled up a chair, and the two of them feasted on Waldorf salad, shrimp scampi, fries, veggies, and cheesecake. Grace ate part of a roll with butter, pulled herself up on the pillows, took the sedative, and closed her eyes.

"I think I walked a hundred miles today without ever leaving the ship." Her voice trailed off.

"Did you hear about the brawl in the bar last night?" Sheldon helped himself to another warm roll. "I guess our little misunderstanding over dinner didn't compare," he continued. "Two old farts had too much to drink and started shoving each other, trying to get in the elevator. Another guy was in one of those motorized wheelchairs and ended up falling down the stairs backwards."

Grace could hardly hear him talking as she drifted into a foggy state. "Uh huh," she murmured.

"Yeah, they had to escort the two guys to the captain's quarters, and the guy who fell down the stairs is in the infirmary."

When Marilyn and Sheldon had eaten all they wanted, Grace lay completely silent. The phone rang and made them both jump. Grace heard, but she did not respond. Marilyn answered after the first ring.

"Yes?"

"No, this is Marilyn Hargrave, her friend. She's asleep now. Can I help you?"

Marilyn was silent as she listened. Grace wondered if she should get up, but her body was so relaxed now, it felt like lead.

"Thank you, Captain. I'll tell her when she wakes up." More silence while Grace started to drift off again until Marilyn's voice brought her back. "Yes, she was given a sedative to take and is resting peacefully." Silence. "I know she'll be glad to hear the Coast Guard has joined the search. She's been very upset, but she's sound asleep now. I'm going to spend the night with her in her cabin." More silence. "Yes, they brought the food. Grace didn't feel like eating much, so she asked us to join her. Thank you so much. I'll give her the message about retracing our route when she wakes up. Thank you."

Marilyn hung up the phone and said to Sheldon, "They're being very thorough. I wonder how the search onboard is going. The captain said we've turned around and are retracing our route. When they're sure they've covered the area, they'll return to the scheduled tour route. He said by noon tomorrow we'll be back on track." Those were the last words Grace heard as she drifted into a deep sleep.

SADIE THANKED JOHN and Nancy over and over. Even though safely back in Highland, the Troudes insisted she and Angel stay with them until Grace and Phil returned home. John took care of getting her car back home, and told Nancy and Sadie that for some reason the tow truck drivers were gone and didn't leave a bill.

The next day wasn't easy on any of them. Nancy helped Sadie get showered and comfortable. Bringing home a preemie made her a little nervous, but she had more experience than Sadie did. She sponged Angel carefully, rubbed lotion gently over her pink skin, and wrapped her like a burrito in a receiving blanket. After placing Angel with Sadie to nurse her, the work began. Nancy worked all day to create a temporary nursery, fix meals, and rock Angel so Sadie could nap. She loved every minute of it.

"This reminds me of when our children were babies. I can't wait for Grace and Phil to get home. They'll be so surprised."

Sadie giggled. "I feel like a little girl who just got a new doll to show off. But when I hold Angel, I know I've entered a new chapter of my life. Just touching my lips to her skin sends chills of joy. She's so silky, soft, and warm. She smells like lotion and mother's milk."

"Grace isn't due until the end of December, but she's going to get some good practice with Angel in the house." Nancy felt lucky to be hosting the two of them. *Thank you God for bringing this baby safely into the world,* she prayed.

Sadie frowned and stuck her fingernail between her teeth. "Hey, you know what? When I was in labor in that tow truck, I saw something weird. I forgot all about it until now."

"What did you see?" Nancy asked as she cradled Angel in her arms.

"I accidentally kicked the glove compartment door. It flew open and some papers fell out. I know I screamed, practically delirious, at that moment, but I could have sworn I saw Grace's driver's license. Could I have been hallucinating? But I'm almost sure I saw it. What would Grace's license be doing in those weird guys' tow truck?"

CHILDERS BOOKED PETE and LeRoy at the Baker jail until he could decide what to do with them. When they were safely in a cell, Childers stood by the counter and marveled. "I can't believe these two characters were smart enough to cook up a plan to pretend to be Mrs. Partian's kidnappers when they'd never set eyes on her. And . . . they almost pulled it off."

The desk sergeant shook his head. "Wasn't the ransom something like five hundred thousand dollars?"

"Yes, and it might have been theirs if the car they 'borrowed' hadn't run out of gas." Childers chuckled. "When I picked them up that first time, I had no idea they'd hatched a much bigger plan than stealing a car. Shoot, when I arrested them, I foiled their plan without knowing it."

Unfortunately he did not have much on them. They had already done some jail time for the car theft. If they picked up Grace's license from the bus wreck debris, there was no law against that. And although they tried to pull off a ransom situation, it fell through. They had posed as kidnappers when they demanded the ransom money, but Childers was not sure it was worth it to try to stick them with attempted kidnapping when they never had the victim. And they never got the ransom money.

"These guys are losers all the way around. Their biggest crime pencils out as stupidity." Childers sighed. "Let's just call it their lucky day and kick 'em loose. They did help the little girl have her Angel baby."

IN JAIL PETE CHIDED LeRoy. "Why'd ya have ta open your big fat mouth and mention gettin' money for the driver's license?"

"He already knew we had it. I thought maybe it'd make sense that we had a plan." He spit in the corner. "We gotta get outa here. I'm running out of tobacco."

"Big dang deal. At least you can chew. I left my cigarettes in the truck. The whole thing sucks. We stopped to help that young lady, and before ya know it, we end up in the hoosegow again. We're the good guys this time. You'd think they'd give us a Good Samaritan award. How will we ever make enough money to buy a new truck? When we get out of here, we're gonna do somethin' really good."

"What are we gonna do, Pete? And what's a Samaritan award?"

"I don't know. It's somethin' 'bout doing' somethin' good for someone. But it's gonna be really good, and people are gonna sit up and take notice. You just wait and see."

CHAPTER 11

Grace awoke with a start and saw the sliding glass door to the balcony standing wide open. She sat up quickly.

"Phil?"

Marilyn stepped in through the slider.

"It's just me, Grace."

"Have you heard anything from the captain?" Grace rubbed her eyes and reached for a tissue.

"He called to check on you shortly after you went to sleep. But there's been no news of Phil. I'm pretty sure we've finished retracing yesterday's path and are moving forward again."

Grace's heart sank, as tears flooded her eyes. "It's been thirty-two hours since he kissed me goodnight. They can't give up looking. What am I going to do without him?"

"Don't start thinking like that," Marilyn said, sitting down on the side of the bed and taking Grace's hand. "You can't give up."

"I know. I know. But it's hard to imagine he disappeared for thirty-two hours and then will miraculously show up."

"Well, *you did* last summer." Marilyn sounded a little perturbed.

Grace shook her head and remembered how she had tried to pull off a disappearing act. At the time she had no intention of appearing again.

"I hope you don't mind, Grace, but I ordered breakfast from room service. When we finish, I'm going to see if the Captain has made any progress and ask him to send someone to sit with you."

Grace nodded slowly. "Yes, I suppose that'll be okay. After all, you and Sheldon need to have some time to enjoy the cruise. There's really nothing you can do for me, or Phil. I don't know what to do next." Grace wiped at the tears that began to roll down her cheeks again.

"I don't imagine there's anything you *can* do until they either give up the search or find him. If they don't find him soon, you might think about getting a flight home when we arrive in Juneau."

After room service arrived, Marilyn ate a light breakfast, and Grace had a piece of toast with a cup of coffee. She insisted Marilyn take some of the food back for Sheldon and enjoy some of the shipboard activities planned for a day at sea.

GRACE DIDN'T WANT TO think about going home yet. But as the hours dragged by, she became less and less hopeful. *Lord, give me a sign or a clue. If Phil is overboard, help the Coast Guard find him.*

Captain Manrova hadn't called all morning, and Grace was anxious to hear from him. Good or bad, he should have called, but since he hadn't, she felt compelled to call him.

The Captain's first mate answered. "This is Grace Partain," she said, "and I wondered if you have any news regarding my husband's disappearance."

"I just started to dial your room. The Coast Guard did find a shirt floating in the water but no sign of a body. Could you come down to the security office and identify it? Mr. Harrison will meet you there."

Grace, still gripping the phone, fell on the bed with heaving sobs.

"Mrs. Partain?" She heard the voice as if from far away. "Mrs. Partain, would you like me to send someone to escort you?"

She took a deep breath and swallowed before answering.

"No, let me . . . get myself together, and I'll . . . I'll come."

Grace trembled from head to toe. This might confirm her worst fears. She wished the shirt would be just some old rag floating on the water. *What if it's Phil's? Will they search more? Will they just assume he's at the bottom of the ocean? Why would the shirt be floating without him in it?* She didn't want to know any of those answers, but the questions kept dancing through her head.

Grace called the Conovers' room. Nobody answered, but she left a message. "Hi, Clarise. I hate to bother you, but I'm going to meet up with the security guy, and I wanted you to know what's happened. The search has been completed, and the Coast Guard found a shirt. I'm going down to identify it. I'm praying it isn't his, and yet, I don't know what to pray for. I don't know what I'll do if it's his, and I don't know what I'll do if it isn't. Call me when you're in."

SADIE SAT CROSS-LEGGED on the floor with Angel cradled between her knees while John and Nancy looked on from their recliners. Angel's little blue eyes opened, and Sadie tested to see if she could track movement. She tried her finger and then a little toy bird. The TV news sounded in the background.

"A passenger on the cruise ship Grand Iris, bound for Alaska, was reported missing at sea. Authorities turned the ship around after a thorough search onboard. They are retracing their path in search of the lost passenger. No other information is available at this time."

Sadie came to attention. "Wait a minute! Did you hear that? Someone's missing off the Grand Iris. That's the ship Grace and Phil are on." Sadie listened for more information, but the reporter went on to another news item.

"That's scary," Nancy commented. "Did you hear a name?"

"No, I just heard Grand Iris, and it caught my ear. I wonder if it's anyone Grace and Phil have met."

John spoke up. "I actually heard of a ship where a passenger fell overboard down by Mexico. Another cruise ship heard the man's cries for help, deployed a lifeboat, and brought him safely back to the ship. It seems impossible, but it happened."

Sadie nodded. "When something like that happens, don't you suppose they try to keep it from the other passengers so they don't freak out? I wonder if Phil and Grace even know what's going on. And I wonder why the reporter didn't give a name. Maybe they still hope he's onboard somewhere. And they wouldn't want to give out a name until the next of kin is notified."

John asked, "Did they even mention whether it was a man or a woman?"

"I don't think so. Not in the part I heard." Sadie went back to dangling the little stuffed bird back and forth in front of Angel's face.

"I guess that's the one in a million," John said as he walked toward the kitchen.

"What? What about one in a million?" Nancy followed, while Sadie remained on the floor but listening in.

"I read someplace that statistically only one in a million cruise passengers go overboard, and it's usually because the person did something irresponsible."

"Really? What did they mean by irresponsible?"

"There were some statistics I've forgotten, but some were alcohol-related, some were suicides, and some were men throwing their wives overboard because they ask too darn many questions."

Nancy chuckled. "You're kidding, aren't you?"

"See what I mean? Another senseless question."

Sadie laughed at their good-natured sparring. She wished she had parents who were funloving like the Troudes.

CHAPTER 12

Head of Security Harrison met Grace at his door. The shirt lay stretched out on a metal table. As Grace feared, it belonged to Phil. It looked shabby and gray from being in the ocean waters, but definitely his. She leaned forward and ran both hands across the fabric. "May I have it?"

"Of course, Mrs. Partain, but not until the investigation is completely over." Harrison hesitated. "But there's something I want you to see." He held out a tiny black box.

"What's this?" Grace took the box and turned it over in her hand.

"I discovered it in the pocket of the shirt. I guess it had just enough air trapped in it to keep the shirt afloat near the surface. We almost missed it."

Grace opened the box slowly. She gasped, snapped the box closed and held it to her breast. "I can't believe it."

The captain stood quietly, waiting for Grace to gather herself.

At last she found her voice. "He must have been planning to give me a new ring to celebrate our twentieth year of marriage. Why didn't he give it to me? What stopped him? How did he end up in the water?"

"Mrs. Partain, was Mr. Partain depressed or sick?"

She shook her head. "No, he actually seemed the happiest he'd ever been. He'd cut back on work and loved the idea of having a baby.

Not only happy, but also very healthy. If you're even hinting that he might have committed suicide . . . *no*, he would *never*."

Silence. Harrison took a deep breath and so did Grace.

"Do you know anyone who would have wanted to hurt Mr. Partain?"

She swallowed and shook her head again. "No, Phil is a great businessman. Honest and thorough and smart. If anyone wanted to hurt him, I don't know who it'd be. And they certainly wouldn't be a guest on the ship, would they?"

"I don't know, but the investigators will ask you these questions over and over. What kind of relationship did you have with your husband?"

Grace thought back to last June when she tried to escape the marriage by taking the Turnaround bus to Las Vegas. But when that whole fiasco came to an end, they had started a new life together. She did not want to muddy the waters with that story again. It had been mentioned at least once before, and it had no bearing on this situation.

"Phil and I have been married twenty years. I teach school, and he's a successful real estate broker. We're both busy with work, but our marriage is solid. We never had any children, and that always frustrated me, so we were both excited about this unexpected pregnancy."

"Would he have celebrated by doing something reckless or irresponsible?"

Grace pulled in her chin and frowned. "Reckless? Like what?"

"Like get up and try to walk on the railing or horseplay with someone?"

"That's ridiculous! Phil is a down-to-earth serious kind of guy. The only person he knew on the ship that he might have been silly with would be his partner, Sheldon. And Sheldon said they never saw Phil after dinner that night."

Harrison got up from his chair and readjusted his jacket. "I hate to say it, but I think we've exhausted what we can do. We searched every inch of this ship with the help of the entire crew, entertainers, and guests. We slowed the ship down and retraced our journey twice, called in the help of the Canadian Coast Guard, contacted local authorities, but other than the shirt, we failed to find a body."

"Body? Wasn't there a chance you could have found Phil alive? Didn't you even consider that?" Grace clasped her hands together and plopped them down in her lap. She wanted to slap someone. She wanted to scream. She wanted to slam a door or throw something against the wall.

"I'm sorry. I should have said, we didn't find your husband anywhere. I had to call off the Coast Guard and put the crew back on regular duty."

"So . . . what am I supposed to do now?" Grace begged.

"You have some choices. I doubt you want to stay onboard. We'll be glad to transport you from Juneau, which is our next port, back to Seattle and from there to LAX. Would that be agreeable? You must be miserable staying onboard."

Grace hung her head. She had to accept the thought that they were giving up. *Did they really search every inch of the ship? If they found a shirt in the water, why didn't they send divers down to find the body? Wasn't there anything else they could do? Does this mean Phil no longer exists? Are they sure he fell in the ocean? How could he have ended up in the water?* Her mind was full of questions, all seemingly without answers.

She sighed. "I guess I don't really have a choice. There's no reason to stay on the cruise, knowing my husband may be dead. I need to get back home with my family. When do we land in the next port?" Grace knew she didn't have any family, just Sadie and the Troudes, but being with them would be better than sitting alone in her stateroom.

"Today's a sea day, so we won't get in until tomorrow morning. That's the earliest. But we'll gladly make all the flight arrangements."

Hot tears stung Grace's eyes yet again. "So is the investigation over? Are you giving up?"

"We've done what we can do, but the investigation will continue. The FBI will take it over from here, and I'm sure you'll be asked all these questions again several times."

"Okay, go ahead and make the flight arrangements. I appreciate that. Is there any way you can contact my home and let someone know what's happened? When you know what time I'll land at LAX, I need to have someone come and get me."

"We'll have a limousine waiting for you. Don't even think about that."

That was better because she wasn't up to talking over the phone right now. Instead she went back to her cabin and started taking the clothes off the hangers and putting them back in her suitcase.

What shall I do with all of Phil's things? She let herself sit down on the bed and cry again. When her tears ran out, she packed up Phil's bag and put it out of the way. She noticed there were messages from both the Hargraves and the Conovers. The Hargraves were going to see a movie in the onboard theater, and the Conovers were having lunch and going to the casino. The reality of living without Phil horrified her, and it was closing in.

THE FIRST MATE CALLED the Partain home phone, but the only answer came from the recording machine. Ship-to-shore phone calls were difficult and usually unreliable. Grace asked him not to leave a message and to keep trying until Sadie answered in person. After several tries without an answer, Grace thought Sadie must be out shopping or checking on classes at the college, but she was determined to make contact with someone.

"Well, if nobody answered there, try Pastor Troude." She gave his number.

The first mate placed the call and handed the phone to Grace.

"Hello, Nancy." Grace's voice cracked and the lump in her throat threatened to become a sob. "A terrible thing has happened. Phil disappeared the night before last."

She heard Nancy gasp. "Oh, no! We heard something about the Grand Iris on the news, and that someone was missing, but we didn't catch it all. What happened?"

"We don't really know. After dinner the night before last, we came back to the room. I crawled into bed, and Phil kissed me goodnight. I didn't see him again. When I woke up, Phil's side of the bed hadn't even been slept in. They turned the ship around, called the Coast Guard, and searched every inch of the ship as well."

"Has anyone seen him? Do they have any idea what happened to him?" Nancy questioned.

"They recovered his shirt from the ocean." She couldn't hold back the tears any longer. "I can't talk anymore. I'll be home tomorrow. They're arranging a flight and a limo to bring me right to Highland."

"Wait, Grace. Things have changed here since you left. I'll tell you about it tomorrow, but Sadie had her baby and she's at our house until you get home, so come here."

"Sadie had her baby?" Grace took the first breath of hope since Phil's disappearance. "Boy or girl?"

"A darling little girl named Angel."

The first mate was beginning to look impatient and reached for the phone.

"Okay, I'll see you tomorrow, and we'll talk more. I can't wait to be home. It's horrible to be here alone."

"What about Sheldon and Marilyn?"

"Of course, they've been a help. Marilyn stayed with me last night, but I can't interrupt the rest of their cruise. They're definitely concerned, but there's nothing they can do. And besides, they've been a little weird on this trip."

The first mate tapped Grace on the shoulder and held out his hand for the phone.

"What about the baby? She's a preemie. Is she okay?" Grace felt her own baby moving inside her belly. She had almost forgotten the child.

"Yes, she's a little fighter, and I think she's going to have red hair."

The first mate cleared his throat and reached for the receiver again. "Please, Ma'am."

"See you tomorrow. I can't talk anymore." She handed the phone back and wiped her eyes. "Thank you," she said and headed for the door, irritated that he was so impatient.

CHAPTER 13

Sadie finally found the time to call Lianne between nursing and naps.

"Lianne, I'm so sorry I forgot to call you. I bet you wondered what happened to me." Sadie was embarrassed by her thoughtlessness.

"Good grief, girl. When you didn't show up, I didn't know who to call. I called the number you gave me, but I only got Grace's answering machine."

"You'll never believe what happened. On my way to see you, my car broke down, and I had my baby in a tow truck. I think the drivers got arrested, and Phil, Grace's husband, has disappeared from a cruise ship . . . and my life is as crazy as ever."

"Wow, that does sound crazy, but I'm glad you're okay. What about Grace? She seemed like such a nice lady when we met at the casino last summer. I couldn't figure out how she ended up working for that creep, Jerry. Maybe you can fill me in on that someday. When you left, I quit. He gave me the creeps."

"The cruise line is flying Grace home tomorrow. I've been staying at the pastor's house. When Grace gets home, we'll move back over to her place. She's expecting in December, and we created a nice nursery there."

"The baby? What about the baby? Girl or boy?"

Sadie felt her heart swell with joy at the mere mention of her baby. "She's a precious girl named Angel."

"That's so cool. You'd better write a book. I've heard of tow trucks delivering cars, but I never heard of them delivering babies. Can't wait to hear more of *that* story."

"Ha! You won't believe it when I tell you. I'll save that for when we make it back to Las Vegas to visit. Meanwhile you've given me an idea. The last few years of my life have been so crazy, I think I'll start writing my story."

"I'll be your first beta reader. I'm glad you and the baby are fine. Scared me to death when you didn't show up, but I didn't know where to call. When you get settled, please keep in touch, Sadie."

SHELDON STOPPED BY to check on Grace. "I'm so sorry to hear the search has been called off. I really thought Phil would show up. It doesn't make sense. How could they find a shirt without finding him?"

"I don't know." Grace shook her head, then invited him to sit down. "They asked me questions about our relationship, his drinking habits, and his behavior."

"What do you mean?"

"They asked me if he drank too much, how we were getting along, if he might be depressed about anything, or if he did irresponsible risky things like walk on the railings. Phil hardly ever drank. I think he was the happiest I've ever seen him since he got the news of the baby. And he didn't do stupid things."

"You didn't tell them about last summer's escapade, did you?"

"A little bit. I'm not sure how much. I think I told them a little. There were moments when I spewed out stuff in a flood of tears. I'm not sure what I told them. I didn't think it relevant since it had a happy ending."

Sheldon shrugged. "I guess that probably didn't have any bearing on this crime."

Grace frowned. "What do you mean by crime?"

Sheldon scratched his head and stammered. "Well, don't you . . . aren't they . . . I mean, when you find a shirt in the water, don't you suppose . . . isn't it logical that someone must have pushed him overboard?"

Grace put her hands over her face. "I don't want to think about it! Nothing seems logical at this point. One day we board a cruise to celebrate our twentieth anniversary and the coming of a child, and the next day I'm alone. I just keep saying, 'It doesn't make any sense.'"

Sheldon laid his hand on her shoulder. "Listen, Grace, if you need us to accompany you home, we will."

She looked at him and sighed, appreciative of his offer but unwilling to accept it. "No. I insist you stay here. Maybe you can keep in touch with the captain just in case another clue or something shows up that'll help figure this out. Phil would have wanted you to enjoy this trip. He planned it for you and Marilyn and wanted to say thank you for being a great partner for all these years." She hung her head.

Sheldon's shoulders slumped. "I sure wasn't very appreciative the other night. I feel really bad now for being so jealous and irritable with him. I embarrassed myself and probably everyone else. I'll never forgive myself."

"Oh, Sheldon, you're forgiven. It was just a tense moment. You know Phil would never hold a grudge against his best friend, or anybody else for that matter."

"Thank you, Grace, for saying that. I didn't behave like a best friend."

She reached over and patted his hand. "Don't worry about that. Just let me know if anything turns up onboard, and I'll see you when you get home."

"Okay, we'll see you off tomorrow."

Grace wondered how Sheldon could be so calm. He obviously hadn't accepted that Phil might be dead. Maybe it just hadn't sunk in. After all, they were like brothers.

Sheldon left and Grace called the Conovers. She told them the bad news and about her trip home in the morning. They exchanged contact information and invited Grace to have dinner with them that evening.

She nodded. "Thank you so much. I really can't be alone this evening, and I would love to be with friends. I just hope I won't be a downer."

Grace had expected the Hargraves to invite her to dinner, but since they didn't, she thought the Conovers would be good company.

AS PROMISED, A CAR was waiting for Grace in Juneau to transport her to the airport. The driver didn't make conversation, and Grace thought maybe he didn't speak English. But he unloaded her luggage, took care of purchasing her ticket, and waited with her until she safely boarded the plane. In Seattle, Grace made her way to her connecting flight to LAX without incident. She didn't feel like eating or exchanging pleasantries with anyone. She wore dark glasses, stuck her face in a magazine, and hoped nobody would notice her. A chatty seatmate wouldn't mix well with her gray mood and periodic tears she'd feel obligated to explain. She felt almost like when she rode the Turnaround bus to Las Vegas, hopeless and sad. The movement of the baby inside her was her only distraction, and even that broke her heart. Going it alone frightened her.

When she arrived in LA, a porter retrieved both her luggage and Phil's and escorted her to the waiting limousine. She sat silently in the backseat with her head back and her eyes closed. *Lord, I've been so distraught I almost forgot you were there. I'm lost in sadness. I miss*

Phil so much. Will I ever love life again? Can you heal my broken heart? What will I do without Phil? Is he alive or dead? I need to know what happened to him.

MARILYN ATE HER SALAD and looked forward to the chocolate chip cookies and ice cream. "Do you think we did the right thing by staying on the ship?"

Sheldon's answer didn't surprise her because she knew how much he hated to waste money. "Phil paid for the whole thing out of the business money, so wouldn't he expect us to stay and enjoy it? It's our business, too."

"I'm not sure what he'd want, but I wanted to stay. We've got a couple of land tours coming up, and we couldn't have done anything to make things easier for Grace." Marilyn looked forward to going kayaking or canoeing. She loved any kind of outdoor sport.

"She said she didn't tell the captain about the stunt she pulled last summer when she ran off to Las Vegas," Sheldon remarked. "It just makes me wonder if she and Phil had really patched things up. Were they as happy as she said they were? If and when the captain questions us – and I bet he or someone will – I'm going to tell them about that charade. She cost us the biggest deal we ever had."

Marilyn set her fork down. "Can we please not talk anymore about business?"

"Okay. Besides, I talked to Grace, and she sincerely forgave me for my behavior and insisted we stay on the cruise. I don't know what else we could do anyway."

"That's right. So let's make the best of it and hope she gets the answers she needs about Phil."

CHAPTER 14

When Childers announced to Pete and LeRoy that he was letting them go, they were greatly relieved.

"Thank you so much," Pete said. "We sure were gettin' tired of starin' at those four cell walls."

Childers shrugged. "Don't think it's because I wanted to go easy on you. I just figured you'd already done your time for the car theft, and your crazy kidnapping scheme turned out to be a ruse that never came to pass, so as far as I'm concerned, you can walk."

Pete lit up a cigarette as soon as they got to the truck. "That's it! Ever' time we go to jail, I miss a meal or two. It ain't happenin' again."

"Yeah, well, this time was dumb. We didn't do nothin' bad." LeRoy accidentally spit his tobacco juice on the side of Pete's boot.

Pete reacted. "Ya stupid jackwagon. Ya better improve your aim. Don't be spittin' on me." He scuffed the side of his boot in the dirt. "We're startin' to look like crim'nals, and that ain't good. We gotta think of somethin' good to do to improve our image."

LeRoy shook his head. "How much better can we do than stoppin' to help a pregnant girl? And lookee where that got us."

Pete had an idea. "What if we took Grace Partain's license back to her? Childers must have forgotten to take it because it's still in the glove compartment." He hadn't thought like this before, but it sure seemed like a good idea now.

"Huh, that ain't a bad idea. Ya always get the good ideas, Pete, but can we wait until we can get some new clothes?"

Pete laughed. They hadn't owned new clothes since they were in high school, when they both asked girls to the senior prom and bought slightly-worn suits at the Barstow Community Thrift Shop. The boys borrowed money from LeRoy's mom, Mamie Ratcliff, to buy flowers and some burgers. They washed Pete's car and buffed out some of the rust to make it look better.

At the last minute, both girls backed out without explanation. LeRoy sat at home and cried all night. Pete spent the money on six burgers and ate them all. Neither of them had a date since or tried to get one.

"Who knows what might happen. Maybe Grace Partain'll be so touched she'll give us a reward." Pete took off his hat and scratched his head. "She don't know we tried to con her husband into paying a ransom for her. But new clothes is a great idea. Think your mom would spot us some cash?"

"Dang, Pete, Mom works too hard and she can barely pay the bills. Can't we just steal a car and make a few bucks?"

Pete swung his hat toward LeRoy's head and missed. "Oh, yeah, that'd sure be a great start to doin' somethin' good. No, you idiot! We'll just borrow some money from your mom. She's always a pushover."

"Oh, yeah, takin' advantage of my mom is okay, right?"

"We'll pay her back . . . some day."

LeRoy shrugged. "Let's see if she'll give us enough to buy some flowers."

GRACE ASKED THE DRIVER to take her home without stopping at the Troudes' house. She wasn't ready to face Sadie and her friends or feel excited about Sadie's new baby. Unpacking her bag would be mindless, but unpacking Phil's bag would be brutal. She couldn't bear to open it; it would break her heart. She pushed his bag, unopened, into the closet, lay down on his side of the bed, and cried into his pillow. As she rolled over, she could smell Phil . . . his hairspray, his aftershave . . . his life.

Grace called the Troudes and apologized to Nancy for holding off. "I just needed to be here by myself for a while. I wasn't ready to face everyone."

Nancy, always forgiving and sweet, responded, "Grace, we totally understand. I'll have John come over and pick you up. You can come have dinner with us, relax, and we'll do what we can to keep things low key."

"I can't stay alone forever," Grace conceded. "It'd be great to be with family, and you're my only family now." Her parents divorced when she was in fifth grade. Her father visited her for a few years and then disappeared out of her life. Her older sisters left home right out of high school, and her mother was busy working and dating a variety of losers. When Grace left home in Indiana, she vowed to get as far away as possible and not return. She looked for a father figure in Phil and a family, and now he was gone. The only family she claimed was the baby growing inside her, Sadie and her baby, and the Troudes.

When John arrived at the door, Grace fell into his arms. He didn't say anything, just held her quietly, waiting for her to speak.

When she finally did, her words were mixed with sobs and tears. "How could this happen? How could God let this happen? We were just going to start a new life together. Why?"

"I don't know the answer to that. I can't answer for God. I just know we have to trust Him."

"How will I ever face Sadie? I want to be thrilled about Angel, and yet my heart is breaking."

John smiled. "I guarantee you won't have to worry about it when you get there. One cooing sound from Angel and you won't have to conjure up a smile. You'll feel joy; take my word."

He was right. Sadie met Grace at the door, holding Angel in her arms. Grace could not contain herself. She took the baby into her own arms and smiled for the first time in three days. Angel became the center of a huge group hug.

"Tell me all about how this sweetheart came into the world. It sounds like a big surprise." Grace determined to keep her spirits up and not allow depression to spoil the evening. The subject of Phil's disappearance and/or death would come soon enough.

"Let's put the food on the table and pray, and then we can talk about Angel . . . and Phil." Nancy acted like an emcee when she entertained friends. She could move people smoothly from one activity to the next. "Let's keep the show going," she urged.

In minutes, Nancy had all the food on the table and everyone seated. Pastor Troude blessed the meal, thanked God for little Angel, and asked for comfort and peace for Grace. Sadie eagerly launched into her story and hardly touched her food. Grace moved hers around the plate and hardly tasted what she actually put in her mouth.

Sadie waved her arms as she told her animated and funny story, exaggerating every part of the event, especially the tow truck drivers. "Can you imagine two greasy tow truck drivers assisting a deputy sheriff and a highway patrolman deliver a baby on the seat of a rusted out old tow truck?" By the time she finished, they were all laughing and wiping tears away. Even Grace joined in.

"You should be a standup comic. You made me laugh like I haven't laughed in a week. I'm afraid my story doesn't have a happy ending, and there won't be tears of joy." Grace took a deep breath and told about Phil's absolute mysterious disappearance. "They recovered his shirt from the sea with a diamond ring in the pocket but nothing else." She paused. "They're still investigating, but I don't know what I'll do without Phil. I thought this baby brought new life to our marriage and that we shared the same excitement, and now it seems like a hopeless situation. Where's the joy without my husband?" She rested her palms warmly on her growing stomach. "It'll just be the two of us."

"No, no, no!" Sadie declared. "There'll be four of us – you, me, Angel, and Rumplestilskin." Everyone laughed through their tears.

Nancy spoke up then, and Grace knew she was trying to brighten the conversation. "The ring is a beautiful token of his love. He must have been planning to give it to you in a special way for your twentieth anniversary."

"Unfortunately they had to keep the ring until the investigation is over."

Pastor Troude spoke up. "This is truly a tragedy, and we can't explain it or understand it. People will tell you God's in control and we can't understand His plan, but that doesn't wipe away the sorrow. Others will even make suggestions about how to fill your time so you don't think about it, and that doesn't work either. You'll have to grieve in your own way. There are grief counselors, grief classes, grief books, and we're all here for you . . . whatever you need."

"But why would God let this happen?" Grace repeated, her tears flowing freely now.

"You may or may not understand that someday," the pastor said, "but for now you can ask Him, you can tell Him how angry you are, you can even tell Him off. God can take it. No matter how you go about it, you're still loved by Him and by all of us."

Grace took a long deep breath. She pushed away from the table, wiped her eyes with her napkin, and said, "Thank you, Nancy, for the nice meal. Sorry I couldn't eat much. And thank you, John, for your prayer and your kind and wise words." She fixed her eyes on Sadie. "Thank you for your amazing and entertaining story. I'm sure you'll tell it a million times through your life, and it'll get funnier every time. Now . . . can I just cuddle Angel for a few minutes?"

Sadie jumped up. "Sure, you hold her and chat with Nancy and John. I'll do the dishes and get our things together. John can move us all back home tonight, so you won't be alone."

It felt good to hear Sadie call the Partains' house her home. Grace would be glad to have Sadie for company and Angel to enjoy. Caring for her would be a wonderful distraction and put some joy in her aching heart.

Angel looked sleepy, but she went to Grace willingly. She felt warm against Grace's expanding belly. Grace wondered if her baby could sense the presence of another infant on the outside. She thought about how much fun it would be to have the two babies grow up together and be best friends forever. What stories they would tell!

THE NEXT DAY THERE was an extensive story in the Highland newspaper about the disappearance of Real Estate Broker Philip Partain from Highland. It had the details of the search and the discovery of the shirt but nothing about the ring.

Several reporters called the Partain home hoping to talk to Grace in order to add to their stories, but she refused. "Sadie, could you act as my advocate for a while and take the calls?" Grace asked. "Either ask them not to call again or take a message. I can't even leave the house without being accosted by reporters." She peeked between the curtains. "Look at all of them out there. If you wouldn't mind, take my car and go for groceries. When you pull out in the street, tell them I won't be making any statements and ask them to go away, please. I'll stay with Angel."

Grace accepted calls from her teacher friends Fran, Janine, and Carol. Janine had planned the cruise for the Partains and Hargraves, so her conversation covered everything from how the crew treated Grace before and after the accident to the systematic onboard search.

She even asked questions about the search at sea and if Grace had observed any of that process.

"Oh, Grace, I never expected anything like this to happen," she said. "I almost feel responsible in some way, but I know that's not realistic."

"You know, Janine, right now I'm not blaming anyone because I have no idea who to blame. It certainly wouldn't be you. Maybe it's best I don't know, but my mind just won't quit trying to figure it out."

Every day there were requests for interviews, appointments with investigators, calls from friends, and sympathy cards. Sadie finally put a sign on the front door that said, "Baby Sleeping. Please do not disturb." She wanted to write in bold letters, GO AWAY! But Grace wouldn't let her.

CHAPTER 15

Pete and LeRoy played pool and drank beer regularly at Buford's Bar in Barstow. If they had any money at all, that's where it got spent. Tonight was no exception. Pete had been the first to suggest going to Buford's, but he wasn't surprised when LeRoy readily agreed.

"Hey, look here." The owner stood behind the bar reading the newspaper. "Remember that woman who was missing after the bus wreck last summer? I can't remember how it all turned out, but she got rescued and went home to Highland." He waited for listeners to recall the event. "Anyway, she and her husband, Philip Partain, were on a cruise ship to Alaska, and the husband disappeared. Isn't that somethin'? They don't know what happened to him, but he's assumed dead at sea. Hmm."

Pete heard the name Partain and perked right up. His brain shifted into second gear, which didn't amount to much. "Hey, LeRoy, let's go out to the truck for a minute."

"No way, Pete. I'm winnin' this game, and I ain't leavin'."

As LeRoy bent over the pool table to take a shot, Pete pulled off his cap and swatted LeRoy on the side of his head.

LeRoy was none too happy. "Dang, Pete, why'd ya do that? Ya made me miss my shot!" Pete wasn't up to patience at the moment. "Outside . . . *now!*" he growled. Pete had always been the boss and didn't give LeRoy much chance to make up his own mind. LeRoy leaned the pool stick against the table and followed him. When they reached the truck, Pete looked around to make sure there wasn't anyone in the parking lot that might hear them.

"What's so danged important?" LeRoy demanded.

Pete's plans were typically impromptu, unrefined, and usually resulted in trouble or jail time. This time he hoped for better results. "Here's our chance to do something good."

"I haven't asked my mom about borrowing money for clothes yet, if that's what this is all about . . . ," LeRoy said.

"Yeah, well, we'll figure that out later. Here's the deal. Did you hear what Buford said about Grace Partain's husband disappearin' from a cruise ship? If they ain't found him by now, he's dead, right? So we'll show up for Mr. Partain's funeral, take some flowers, and give Mrs. Partain back her driver's license. Wouldn't that be nice?"

"But she don't know us."

"Don't ya see how that would look in the papers? In fact, we could skip the new clothes. Just think of it. Two poor tow truck drivers who found Grace's license last summer have traveled all the way from Barstow to pay their respects, return the license, and maybe receive a reward."

"But she don't know the whole story."

"Don't ya get it? It's a human-interest story. It's like when someone finds a letter that belonged to someone fifty years ago, and it finally gets delivered. Stories like that always make the newspaper. People love that stuff. We might get a little famous even."

LeRoy grinned, and Pete got a warm, fuzzy feeling just thinking about what a nice thing they were going to do.

MEMORIAL ARRANGEMENTS were difficult for Grace. She felt certain she needed to set the date for a couple of days after the Hargraves' return. She thought Sheldon would want to speak. Pastor Troude would do the service, and Nancy could help plan the details. It seemed strange to have a memorial service for a missing person, but everyone else believed there were too many clues that determined his death. Waiting, wondering, and lingering would only make it more painful. Maybe this would bring some closure.

She hadn't heard a word from the Hargraves, but a ship-to-shore call wasn't something she expected. When they did arrive home, Sheldon called immediately to find out the details.

"Yes, Grace, of course, I'll be glad to speak," he said when she asked. "I've been thinking about it ever since you left the ship."

"So how was the rest of the cruise?" Grace felt obligated to ask, though she really didn't care to know.

"Pretty hard to enjoy anything, knowing Phil was gone. I wanted to call it quits and come home when you did, but Marilyn insisted we carry on. She thought Phil would have wanted it that way."

"That's okay," Grace agreed. "We all grieve and adjust in our own ways." She said it because Pastor Troude said it, but she wasn't sure how much of it she believed.

"Marilyn got so angry when the ship's security officers came around after you left."

Grace perked up. "Why? What did they want?"

"They interrogated us for three hours. They even took swabs of our mouths for DNA."

"What? They couldn't possibly think you had anything to do with Phil's disappearance. I'm so sorry about that."

"Maybe it is just normal procedure. They probably don't have a death onboard or overboard very often and have to err on the side of caution. They weren't rude about it, but we were surprised."

Grace's curiosity was running full-tilt now. "I wonder if they did that to all the passengers. I mean, they're working at a disadvantage because in a few days all those hundreds of passengers disembark and go their separate ways. How in the world would they ever keep track of them if it was a crime situation?"

GRACE OPTED FOR A SIMPLE memorial service outside at the cemetery. Because Phil's body had not been recovered, she had a plaque put at the gravesite. The service went smoothly. Pastor Troude gladly officiated. Besides marrying her and Phil twenty years earlier, he and Phil had become very close.

Sheldon gave a heart-wrenching speech and recalled all the victories he and Phil experienced together, from high school football to real estate sales. "Phil became my hero in high school, and every success I ever had since then I owe to him."

At the end Pastor Troude talked about the saving grace of Jesus and invited anyone who wanted to say the sinner's prayer and accept Jesus as Savior to come forward for prayer.

LEROY AND PETE WENT to the Salvation Army store and bought some new used clothes that were close to their sizes. LeRoy's sleeves were too short, and Pete couldn't get his jacket buttoned around his belly. Their grease-stained caps topped off their strange outfits. They didn't get to Highland in time for the service but arrived just as people were beginning to leave.

Pete was getting nervous. "Dang, LeRoy, looks like we almost missed it. Can you see Mrs. Partain?" They skulked around behind the people until they could see Grace seated in the front by the gravesite.

They spotted people filing by her, as she sat between a red-headed woman and a couple, none of whom Pete or LeRoy recognized. At the tail end of the line, Pete pushed LeRoy up first.

"Ma'am, we're so sorry your husband jumped off that ship," LeRoy mumbled just before Pete slapped him in the back of the head.

"LeRoy didn't mean that, ma'am," he said quickly. "We're just sorry about whatever made him die."

Grace's mouth dropped open, and a look of horror crossed her face. Pete wondered if he too might have said the wrong thing.

"AND HOW DID YOU KNOW my husband?" Grace asked, trying to control her anger.

Pete and LeRoy looked at each other, obviously searching for an answer. Finally Pete blurted out, "We didn't really know him. We just read about him in the newspaper. But we found something of yours last summer and wanted to give it back to you."

"What's that?"

Pete dug around in his pocket and pulled out the driver's license, then held it out to her.

"My driver's license? Where on earth . . . ?" Grace hesitated and then accepted the dirty license, turning it over in her hand.

Sadie lifted her head with a jerk and widened her eyes. "Are you kidding me? You're the two tow truck guys! Grace, these are the guys who stopped to help me on the freeway." Sadie jumped to her feet and hugged Pete and then LeRoy.

Grace gasped. "Wait . . . these are the guys?"

"Yes," Sadie said, smiling at them. "I thought they went to jail."

Grace was taken aback by their ill-fitting clothes, oil-stained hands, and uncouth behavior.

"Oh no, that was just a misunderstandin'" Pete said. "That Officer Childers was glad to hear we were gonna return the license."

"I never got to thank you for letting me use your tow truck for a delivery room." Sadie giggled.

"And we were thinkin', if there's a reward . . ."

"Shut up, LeRoy," Pete cut in. "Don't mind him. We're just here out of the goodness of our hearts. We don't need nothin' in return." Pete tipped his greasy baseball cap, and dust flew off.

Apparently LeRoy wasn't finished. "But, Pete, I thought you said this would be like a interestin' 'humane story,' and it would be in the papers."

Pete slapped LeRoy in the back of his head again, obviously annoyed with his friend.

Grace was still puzzled over the driver's license and their connection with Sadie.

"Don't mind him," the one named Pete said. "I don't know where he gets these crazy ideas."

Grace didn't know what to think of the two men. Were they for real? Pushing the thought aside and knowing it was time to move on, she stood up and started to walk toward the cars. Everyone followed. Sadie, LeRoy, and Pete chatted away about their meeting on the desert. "Listen, fellas," Sadie said. "You were kind to me when I needed help. How about coming to church when we have Angel dedicated? You did have a hand in her birth."

LeRoy kicked the dirt and Pete stammered, "We ain't never . . . I mean we don't . . . well, I guess we could. "

LeRoy added, "The church won't fall down, will it? My mama always said it'd fall down if she walked in."

Sadie giggled again. "No, it won't fall down. I promise."

"What's a dedication, anyways?" Pete asked. "I called the radio station and dedicated a song to a girl once, but that didn't turn out too good. She stood me up for the prom."

"Oh, that's terrible," Sadie said. "But this kind of dedication is a little different. The child is presented to the church, and the parents and the people make a promise to raise her in the Christian tradition," Sadie explained.

"Would it be a 'good' thing if we come?" LeRoy asked.

"It would be a real good thing," Sadie said and gave each of them another hug.

So arrangements were made for them to attend the dedication. Grace thanked them for coming and returning the license but wondered if Sadie had made a wise decision by inviting them to come back. And how they had possession of her license was still a mystery.

CHAPTER 16

When summer vacation ended, Grace didn't have it in her to go back to school, so she took a leave of absence. Paperwork regarding Phil's supposed death mounted daily. Life insurance, the real estate business, working with estate trustees, and taking Phil's name off of documents was tedious. In fact, it was overwhelming. Everyone assumed Philip Partain was dead except Grace. She held on to a glimmer of hope that somewhere, somehow, sometime soon, he would show up.

Sheldon went right back to work, and according to what Grace heard, with great determination. He had never given up on the Wilburn deal and worked hard to reestablish their relationship. Grace wondered if Phil would have agreed with his tactics, but she wasn't privy to his private dealings, so she just hoped for the best.

"Well, Grace," Sheldon said to her one day, "I just added another million to the coffers. I don't know if you realize what a rich lady you are with half of this business."

Grace found herself constantly confronted with money matters she had never dealt with before – more money than she could imagine. It frightened her to have so much responsibility. In the past Phil took care of all their finances and bills. She hardly had to write a check and did most of her business by credit card, which he paid each month. Now paying bills and keeping track of expenses kept her awake at night, even though she had more than enough money.

"Sheldon, I simply don't know how to make decisions regarding money. Phil always took care of that. I'd like to have you buy me out, and I'll retire from teaching. I'm going to have my hands full with the baby and managing our household. I have so much to do with Phil gone."

"I can't buy you out completely," he said, "but I can pay you enough so you'll be comfortable and give you a percentage of future sales until I can pay off the rest."

Grace nodded. "I'll have my own retirement someday, but that's a long way off. With only twenty years of teaching, it won't be much, so that sounds like a perfect deal for both of us."

When Grace's leave was up, she decided to retire altogether. The money Sheldon gave her would supply all her needs abundantly.

ADMINISTRATION RECEIVED Grace's resignation without resistance. She had given everything she had to teaching and earned the respect of all the teachers and administrators, and she knew they wanted the best for her. With the loss of her husband and the coming baby, they understood her life had changed drastically and would require her full attention. Janine, Fran, and Carol made sure the staff had a pregnant/retirement party and made it a lot of fun. Grace, her heart still heavy, enjoyed it as best she could, though she could see the men hated it. With a little prodding from Fran, they participated grudgingly.

Grace appreciated all the work the women had done, decorating with yellow and green balloons and planning silly games. They had soaked the labels off baby food jars and had everyone taste and guess what food was inside. Grace's classroom aide brought notes of congratulations from Grace's students and suggestions for baby names, both boys' and girls'. They got some great laughs.

All in all it was a lovely gesture, but Grace was more than ready to go home when the party ended. "Thank you so much – all of you – for honoring me in this way. I'll miss you, but I'll bring the baby by when Mergatroid, Methusaleh, or Whatshername is born." They all laughed at the way she had incorporated some of the funny names the kids had suggested.

SADIE WAS PROUD OF Grace, who had fired the landscaper as her first independent household decision. He had let the yard get completely out of control and only showed up sporadically. Then she asked Fran and Janine if either of them used a good lawn service or landscaper. Fran promised to send over her guy.

The next day Sadie heard a gentle knock at the door. Grace had gone shopping, so Sadie answered. Breathless, as a result of her dash from the nursery to the front door, she didn't bother to look through the peek hole.

"Uh, hello." Sadie was shocked to meet face-to-face with a handsome young man with wavy black hair, tanned skin, brown luminous eyes, and a dimpled smile.

"Hi. Are you Mrs. Partain?"

Sadie laughed and caught her breath.

"No, I'm Sadie McClarron, but this is Grace Partain's home."

"I'm Blaine Markem. Fran sent me over. She said Mrs. Partain needed a new gardener, and I have an opening in my schedule."

"Want to come in and wait for her?" As soon as the words came out of her mouth, she thought, *What in the world am I doing inviting a perfect stranger into the house?* Maybe *perfect* was the opporitive word. He couldn't have known how much Sadie hoped he would accept.

"I can't." He looked almost as disappointed as Sadie felt. Or was it wishful thinking on her part? "I've got a class at Cal State San

Bernardino," he said, "and I don't want to be late. Can I just leave my business card? She can call me, and we can figure out which day works best for her."

Sadie took the card and read aloud, "Blaine Markem." She looked up and smiled. "I'll give it to Grace."

"Thanks, Sadie." He grinned again and hopped off the porch. Halfway down the sidewalk, he stopped and turned back. "Miss Sadie, if she hires me, will you be here again?"

Sadie responded quickly. "Yes. I live here."

"Great. Then I hope you'll put in a good word for me, and I'll see you again." He headed for his vehicle.

"Blaine?" she called after him. He stopped again and looked back. "Even if she doesn't hire you, I'll be here."

He waved, smiled with full dimples, and nodded his head in agreement.

Sadie, shocked at her forwardness, felt her face turn fire red.

She hadn't met anyone that made her heart go pit-a-pat since Scott. Not until now anyway. She watched Blaine get into his pickup truck and drive away. Leaning against the door, fanning herself, she prayed Grace would hire him.

———⊙⊙———

AS GRACE'S PREGNANCY advanced, so did the mammoth pile of paperwork and disagreements with Sheldon over the business. Phil was never out of her mind, and she called the cruise company every few days in hopes they had found another clue.

As it turned out Grace hired Blaine, and she sensed Sadie was pleased. He always seemed to finish his work about dinnertime when Sadie was busy helping Grace with dinner or changing Angel's diaper. On his third visit, Sadie asked if she could invite him for dinner.

Of course Grace agreed, but she noticed Sadie seemed a bit hesitant.

"Everything okay?" she asked.

Sadie appeared surprised at the question, then nodded. "I'm fine," she said. "Just wondered about . . ." She took a deep breath. "I'm just wondering how I should introduce Angel to Blaine. I mean, I know shes' still a baby, but I think it's important to get off on the right foot."

Grace nodded. "True, though I can't imagine our little Angel will wonder who he is. So why are you concerned?"

"I guess the real problem is what to tell Blaine about Angel. At first glance he'll undoubtedly figure out I'm a single Mom. But . . ."

Grace reached across the table and laid her hand on Sadie's. "Stop worrying. It'll all work out just fine."

Later that day, as Blaine worked in the yard, Grace encouraged Sadie to accompany her to the patio and to bring Angel along. The moment Blaine caught sight of them, he grinned and came right over to the patio.

"Okay, and who is this little miss?"

"This is my daughter, Angel," Sadie said, her cheeks turning rosy.

"She's a cutie. I'd hold her if I wasn't covered with dirt and grass."

"Maybe when you're done," Sadie said. "Can you stay for dinner?"

Blaine hesitated briefly, then nodded, his warm smile broader than ever. "Sure." He looked toward Grace. "That is, if you don't mind if I clean up in your bathroom when I'm done."

Grace smiled. "I wouldn't mind a bit. Looking forward to having you join us this evening. It'll be nice to have a man at the table."

THE EVENING WENT SO well that Blaine quickly became a dinner guest whenever he came to do Grace's yardwork. It was obvious he loved Angel and would hold her and talk baby talk to her while Sadie and Grace prepared dinner.

"If I ever hope to be married," Sadie whipered, "I'd better learn how to cook something besides macaroni and cheese."

Grace whispered back, thinking the reason for whispering was so Blaine didn't hear Sadie mention marriage. "I can teach you." Carrying the food to the table, they giggled at their little secret.

"Blaine, where did you grow up?" Grace asked, later as they were enjoying a light dessert. She felt obligated to learn more about him if he had designs on Sadie. She could already see that Sadie had designs on him.

"I grew up in the San Joaquin Valley. It's a long drive, so I don't go home often. With my lawn business and studies, I don't have much time off, but I miss my family."

Grace liked that he was so industrious. Sometimes he'd bring his books to study after dinner. Grace could tell Sadie loved to hear him talk about the theater and his hopes of getting into TV production. One night, however, as Grace lingered at the table while Blaine and Sadie cleaned up in the kitchen, she heard Blaine clear his throat and ask, "Sadie, how did you end up as a single mom living with Grace? You don't have to tell me if you don't want to, but I'd like to know."

Sadie told him the whole story about her family, the dark time in her life, hitchhiking to Las Vegas, and Scott' death. She also told him how she and Grace ended up being friends and escaping danger together.

"Wow! You women are lucky to be alive. And I'm lucky I found you."

Though Grace couldn't see them, she heard the emotion in his voice, and she knew Blaine was indeed beginning to care deeply about Sadie and Angel.

Grace quietly left the table and went to her room to give them privacy. She knew Sadie was crazy about Blaine, even though she tried not to show it. Grace chuckled to herself because she had noticed Sadie had put on full make-up and her fake eyelashes before Blaine arrived.

WITH GRACE AT HOME to help care for Angel, Sadie got a part-time job as a waitress. It was a nice place and she made good money in tips, but Grace wouldn't let her pay rent. Sadie wanted to do her part by chipping in on groceries, helping out with the cooking as her skills improved, and doing what she could around the house.

One night, dinner seemed different. Blaine was usually chatty and full of life, but he ate quietly and seemed pensive. After they cleaned up the dishes, Grace went to her bedroom to watch TV.

"Sadie, the next time you have a night off, do you think Grace would mind if I took you out to dinner and a movie?" Blaine had taken so long to ask, Sadie had given up hope and thought maybe he only wanted to be friends and get free meals.

"I know she wouldn't mind, but I'll ask her." She didn't waste any time and went right into the bedroom to ask Grace. Grinning from ear to ear, she posed the question.

"Blaine has asked me to go to a movie and dinner next time I get a night off. Would you be okay with babysitting Angel?"

"I guess you know the answer is yes, of course. Angel and I will be just fine." Grace gave her a big hug. "And when will that be?"

"I'll ask the boss for a night off as soon as possible," she said with a giggle.

Sadie nearly danced back into the room to Blaine. "She said yes, I say yes, and when the boss says yes, you've got a date! I feel like a little kid asking for permission to go have an ice cream cone."

Blaine pulled Sadie into his arms and held her close while she submitted to the comfort of his embrace.

CHAPTER 17

"When are we dedicating that little Angel of yours?" Pastor Troude inquired of Sadie one Sunday as they exited the church.

"We could do it any time, but wouldn't it be cool if we wait until Grace's baby is born and dedicate them both in the same service? We, two single moms and our babies, would kinda be like a family up there together. What do you think?"

The pastor smiled. "I think that's a wonderful idea. And I'm sure Grace will agree. She's supposed to deliver in December, so we'll plan to do it in January. How about that? I'm hoping to see you bring that young man you've been seeing to Sunday service."

Sadie hadn't wanted to push, but every day she thought of inviting Blaine to church. She needed to know a little more about his intentions and beliefs before that happened. What were his thoughts about a future with a single mom? If he wasn't serious about a future, then she would have to cut him loose, and that would be painful. They had grown close over the weeks and enjoyed each other's company, not to mention how attached Angel had become to Blaine and looked forward to his visits.

One night after dinner Grace took Angel to bed while Blaine and Sadie took their iced lemonade and went out on the patio. Before Sadie could bring up the subject, Blaine blurted out, "Could you see me being a father to Angel?" Sadie felt her eyes widen and her heart jump for joy.

"Wow! Is that a proposal?" She jumped into his arms and burrowed her red curls into his chest.

Blaine laughed. "Hey, wait a minute. I only asked. Don't get ahead of me. It could have been a hypothetical question."

Sadie felt the red flush come from her neck to her face. "I guess I jumped the gun. Sorry. But I've been wanting to ask you how you felt about dating an unwed mother."

"I haven't been coming over here or asking you out because I like macaroni and cheese," he chuckled, "or because I like to keep an eye on the lawns I mow. I love you, and I've thought a lot about what it'd be like to be married to you with Angel as our starter child."

Sadie could not contain herself. She kissed Blaine with such passion it surprised them both. Then she pushed away, jumped up, and did a happy dance around the patio.

When she finished she said, "There's just one other thing I need to know. How do you feel about going to church? You know I'm a Christian." She hadn't forgotten the importance of her faith and marrying a man of like-mind.

"I know. I've thought about that, too. I grew up in a pretty strict Mennonite home, so I'm definitely a believer. I just couldn't keep all the requirements of that faith. I'm glad I grew up with the values and belief, but I need to get recharged. I wouldn't want to raise a child without a belief in Jesus."

Sadie felt like her heart would burst out of her chest and fly around the room with joy. "So you'll go with me?"

"Sure, but let me take it at my own pace. Okay?"

GRACE COULDN'T HELP but notice Blaine's pace for getting back into church was comparable to the rate at which he fell in love with Sadie. No hesitation, full-steam ahead. By November, they were both involved in practicing for the Christmas play. Blaine rehearsed the part of Joseph, and Sadie accepted the part of Mary. Angel played the baby Jesus. She didn't have much hair yet, so the audience wouldn't be able to distinguish between a darling little girl or a darling little Messiah. Grace was especially pleased that Sadie and Blaine were going to Pastor Troude for pre-marital counseling, and also getting connected with other couples their age.

Grace waddled around wondering why she was so happy about being pregnant last summer. Her life had changed so much since then. A rich widow with a big belly seemed ridiculous now. She had finally parted company with Sheldon and was financially independent even though he agreed to keep giving her a percentage of new sales.

Sadly, there were no answers about Phil's disappearance, and she quietly grieved her loss and worried about the future.

THE NIGHT OF THE CHRISTMAS program, Grace felt physically miserable, but she dragged herself to the church anyway. She couldn't miss seeing Sadie, Blaine, and Angel in the pageant.

The choir sang, and Pastor Troude read the Christmas story.

Mary entered alone and looked around innocently. As the story began, an angel appeared from off stage.

"God sent the angel Gabriel to Nazareth," the pastor read, "a town in Galilee, to a virgin pledged to be married to a man named Joseph, a descendant of David. The virgin's name was Mary. The angel went to her and said, 'Greetings, you who are highly favored!'"

He went on with the story, then the lights went out for a few moments. When they came back on, Joseph and Mary stood over Angel, who was swaddled in a blue blanket in the manger. Grace thought her heart would burst with so many emotions: love, pride, grief, and sorrow all at the same time. Meanwhile, the pain in her back elevated until she could hardly sit.

The wise men entered as the pastor continued reading. "And they came with haste, and found Mary, and Joseph, and the babe lying in a manger."

Grace thought Mary and Joseph looked at each other with a heavenly spark, and she smiled in spite of the pain in her back. "They brought gifts of gold, frankincense, and myrrh and bowed down and worshiped him, Christ the Lord." The wise men went through the motions and knelt.

The play ended with the congregation standing to sing "Hark the Herald Angels Sing." Everyone clapped and cheered. Suddenly Joseph turned and motioned for Pastor Troude to hand him the microphone.

"Please be seated," Blaine said to the audience. The congregation murmured among themselves as they sat down. Joseph wasn't expected to make an announcement. When it got quiet, he kneeled in front of Mary, who was now holding Angel in her arms.

"Mary – Sadie McClarron – will you marry me?"

The whole church broke into cheers and clapping. Sadie turned away, settled Angel in the manger, dropped to her knees, wrested the microphone from "Joseph" and said, "Yes, yes, yes!" Again the congregation filled the church with wild cheers.

The Christmas reception in the community hall seemed more like an engagement party. Everyone congratulated the young couple while they enjoyed refreshments and hot cocoa.

By that time, Grace was experiencing what she thought was false labor and asked Blaine if he would drive them all home in her car. He agreed, and she climbed into the backseat and lay down.

When they arrived home the recording machine flashed a red light, indicating someone had left a message. Grace was in such pain she could hardly stand up long enough to retrieve it.

"This is Sergeant Collins calling from Wrangell, Alaska," the voice said. "I'm trying to reach Mrs. Philip Partain. It's of utmost importance. Please call me at . . ." and he left his number.

It was after ten o'clock, and Grace couldn't handle returning a call. *What on earth could he be calling about? I didn't even get off the ship in Wrangell.*

Sadie and Blaine were putting Angel to bed and hadn't heard the message, so Grace thought she'd keep it to herself until she heard more. She certainly didn't want to spoil their high-spirited evening. They were probably necking crib-side as they rocked Baby Jesus to sleep.

A SCREAM FROM THE KITCHEN brought Sadie to a shocked wakefulness. She jumped out of bed thinking Grace had fallen, given birth in the kitchen, or was fighting off an intruder. She ran through the house without a robe or slippers. "Grace? Grace? Where are you?"

Sadie found her slumped in a pile on the kitchen floor, screaming at the top of her lungs. Sadie knelt beside her, patted her on the back, and tried to console her.

"Grace. Grace! What's wrong? Are you okay? Please tell me how I can help."

"No, no, no! It can't be!" The phone lay on the floor beside her. She picked up the receiver and threw it against the refrigerator. Her body shook with every sob.

"Come on, Grace. Tell me . . ."

Grace seemed unable to formulate a sentence. She tore at her hair and screamed, "This can't be! No, no, no! I don't believe it!" Her hysteria could not be quelled.

Sadie sat all the way down on the floor and put her arms around Grace, but she lost her balance, and the two of them tumbled over and sprawled out on the tile.

"Please, Grace. Let me help you."

Grace's tears mixed with the mucus from her nose as she wailed. When she finally cried herself out, silence surrounded the two women as they lay panting quietly in each other's arms.

"They found Phil's body in a container in the town of Wrangell where we made our second stop on the cruise," she finally whispered.

"How do they know?"

"He had no shirt, but his wallet was still in his pants pocket."

"Oh, Grace. That's horrible. How in the world did he end up there?"

"I don't know. We didn't even get off the ship there. And the cruise employees said he never left the ship."

The news seemed ludicrous to Sadie, and she could only imagine how it must seem to Grace. "That's crazy."

Grace nodded. "This'll rev up the investigation, and they'll be questioning me again, and probably everyone in that little town. I don't know how they'll question the hundreds of employees and guests from the cruise ship."

―――― ⚜ ――――

WHEN GRACE HAD COMPOSED herself, she called Sergeant Collins back for more information.

"We're a very small department," he explained. "There's just two of us here, and we don't have the tools to do much more than what we've done."

"So how will you figure out how he died and who did this?" Grace could feel her mind creating horrible pictures of what he must look like after four months in a container.

"Ma'am, I doubt if we can do that. It does look like someone hit him over the head with a heavy instrument. But other than that, we turned over our findings to the cruise line and the F.B.I."

Grace began to tremble. "What kind of a container was it?"

"It was a large plastic container that cruise ships often use to carry life jackets or supplies on and off the ship. Whoever did it put a tarp over the container and shoved it behind a building near the dock. It just didn't get noticed until a couple of days ago."

Grace couldn't control the shaking. "What happens now?"

"Identifying the body is the extent of our ability here, and his wallet made that easy. I'm so sorry for your loss. A medical examiner from Juneau came down to help with the investigation. We contacted the FBI, and they'll be in contact with you when the body's released."

"How does . . . what do I . . ." Grace tried to keep from sobbing, but she couldn't get control. She handed the phone to Sadie.

"Ask them how we . . . get Phil back here." Grace's voice cracked as she spoke.

"Hello, Sir, this is her . . . daughter . . . friend . . . . She needs to know how to get Phil's body back to California."

Sadie listened for quite a while, asked a few more questions, thanked the man, and hung up.

"When they're done with all of their investigation," Sadie explained, "and the body's released, you'll be contacted. You can have it transported to a local mortuary at your expense, or you can have them transport it to Ketchikan where there's a crematorium. They can send you the ashes. You don't have to think about it yet."

The room was still, but Grace's heart raced. She could feel it pounding and hear her ears ringing over the sound of the clock ticking in the living room. The thought of Phil being left in a box sickened her, and she felt the bile coming up in her throat.

When she had pulled herself together, Grace called Sheldon to tell him about the discovery. Both of them had given up hope of Phil's body being found. Their conversation was brief, and Grace imagined it was because they had to completely readjust their thinking about the crime and each other. Words just couldn't make sense of it. She knew they both had questions that couldn't be answered.

Sheldon had, in fact, asked a few right before hanging up. "Who would have killed him? And how? How would they have transported him to shore without anyone knowing about it?" Grace, of course, was unable to answer. They were both left with more questions than before.

"I'm so sorry, Grace," Sheldon said just before hanging up. "This doesn't make it any easier."

"No, I think it's worse. I'd almost accepted that he might have fallen overboard by accident, but to think someone purposely murdered him seems even more horrible."

WHEN THE FBI CALLED a few days later to discuss getting Phil's body released, Grace made arrangements to have it sent to the morgue in San Bernardino where she could come and identify it. As much as she hated the idea, she needed to see for herself in order to believe the report.

Grace called the Conovers in Branson. They had kept in touch and asked Grace to keep them up-to-date if anything changed. They exchanged brief greetings, and Grace continued. "They found Phil's body in a carton in Wrangell."

Grace heard Clarise moan, but she went on. "I just talked to Sheldon, and all we could do was ask one question after another. Who did this? How did they do it? How did they get him into the port?"

Silence, and then Clarise gasped. "Oh, my goodness, Grace. Wrangell was the second place we stopped, right? Remember when we went down to the place where people were checking through with their keycard to go ashore?"

"Sort of. By that time the worry had me so frazzled I couldn't think straight."

"Remember how the line got all backed up? A couple of deck hands were rolling a big heavy container down the gangplank, and they made all of us wait." She hesitated. "I can't believe I'm thinking and saying this, but I wonder if Phil was in that container."

Grace caught her breath. In her mind's eye she could now see the two men struggling to roll that heavy black trunk down the ramp. Guests were getting impatient, and she anxiously spoke to the steward about Phil's disappearance. He made a dumb joke about maybe he jumped overboard, so the container didn't get a second thought.

"Could we have been looking right at Phil's coffin?" Grace was horrified, and her gut tied in knots as her baby kicked furiously from inside.

"What about this? If he *was* in the trunk, how did his shirt get in the water?" Clarise asked.

More questions....

CHAPTER 18

On Christmas Day Miss Partain, a baby girl, came into the world without fanfare. Complications necessitated the baby be delivered by an emergency cesarean.

Grace lay quietly waiting for the doctor to come in to see her. She expected to have her baby brought to her by now, but the doctor came in empty-handed.

"Grace, the cesarean went well, but your baby is struggling." He looked at her chart, but Grace felt sure he knew what was on the chart and was stalling as he figured out what to say next. "There is a condition called placental hemangioma."

Before he could finish Grace interrupted. "That sounds awful. What does it mean?" *Oh, please, Lord, don't let this be something serious.*

The doctor went on. "It's a rare condition where the blood veins to the placenta are tangled and the baby's heart has to beat too hard to get nourishment. It has left her very weak and her heart is enlarged. She is holding her own, and we are doing everything we can." He patted Grace's hand. "Do you have any questions?"

Grace wanted to ask the doctor if he thought her baby would live, but she was afraid the answer would be too difficult to hear. Her voice cracked as she whispered, "Can I see her?" She tried to hold back the tears, but they were demanding freedom.

"Of course. I'll have a nurse come and help you walk down to the NICU (neonatal intensive care unit). You can see her through the glass." He tapped the end of the bed as he left, as if to signal the visit was over.

As soon as Grace could get out of bed, she walked down the hallway to look through the glass at her baby. She desperately wanted to hold the infant, but tubes and electrodes made it impossible to take her from the incubator. Day after day the baby remained dependent on life support, and everyone prayed.

Grace would not leave the hospital. When Blaine could be available to watch Angel, Sadie went to the hospital to beg Grace to come home for a rest. She refused and slept in a recliner the nurses fixed up for her with sheets, blankets, and a pillow.

"I'm naming her Philisity Noel," she announced to Sadie, "after Philip and Christmas."

"That's a cool name," Sadie said, trying to sound encouraging.

"The Book of Names says Philisity means good fortune[1] and happiness," Grace told her. "A beautiful girl who is very high energy[2] and knows what to say to make you laugh and smile." She forced a smile she knew was weak and hoped it covered the pain in her heart. But it couldn't stop the tears that spilled over and down her cheeks. "It also says she has many friends but yet is very independent. She's poised but loves a good fight[3]." The words had no sooner left her mouth than Grace put her hands over her face and broke down in sobs.

It was a grim beginning and a fight Philisity could not win. She clung to life for eight days, but no amount of medical science could save her. When the doctor gave the sad news that Philisity had lost the battle, Sadie stood silently holding Grace steady.

"No, no, no," Grace wailed, her heart breaking yet again. "First Phil, and now my darling baby girl. It can't be. I can't bear it."

---

1. https://www.urbandictionary.com/define.php?term=fortune
2. https://www.urbandictionary.com/define.php?term=high%20energy
3. https://www.urbandictionary.com/define.php?term=good%20fight

ONLY BLAINE, SADIE, Angel, and Pastor and Mrs. Troude attended the brief funeral service. John said a few words and committed Philisity to Heaven because Grace wanted it that way.

No amount of love or support consoled her. She pulled the curtains, made the house as dark as possible, curled up on the sofa in the fetal position, and refused to eat or talk. She knew Sadie and Blaine wanted to help, but no doubt, didn't know what to do. They took Angel out in the stroller in order to keep the house quiet. When they were in the house, they tip-toed around as if on eggshells.

Grace's heart was broken and her head reeling. *God, why would you do this? You couldn't be the God I've loved and I thought loved me. What about all your promises to love me and keep me and bless me abundantly? What happened to all that? Here's Sadie, an unwed mother, and you've blessed her with a beautiful baby and a fiancé who loves her dearly. You've taken everything from me. How can I praise you or trust you?*

PASTOR TROUDE HAD TRIED to contact Grace, but Sadie always answered, and Grace refused to come to the phone. After the pastor's most recent – and rejected – call, Sadie and Blaine were worried.

"We have to get her out of this depression," Blaine said. "It's unhealthy and a little scary. Isn't there something you can think of that might cheer her up?"

Sadie shook her head, discouraged. "No, it just gets worse. Now she's locked in her bedroom and won't come out. Today an investigator called to tell her they'd pulled two or three samples of DNA off of the corpse, which confirms Phil's identity. When I told her, she just started crying again and slammed the door to her bedroom. I'm really worried about her."

"Me, too. I thought they'd already made a positive ID. Were they just confirming his identity, or did they have DNA of others? If so I wonder when the DNA testing will be complete."

"I think he said they were trying to make a match, but they didn't know anything yet. He said they'll call us when there's more information."

"I wonder if Grace would pull out of her funk if you asked her to help with our wedding," Blaine suggested. "She used to put all kinds of events together at the school, right?"

Sadie brightened. "Yes, that's a great idea. I really do need her help."

Blaine shrugged. "Worse-case scenario, maybe she'd take care of Angel while you get things ready. I know she loves that baby."

Sadie liked that idea. "I'll try. I'll really try."

THE BAR WAS ALMOST deserted. Pete and LeRoy had just finished a game of pool and sat down in a booth to have a beer. Pete's throat was parched, and he imagined LeRoy's was as well.

The bartender called out, "D'you see the news? They found the body of that real estate guy from San Bernardino, or Highland or wherever, that fell off the cruise ship. Very weird. I wonder if someone shoved him."

Pete never read the paper, but Buford the owner/bartender kept them up-to-date on anything interesting.

Pete leaned in and spoke quietly to LeRoy. "That must be Mrs. Partain's husband. Poor lady. It's weird that we stopped to help that Sadie girl and turns out she lives with Mrs. Partain." The ash on Pete's cigarette dropped off on the table. "Makes me sad for her, but if her husband turned up alive, he might have asked questions about how we happened to have Grace's driver's license."

"Grace and Sadie and all them people was really nice to us," LeRoy said. "They even said we could come to the delegation of their babies."

"It's a dedication, stupid."

"Oh, yeah, dedication."

"I think I'll call her and see if she had a boy or a girl. That'll remind her we were invited, and maybe it'll cheer her up." Pete went to the pay phone at the far end of the bar, glad the girl named Sadie had given them the number.

"Hey, Pete," Sadie said when she answered the phone and he identified himself. "How have you been?"

"We're good. We just wanted to say hey."

"I'm glad you called. We're having Angel dedicated the second Sunday of January. Can you come?"

"What about Mrs. Partain? We saw in the news that her husband's body got found. Do they know who whacked him?" He fidgeted a bit while waiting for her answer.

"Not yet. They do have DNA samples to work with. It's all very sad. Grace is heartbroken and not doing well."

Pete had heard of DNA but didn't know much about it, so he decided to let that go. "What about the baby? Did she have a boy or a girl?"

"Pete, . . . she had a little girl, but . . . the baby didn't survive."

"Ahh, you mean she died?" Pete didn't know what else to say.

"She had a rare condition, and she just got weaker and weaker even though the doctors tried everything."

"That's terrible. We're sorry, but can we still come?" He and LeRoy hadn't been invited to anything since high school, and he didn't want to let this opportunity slip away. Their circle of friends consisted mostly of thieves and no-goods that hung out at Buford's Bar.

"Sure. Maybe that'll cheer up Grace."

Pete was surprised. He had the feeling Grace wasn't all that happy with them around. Maybe he was wrong. Either way he was determined to be at the baby event.

Sadie repeated the date and the address of the church. "You can join us for lunch afterward," she said.

Well, now, Pete thought, *this is getting better all the time.*

GRACE AGREED TO HELP with the wedding, but her heart and mind weren't in it. As hard as she tried, she constantly waited for the call that would uncover Phil's killer. If she wasn't thinking about that, she was thinking about Philisity. Grief clutched her heart in both cases. *How could you do this to me, Lord?*

Her experience as a teacher helped her plan and execute in spite of her dark mood. *One foot in front of the other* became her motto. She knew Sadie kept doling out tasks to keep her going, and she appreciated it.

The day of the wedding, Grace managed a smile and put on her makeup for the first time in weeks. She helped Sadie get dressed as if she were her daughter, and it made both of them smile. Sadie's joy and excitement were contagious and spilled over on everyone.

Sadie's friend Lianne drove down from Las Vegas, and Grace was happy to see her. They had worked together briefly in the casino during her crazy episode, and she knew Lianne would be a help to all of them.

When Lianne arrived, Grace ushered her into the room where Sadie was ready and waiting.

"Sadie, you look like a doll!" Lianne exclaimed, her face lighting up. "I'm so glad you invited me."

Grace held her breath as the two girls came together. She hoped Lianne would resist hugging Sadie, because she didn't want her to mess up her make-up or tug on the veil by accident. Lianne widely encircled Sadie with her arms, and without the slightest touch, gently kissed her on the cheek.

Sadie's dress was simple with a brocade bodice and satin skirt. The flowered halo sat on her long curly red hair with the short veil fluttering behind.

Lianne took charge of Angel, Nancy Troude took care of the flowers and set up for the reception, and Grace walked Sadie down the aisle. Blaine's tears and smile reflected the bride's beauty.

Fran, Janine, Carol, and many of Grace's teacher friends attended. Sadie invited her parents, but they evidently preferred to maintain their estrangement, which Grace could not understand but accepted. Blaine's parents, siblings, and a few friends came down from Fresno.

The Hargraves had RSVP'd they were coming, but at the last minute they left town, leaving a cryptic apology and something about an extended trip. They hadn't been any support to Grace through this difficult time except for a couple of brief calls to Sadie, voicing their condolences, concern, and asking about the investigation.

Pastor Troude officiated a beautiful, simple, and very personalized wedding for the two young adults, who Grace knew he hoped would flourish in their relationship as parents of Angel. When he pronounced them man and wife, Lianne brought Angel up and put her in Sadie's arms. The pastor followed with, "I now present to you the Blaine Markem family."

Everyone cheered and clapped. Truly a joyful occasion, and even Grace shook off the gloom and rejoiced for a while during the reception.

BLAINE MOVED INTO GRACE'S house with Sadie and Angel. With classes and his lawn service, he and Sadie decided not to take a honeymoon until summer.

"Sadie, I have a great idea." Blaine suggested one day. "Let's see if Grace'll keep Angel in the house, and we'll pitch a tent in the backyard for a couple of nights. We'll call it 'hamping' for Honeymoon Camping. What do you think?"

Sadie laughed and then stopped short. She was so grateful for her creative husband. "Hey, ya know what? That'll be great fun! Of course you must carry me over the threshold, and I'm not sure how that'll work."

"I'll donate a king-sized air mattress to the honeymoon, and I'm more than happy to keep Angel with me in the house," Grace said, walking into the room. "Sleeping in the yard, smelling new mown grass, will be like a busman's holiday for Blaine," she teased. They all smiled at Grace's attempt at humor for the first time in months.

The tenderness inside the tent made it a honeymoon to be remembered, and Sadie thought she could never be happier. Nothing they had ever done followed tradition. This suited them and would provide great stories in years to come. She was sure Blaine hardly noticed the smell of new-mown grass, and Sadie didn't miss being carried over the threshold when they agreed it was safer to crawl in together.

CHAPTER 19

"Iffin we're gonna make it to that there dedication, we'd better get to goin," LeRoy said, getting excited about going to Highland. They borrowed a car from a friend and were going in style. A 1964 Chevy Impala painted with black and white zebra stripes would definitely get them noticed. They had helped restore and paint the car and were quite proud of their work.

LeRoy grinned in anticipation as they barreled down the road. "Wait till they see us comin.'"

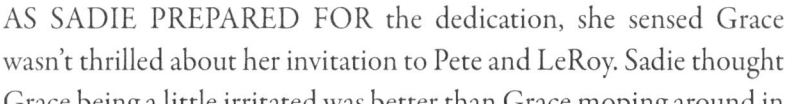

AS SADIE PREPARED FOR the dedication, she sensed Grace wasn't thrilled about her invitation to Pete and LeRoy. Sadie thought Grace being a little irritated was better than Grace moping around in sorrow. She did seem to cheer up a bit during the wedding planning and preparation.

On the day of the dedication, all heads turned when Pete and LeRoy drove into the parking lot of the church. It was, after all, pretty hard to miss a car hand-painted with black and white stripes.

As Pete turned off the engine, an explosive backfire caused everyone to jump, and a cloud of smoke rolled out from the rusty exhaust pipe. Sadie watched in both gratitude and amazement that her two tow truck heroes had come. She saw Grace shake her head in apparent disgust.

"My stars," Nancy Troude exclaimed. "Will you look at that! I don't know whether to laugh or pay admission." Everyone who heard her laughed.

If the zebra-striped car belching smoke wasn't enough, Pete sounded the ooga ooga horn and grinned.

Sadie, with Angel in her arms, sauntered up to Nancy. "Looks like LeRoy and Pete are stepping up in the world. Ha! Those are the guys who provided a delivery room when I had Angel. Can you believe it?"

"Oh, yeah, the tow truck guys. I remember them from the funeral. Glad they could come," Nancy said.

"Hi, guys," Sadie said as Pete and LeRoy walked up to them. She gave each one a hug and thanked them for coming.

In response, LeRoy gave Angel a little poke in the tummy and held out his grease-stained finger toward her. To his visible surprise, she grabbed onto it in a baby-strong grip.

LeRoy gasped. "I ain't ever touched a baby before. Her fingers are tiny and soft, but lookee how she holds on to me like I was her friend. I think she likes me."

"Of course she does." Sadie wished she had an extra moment to take a photo of Angel clinging to LeRoy's finger. "We'd better get inside before the service starts."

"I wonder what they're servin'," LeRoy whispered to Pete as they followed Sadie and the group into the church. Sadie chuckled, truly pleased they had come.

Blaine ushered them into the front row seats, but everytime Sadie turned around to look at them, LeRoy seemed to be staring at Angel in awe.

PASTOR TROUDE STARTED the service. When it came time to dedicate Angel, Sadie motioned for the family to come up on stage.

She looked for Grace, Blaine, and Nancy to follow. She didn't expect LeRoy and Pete to come along too, but to her surprise, they did. So there they stood – Blaine with Angel in his arms, Sadie, Grace, Nancy, Pete, and LeRoy. Sadie wondered if she should have invited Sergeant Childers and Officer Purcell. After all Childers was the one who delivered Angel, and Purcell assisted. Might as well have the whole crew there, she thought. But it was too late now.

"Wow, Angel, you have quite a large family," Pastor Troude commented. Then he read the dedication out of a book and asked everyone on the stage and in the congregation to raise their right hands and promise they would help Angel grow up to be a good Christian woman.

"I will," they all answered in unison, and Pastor Troude closed with a prayer of blessing over all of them.

After the service, LeRoy offered his finger to Angel again, and when she grabbed it, he asked if he could hold her. Sadie didn't hesitate, but she noticed Grace seemed horrified. LeRoy's grease-stained hands could not be hidden by Angel's ruffled yellow dress. She put her hand on his whiskered cheek and frowned as if she had just touched a scrub brush for the first time.

"What a picture that is," Nancy said. "The only thing better would be for you to take her and go stand in front of that zebra car." Everyone laughed and moved toward the car for some photos. Even Grace smiled, no doubt at the oddity of it all. Sadie took it all in and filed it away for future memories.

After the pictures, they talked about where they were going for lunch. Grace had extended the invitation to all of them, but Sadie noticed LeRoy and Pete lagged behind.

Sadie turned back to encourage them to come along. Before she could say anything, she overheard their conversation. Apparently they hadn't noticed her yet.

"Do ya think we were invited?" LeRoy asked cautiously.

"Sure we are. Never turn down a free meal."

"I know, but I promised to help Angel be a good Christian. How am I gonna do that?"

"Don't worry about it. Maybe Sadie can tell us . . . or maybe we can ask somebody in Barstow. They got churches there."

"Is God gonna get mad if I promised somethin' I can't do?" LeRoy asked.

Pete took off his dirty cap and slapped LeRoy across the head.

"I don't know what God does, ya dipstick. Let's just eat."

Sadie swallowed a giggle and turned back to the group waiting by the cars. It was obvious Pete and LeRoy would be joining them.

SADIE SENT LEROY HOME with a few cartoon gospel tracts. On the way, he read every single tract out loud to Pete and nagged him until he promised they would go to church somewhere in Barstow.

"Sure, sure," Pete finally agreed.

LeRoy wasn't satisfied. "I don't like it when you say, 'sure, sure' cuz that isn't a yes, yes."

"Okay, okay, we'll go," Pete promised, and LeRoy smiled, satisfied and reassured.

"GRACE, THERE'S A CALL for you." Sadie held out the phone.

"Who is it?"

"Another detective or investigator guy."

Grace took the phone fearfully. She hesitated to speak, wondering what other bad news could come her way. Finally she said, "Yes, hello."

"Mrs. Partain, I'm Detective Watkins with the FBI. We're trying to locate Mr. and Mrs. Hargrave. Would you have any idea how we could contact them?"

Grace gave him their home phone and the office numbers. She didn't know anything else about how to reach them. It almost seemed like the Hargraves had disappeared.

"I think they're out of town," she told him. "They said something about an extended vacation, but I don't know where. Sorry."

When she hung up, she wondered why the FBI would want to find Sheldon. Then she reminded herself that they were no doubt questioning everyone from the cruise ship, especially those who were friends of Phil's and knew him before.

THE SEMESTER AT CAL State San Bernardino ended and Blaine had enough units to graduate mid-year. He pursued an internship, hoping it would give him some credibility and get him into the movie production industry. When the offer came through, he wasn't sure how to break the news to Sadie.

"Sadie, where are you?" He repeated in a sing-song tune as he meandered through the house. "Sadie, where are you?"

"I'm in the baby's room," she sang back.

Blaine hid the papers behind his back and crept up on Sadie as she changed Angel's diaper. He slipped his arms around her waist and held his body against hers.

"I've got big news," he sang again.

"Is it more important than changing this diaper?" Sadie continued to wet-wipe Angel's stinky bottom.

"Oh, wow! Did my pretty Angel do that stinky?" Blaine curled up his nose and made a funny face. Angel giggled as Sadie finished sticking the tab of the diaper securely. She left the baby lying safely in the crib and pivoted in Blaine's arms, encircling him with hers.

"Okay, now. What is this big news? Does it have anything to do with the papers you're hiding behind your back?"

He was grinning ear to ear now. "You won't believe what just came in the mail."

"A check for a million dollars?" she joked.

"I wish. It's an offer for a paid internship in India." He kissed her forehead. "Did you hear me say *paid*?"

"I heard you say *India*. Are you kidding me?"

"Can you believe that? Eros International, one of the biggest movie producers in India. That's where Bollywood originated."

Blaine watched Sadie's eyes go wide as her lips moved, but she didn't speak. He imagined she was as surprised and thrilled as he was.

"Sadie, can you imagine what I could learn?" he asked. "India's the biggest producer of movies in the world. Just think how that'll look on my resume."

"I . . . I . . ."

It appeared Sadie was still speechless, so he went ahead. "Sadie, just think. We'll be able to see India and learn about another culture."

Sadie finally found her words. "I don't want to burst your bubble. I want to be supportive, but I'm concerned."

"Sadie, just think what a great adventure this will be. We'll be in Mumbai, the largest city in India."

"Mumbai?" she said weakly.

"It used to be called Bombay," Blaine offered, thinking maybe she didn't know that particular fact, "until 1995."

She nodded and swallowed, then finally spoke again. "Let me think about this. I want to be excited, but I'm afraid."

Blaine appreciated her honesty, but he wanted to reassure her. "Sadie, don't be afraid. You left home all by yourself and went to Las Vegas. Talk about a culture shock. And you managed, right?"

She nodded. "Right, but my parents were only one state away, even though I had no plans to return. And I was also young and stupid. Now I'm a wife and a mother, and I hope I'm a little smarter. India is on the other side of the world. We don't know the language or anything."

Blaine smiled, touched by the fear in her eyes. "They speak English, and we'll get help from the American Embassy to find temporary housing. We'll only be there for six months. It'll be the greatest adventure of our lives. Much bigger than camping out in the backyard for sure. Please pray about this and see if God'll give you peace concerning your fears."

"You know that being with you is the most important thing in my life," she said, her eyes moist now. "Wherever you are, I want to be there too. I just don't want to put Angel or us in danger. Maybe you could connect with one of the Indian students and learn more about the area we'd be going to, and find out what we need to know before we go."

Blaine felt his smile widen, if that was possible. "That's my girl. Now you're thinking positively. We can do this. And that's a brilliant idea, by the way."

Sadie sighed. "I guess, if I expect you to be the leader of our family, I'd better be ready to follow, huh?"

Blaine pulled Sadie closer and kissed her tenderly.

GRACE DID NOT RECEIVE the news of Blaine's internship with enthusiasm. Her heart sank once again. She could not bring herself to rejoice, but she agreed to welcome an Indian student for dinner. She decided to take a stab at appearing supportive, even though she struggled inside herself.

Blaine didn't waste any time. He invited one of his Indian classmates for dinner. Ashish Khatri, a fellow drama student, gladly accepted the invitation.

Before dinner was on the table, Grace became captivated by Ashish Khatri, whose name she discovered means blessing. He seemed to enjoy the interaction as Blaine, Sadie, and Grace pelted him with one question after another. He made India sound absolutely exotic and inviting. He even had relatives who were quite rich and lived in the area of the production company.

"Lots of the people are vegetarians, but I am not." Ashish seemed quite at home eating the chicken with his fingers. "Most of the people are Hindu."

"Are there Christians there?" Sadie asked.

"Not many. Life is difficult for Christians."

"Why?" Blaine frowned.

"There are often attacks against them." Ashish lowered his eyes as if embarrassed.

"What?" Sadie shot a look at Blaine, and Grace nearly jumped out of her chair.

An unsettling moment hung in the air, and Grace imagined, like her, no one knew what to say. She saw Sadie tighten her lips, and Grace knew she was struggling.

Almost in a whisper, Sadie asked, "Who attacks Christians?"

"Extremists. People who don't want them in the country."

Tears glistened in Sadie's eyes. "That's terrible."

"Yes, but there are extremists in the United States and other countries as well. Those who take extreme action against others because of their fanatical religious or political ideas exist in every country. Don't you know there are people in the United States who do not welcome me and shout for me to go back home where I belong?"

"I guess that's true," Blaine admitted.

"Will they hurt us when we go there?" Sadie asked, her voice trembling slightly as she voiced the question that burned in Grace's heart.

"You are going to learn about film production," their guest explained. "You are not going as missionaries to proselytize. They will not see you as a threat, and you will be just fine. Mumbai is a wonderful place."

"You're sure?"

"You are going to a metropolitan area where people are hustling and bustling. They will not even notice you."

They all laughed as Grace realized he was joking. Sadie might be the only redheaded white woman in the whole country, and all her curls would be hard to hide.

Ashish assured Sadie she would love India, and she would not be in danger. When he left he promised to contact his family about housing possibilities, leaving both Blaine and Sadie ready to start packing – and Grace wondering how she would deal with yet another broken heart.

AS SHE EXPECTED, GRACE did indeed mourn another loss. *What will I do without Sadie . . . and Angel . . . and Blaine?* They were her only family, and she would be alone. *Lord, you've taken everything away from me. What have I done?*

She thought about Job of the Bible and how Satan stripped him of everything. She thought about how she had run off to Las Vegas and disappeared without any intention of returning, without appreciating what she had in her home, her husband, and her career. How selfish she had been, all because things were not suiting her. She even harbored jealousy at families who had their own children. Philip would not give her enough attention, and she resented the long hours he worked. She had money enough to buy anything she wanted and yet, she had not been satisfied.

When she came back home, she and Phil had found rekindled love. They both had a personal relationship with Jesus, and they expected a baby. A gift from God. She would finally be happy. She would finally have everything she wanted.

It didn't make sense that God would take it all away. First Phil, then her newborn baby girl Philisity, now Sadie, Blaine, and Angel. Sadie had been like a daughter to her, Blaine like a son, and little Angel like a granddaughter. How could she bear it? *The world is caving in on me. Please, God, don't let this happen.*

Even in her prayers, Grace felt guilty for praying against the India Internship, but she could not bear to see them go. She tried to enlist Pastor Troude's help on the phone. "John, can you talk to the kids? They're planning on moving to India for six months. I'll be alone. Can't you help me talk them out of it?"

Pastor Troude paused, then said exactly what she did not want to hear. "Grace, Sadie and Blaine are young and ambitious. I'm sure they've prayed about this and will make a wise decision. When you and Phil got married, did you expect your parents or your pastor to tell you what to do?"

She felt her shoulders slump as she answered. "No, but we weren't thinking about going to India. What will I do without them?"

John paused before answering. "Grace, maybe it's time to create your own life. The last eight months have been a roller coaster ride for you. Think about it. Last summer you were convinced you could happily leave Phil, but after getting in a terrible mess, you discovered how much you loved him and wanted to come home."

She sighed. "I know. How stupid it all seems now."

"You found yourself pregnant at forty, which you'd desperately wanted for twenty years and thought that would make you happy.

Sadie moved in, and that created a new distraction for you as her pregnancy advanced. Then Phil planned an exotic cruise vacation. Just when you were riding high with everything going your way, Phil disappeared. Down in the pit you went again."

"Yes, for good reason," she answered, somewhat defensively.

"You came home to find Sadie had her baby, and your spirits were buoyed. Then the news came of Phil's murder and how his body was found in a crate behind a shed, and you lost the baby to a rare complication. That sent you spiraling out of control and into another nosedive."

"Who wouldn't?" Her defenses were now in over-drive.

"You're right. Anyone would have a struggle slogging through such horrific circumstances."

The familiar feeling of an elephant sitting on her chest was back. "I don't think I can bear another loss."

"Hear me out. The kids got married and dedicated Angel, and you soared again until the news comes that they're going to India for six months. Anyone would feel the loss, and you did. But here's the part you often forget. God knows all this, and his eye is on you. None of this has come as a surprise to him. He knows what's happening in every life. We grow when we live through hard stuff. It isn't easy, but this is when your faith has to see you through. It's easy to be faithful when everything is going well, but the real test is when times are hard. You've come this far without giving up; you can make it through six months on your own."

She swallowed a sob. "It's been tough."

"I know it has, and I understand, believe me. But God has a plan, and your life isn't over. There's more to come."

She struggled to speak. "I've quit teaching and poured myself into Angel and the kids. What will I do without them?"

"For right now, what do you think would be the right thing to do? Name three things you're willing to do."

Grace paused. "You just took off your pastor's hat and put on your coach's hat, didn't you?"

John chuckled softly. "Yes, and in a minute, I'm going to put on my friend hat and tell you my opinion."

A long silence gave Grace a chance to gather her thoughts. Slowly she began. "Hmm. Okay, three things I'm willing to do. First, the right thing to do would be to pray for the kids to have a safe and productive adventure in India." Long pause. "Uh . . . second, I can afford to whisk them off with some serious cash that I'm sure they aren't expecting. And third . . . I probably need to find a new hobby, or job, or volunteer at the church. How am I doing, Coach?"

"As your friend, I think I can say you've come to the perfect solution. See, it wasn't that hard. Now quit the pity party and get on with life. Don't let yourself sit there alone when they leave and feel sorry for yourself. Sounds like you already have a plan, so execute your plan and see what God has for you."

Tears threatened her eyes once again, but she blinked them away. "What would I do without you and Nancy? You've been so good to me."

"I don't know about Nancy, but you've kept me busy with funerals, dedications, weddings, and last summer's crime adventure." He chuckled again.

It wasn't really funny, but she had to admit it was true. "I guess you're right. You've been a pastor, coach, counselor, and friend. Not to mention babysitting for Angel once in a while." Grace managed a chuckle and promised to move ahead. John hung up and Grace felt good about the results of their conversation. She hoped John did too. She had needed his straight talk and probably would again.

CHAPTER 20

It was the beginning of a new year and Pete worried about how they were going to make money when their old tow truck breathed its last. They sat on the porch at Pete's house and while Pete was trying to think, LeRoy persisted, "Pete, ya said we'd go to church. When's that gonna be?"

LeRoy asked Pete this question nearly every day since the dedication, and it was starting to get on Pete's nerves. "I'm sick of you buggin' me about it. We'll go when I say."

"Okay, then I'll just go my ownself." LeRoy got up from the porch step and started walking down the dusty road.

Pete shook his head. He usually called the shots in their relationship, but occasionally LeRoy got stubborn, and they had to compromise. "Come back here, LeRoy. Today's Saturday, and church is on Sunday. I promise we'll put on our good clothes and go tomorrow."

LeRoy stopped and turned back to face him. "Sadie told me when we went in the restaurant that it's the right thing to do to take your hat off inside eatin' places and churches and stuff. I'm gonna try to remember that."

Pete laughed. "I figure if the church is gonna fall down, I want my head to be protected."

LeRoy looked serious as he walked back toward Pete. "Was you really thinkin' the church was gonna fall down?"

Pete took off his greasy cap and slapped LeRoy across the back of the head. "You're so stupid, boy."

SADIE FELT A LITTLE guilty for picking Ashish's brain, but he seemed to love her questions and accepted her invitation to come for lemonade so she could ask a few more. They sat inside where it was cool, and Sadie brought out her list. "I want to know everything."

She watched Ashish take a deep breath, as if preparing for the interrogation. "I've already contacted my relatives," he explained, "and they want to help you find living accommodations."

"That's very kind, Ashish. I can't wait to meet them." Sadie settled into the chair and took a sip of the cold lemonade before asking her first question. "What about clothes? What do the women wear?"

Ashish grinned. "It is very hot there, but women must dress modestly."

"What is modest?" Sadie wrinkled her nose and didn't like the sound of that. "No shorts and tank tops?"

His eyes widened and he shook his head. "No. No shorts or tank tops. You must cover your whole body, but with loose clothing."

Sadie thought about her present wardrobe, which consisted mostly of shorts and tank tops. "I'll have to ask Grace for help."

"Don't worry. I'll bring you some photos of my family, and then you will see."

"Okay, I appreciate that. Blaine and I don't own much, but Angel and all her clothes and toys will be the biggest part of the luggage. We'll figure it out."

Sadie still worried about their safety, but she would have to leave that to the Lord. Ashish gave her contact information for his cousins and family friends. "I've made arrangements for some of my cousins to meet you when you arrive."

Sadie felt the knot in her stomach loosen its grip. "That's so sweet. I think I'll feel a lot safer if I know someone will meet us. I know I'm being kind of a baby about being in a foreign country, but you've really helped me."

They continued with their questions and answers until they finished their lemonade. As Ashish rose to leave, the phone rang, so he let himself out so Sadie could answer.

Numerous calls regarding Phil's murder came on a regular basis now, none of which had any further information. Sadie was used to taking messages and ending the calls quickly when Grace was away from home, but this call turned out to be from Blaine.

Sadie was surprised because she knew he was doing a project on campus. "What's up, Honey?"

The excitement in his voice was evident. "I just hired the perfect replacement for my landscaping business while we're away. His name's Bernard."

"Like Saint Bernard? Is he coming to rescue us? Ha!" Sadie thought that was funny, but Blaine went on.

"He's a big, strong football player and definitely sounds like he could be trusted. I told him he could make some serious money if he keeps all my customers happy, and he appreciated the offer."

Plans were falling into place, and Sadie thought Grace might be happier about their departure if she asked her to help with the wardrobe. Sadie knew how Grace loved clothes and would probably welcome the chance to help out; anything to occupy her mind would keep her from worrying about being alone.

In the middle of planning and preparing for their trip, Sadie was amazed when Grace announced, "I've started doing research to see what a forty-year old widow with plenty of money could do to make a difference in the world."

"You make a difference to us!" Sadie said as she finished folding one of Angel's outfits and picked up another one. From the corner of her eye, she noticed Grace slip an envelope full of what looked like traveler's checks in the bottom of Sadie's purse. She pretended not to see because she didn't want to spoil Grace's surprise or rob her of the blessing of giving. She and Blaine could be surprised together later.

THE MARKEMS LEFT IN a flurry, and the house fell silent. Sadie had acted as Grace's assistant in so many ways, and now all that assistance was gone – at least for several months. Besides housekeeping, Sadie helped with the cooking, shopped for groceries, answered the phone, and sorted the mail. When the phone rang, Grace reminded herself she had to learn to respond to the ring again and hustle to the phone.

"Hello," she said, placing the receiver against her ear. She grew tired of hearing from advertisers and almost always hung up if she heard a click, which meant they were calling from a group-dialing system. For some reason, this time, she waited.

"Hey, Grace," said a vaguely familiar male voice. "How are you doin' these days? I heard Mr. Partain was murdered."

She felt her stomach turn in pain at the graceless greeting. "Who is this?" she demanded.

"Oh, come on, honey. How could you forget me?"

Grace wanted to hang up, but something about that voice made her stay on the line without saying a word.

"I was your employer and landlord for a couple of days until you stole something from me, and I ended up in jail for six months."

The hair on the back of her neck stood on end . . . Jerry Hodges.

"What do you want?" Her heart raced as she remembered her encounter with Jerry. Grace had gone on a turnaround bus to Las Vegas. When she hurried to return to the bus, Isabel Hodges, Jerry's mother, fell to the floor with chest pains. Grace stopped to help her and missed the return bus. When people assumed she was Isabel's daughter, and the news reported her missing in the bus accident, she decided to change her identity and not go home. She accompanied Isabel to the hospital in the ambulance, and when Isabel got discharged, the grateful woman invited Grace to come home with her. Grace's belongings were on the bus, so she had no money, clothes, or identification. Isabel's son, Jerry, offered her a job at the casino he managed, no questions asked. That's where she met Sadie who worked as a cocktail waitress.

Within two days, Jerry accused Grace of stealing drugs he had stashed in her locker, and his girlfriend beat her with a broom handle. If it hadn't been for Sadie, Grace might have been killed. They escaped together. The cops brought an end to the whole episode, and Jerry went to jail. Now, apparently, he was out and no doubt looking for revenge.

"I hear you're pretty well-heeled now that you inherited the family business."

Grace cringed at the sarcasm in his menacing voice. "Pretty well-heeled?"

"You've got plenty of money to share with an old friend like me. I took you into my home, gave you a job, and gave you a bag of drugs to keep for me."

Fear melted away as anger took its place. "What? You're crazy. Your mother invited me into your home. You didn't give me anything except my meager paycheck. And that only because Sadie picked it up when I was afraid Madeline would hit me again. I had nothing to do with any drugs, and I don't know why you're calling me. I don't owe you anything."

"I'm thinking about sending a photo of you to the Highland newspaper, or how about the *L.A. Times*? A shot of you in that sexy red satin blouse and tight black jeans you wore while serving drinks in the casino. Remember? That'll make a nice story. Something like that might make you a suspect in your husband's murder. Unhappy wife . . . school teacher . . . wife of big real-estate broker . . . changes her identity and goes to work as a barmaid in a shabby Las Vegas Casino. That'll make interesting reading."

The fear was back. Grace couldn't get her breath, and she could taste the bile coming up in her mouth. Tears welled up in her eyes, but she had no idea what to say. She had kept what happened in Las Vegas a secret that only Sadie knew. What happens in Vegas should have stayed in Vegas, as far as she was concerned. *Is this blackmail? Would he really do such a thing?* She remembered Jerry taking a photo of Lianne, Madeline, Sadie, and her in their red satin uniform shirts and tight black pants, and her stomach churned. "Jerry, you can't get away with this. If I'm not mistaken, this is blackmail."

"What do I care what it's called? Do you want me to send the photo to your local newspaper, or do I hear you counting out some serious cash?"

"You can't do this. It's insane. I'll call the police."

"I could drop that photo with the story in the mail to the newspaper today. I may not get my money, but you'll hit the front pages as a murder suspect within twenty-four hours. What good will the cops do for you then?"

Grace trembled in fear, as the idea of being suspected of Phil's murder terrified her. "How much cash are you talking about?"

"Well, my mother and I should have gotten the fifty-thousand dollar reward for finding you in Las Vegas, and since there are two of us, I figure it should be a hundred thousand dollars."

Grace slammed down the receiver, trembling from head to toe. Only minutes passed before the phone rang again and Grace, always afraid of missing a call from Sadie or the FBI, picked it up.

"Don't you dare hang up on me again, or my next stop will be the post office." Jerry then set the date and time for Grace to meet him to exchange the photo for the money. She agreed to come if they would meet halfway in Baker. That would be neutral territory, and she knew he would come at least that far for one hundred thousand dollars.

CHAPTER 21

Phone connections between India and Southern California were expensive, unreliable, and difficult to make. Grace wanted to talk to Sadie about Jerry's call, but there wasn't really anything Sadie could do. She had told Grace from the beginning to be careful of Jerry because he spelled trouble. But Sadie remained the only one who knew the whole story of what Grace had gone through in Las Vegas. Strangely enough, though, nobody really knew the whole story, not even Grace.

As the meeting date approached, Grace tried to hatch a plan to get the photo away from Jerry. She decided that meeting him would be the only way to put an end to this. It would be a very dangerous situation, but there wasn't anyone she could tell about last summer. Jerry was indeed a dangerous guy, and the situation seemed hopeless. He could make her look horrible to her community, her church, and worse than anything, it would make her look guilty. She decided to make a call.

"Hi, Pete," she said when she heard the familiar voice. "This is Grace Partain. I called because I need your help."

He hesitated before answering, and Grace imagined he was more than a little surprised to hear from her. "Hey, Mrs. Partain . . . umm, what's up? Is Sadie okay?"

"Yes," she answered, "but she and Blaine and the baby are in India for six months."

"Wow, India. Isn't that next door to Illinois?"

Grace smiled. "No, you're thinking of Indiana. India is in Asia."

"Wow, that's another country, ain't it?"

"Well, yes, it's another country on the other side of the world. Listen, I have a problem, and I think you might be able to help me."

"We'd do anything for you and your family," Pete replied.

Grace sensed he meant what he said, and it confirmed her judgment in approaching him about this matter. "Well, this really doesn't have anything to do with my family. It's just me."

Without hesitation, he replied, "Okay. What can we do?"

She didn't want to tell him about the photo, but she let him know she had to meet with a very dangerous person, and she wanted Pete and LeRoy to accompany and protect her.

"Oh, man, that sounds great," Pete answered. "Right up our alley. We could be your bodyguards. We ain't never done that before, but we did win a bar fight with a motorcycle gang once down at Buford's. Should we wear our good suits so we look like FBI agents?"

Grace could still see Pete and LeRoy in their ill-fitting suits, and she swallowed a grin. "Sure. That would be great. Could I ask you to do something else for me? While you're on duty, could you not smoke and ask LeRoy not to spit, and I promise I'll pay you for your services."

Pete readily agreed, and when Grace was satisfied the instructions were understood, she ended the conversation, only slightly relieved about the upcoming meeting with Jerry.

AS SOON AS HE HUNG up the phone, Pete ran out of the house to find LeRoy. On his way to the truck, where he knew LeRoy would be working under the hood, he lit a cigarette, and then suddenly remembered he wasn't supposed to smoke on duty. He threw the cigarette down and stomped it out.

"LeRoy, we been called into duty by that nice Mrs. Partain," he announced when he spotted him right where he figured he would be. "She's doin' somethin' dangerous, and she wants us to protect her."

LeRoy looked up from where he'd been tinkering on their truck. "Protect her? Like FBI guys or bodyguards or somthin'?"

"Yeah, and she wants us to wear our good suits. No smokin' or spittin', and I bet we prob'ly ain't supposed to wear our ball caps either."

LeRoy's eyes widened. "Zowie, I'm gettin' me a haircut and takin' a bath. We're gonna be like superheroes!" LeRoy spit on the ground and quickly covered it up by kicking dirt over it. "Okay, no spittin'. Guess I'll just have to swaller it."

"LeRoy, this is a really good thing we're gonna do."

LeRoy nodded solemnly, a look of wonder and excitement on his dirty face.

THANKFUL FOR ANGEL'S naptime, Sadie scooped up a pen and paper and sat down at the kitchen table preparing to write a letter to Grace. She wished Grace was sitting next to her so they could share a cold drink and chat about Angel, India, and home. She missed 'home.'

> Dear Grace,
>
> Blaine, Angel, and I miss you a lot.
>
> We love it in Mumbai. Living is cheap, and for almost nothing we could have a cook and a housekeeper. We were so surprised to find the envelope of traveler's checks in the bottom of my purse. Wow!! Thank you so much. We've already decided to save as much of it as we can so when we get home, we can get our own place.

I've been working in a school as a classroom assistant, and they let me bring Angel. They love that I speak English and can help them.

The country is beautiful, and Ashish's friends and family have made us feel very welcome. They met us at the airport and had already scoped out many housing options for us.

Angel is growing so fast! You'll be so surprised when we get home. I'll send a photo with my next letter if I can get one developed.

I wonder what you're doing without us there. I hope you are doing something fun. You deserve something fun, my dear friend.

Have you heard anything from Pete and LeRoy? I'd love it if they'd actually go to church. It would help them lead a better life. I told LeRoy that polite men don't wear their hats in church or restaurants. I wonder if he listened to me. Ha!

Well, I need to go now. Say hello to the Troudes for me. Please write. We love you.

Sadie

Sadie had been careful not to let on that she knew about the traveler's checks ahead of time. She wanted to ask if they found out who killed Phil, but she worried it would just make Grace sad again. Besides, Grace would no doubt bring it up if they had. Surely by now they had given up.

She wanted to ask if Bernard had done a good job keeping Blaine's business going, but she didn't want to know if he wasn't. Blaine chose Bernard, and she trusted Blaine's judgment.

Sadie also wanted to ask if Grace had seen a counselor to help her get over losing her baby and husband, but she didn't ask that either. That was Grace's business, and she might not want to share it.

SADIE'S LETTER TOOK two weeks to get to Grace, and when it finally arrived, it buoyed Grace's spirits for a few minutes. She desperately wanted to hear they were doing fine.

She sat down to write back, but stared at the blank stationery and tried to figure out what to say. She thought about telling Sadie she still didn't know who murdered Phil, but she didn't want her to be sad. She wanted to tell her the depression had become worse and threatened to kill her spirit all together, but she didn't. And now Jerry had come into the picture with a horrible threat, but she didn't tell here that either. No sense worrying Sadie about any of it. She wanted to tell her she would be meeting Jerry to give him one hundred thousand dollars and taking LeRoy and Pete as bodyguards, but she didn't. So what was left to say?

Uncertainty gripped her as she thought about how that situation might end. She wanted to tell Sadie that Pastor Troude had told her to create a new life for herself, but she hadn't, so she didn't. She wanted to tell her she had found an organization called MTI - Mission Training International – that did missionary work in India, but going there seemed crazy at her age. She wanted to tell Blaine that Bernard was doing a terrific job keeping his business going, but she didn't. There just wasn't much she wanted to say without putting a burden on Sadie. Finally she wrote:

Dear Sadie, Blaine, and Angel,

I miss you, but I'm doing fine.

I'll be visiting Pete and LeRoy soon. We've planned a meeting to see if we can work together on a project. I'll let you know how it works out in my next letter.

Pastor Troude has encouraged me to take a trip or start a new hobby, so I'm going to invest in something I hope will have good results. I can't tell you about it yet.

Love you all,

Grace

P.S. Sorry this is so short, but I'll write more next time.

IT HAD BEEN A WHILE since Grace felt like dressing up and going out in public, but for some reason drawing out one hundred thousand dollars from her bank account made her feel like she should be dressed accordingly. It was too hot for one of her knit suits, but she dug out a classy lightweight dress she hadn't worn for over a year. She selected some attractive jewelry, spent extra time on her makeup and hair, and when she finished she looked in the mirror and liked the transformation. *Well, look at you,* she said to her reflection. *A-banking we will go!*

Grace felt a wave of confidence as she drove, but all that changed when she entered the bank and walked up to the counter.

She smiled and greeted the teller. "Good morning. I'm Grace Partain, and I'd like to draw out one hundred thousand dollars in one-hundred-dollar bills."

The teller smiled back and replied, "Mrs. Partain, it's my pleasure to serve you; however, you aren't allowed to draw out more than ten thousand dollars without signing some papers and waiting a few days."

Grace felt her confidence melt away. "But I have plenty of money in your bank. Why is this a problem?"

The teller motioned to a woman in one of the private offices surrounded by glass windows. "Let me get one of the managers to speak with you."

Grace could only think about her conversation with Jerry. *I set a date and time with him. If I don't show up with the money, he'll send the photo to the press.*

The manager beckoned Grace into her glass office and shut the door. "I understand you'd like to withdraw a hundred thousand dollars. Is that correct?"

Grace wondered if they were going to question the reason for her large withdrawal. "Yes, that's my intention." She felt the perspiration forming on her forehead. "There's plenty of money in my accounts." Grace was sure they knew her name because Phil did all his business there.

"Yes, Mrs. Partain, you have several large accounts, but I can only give you ten thousand today. You'll have to sign a request for the remainder, and I'd be glad to help you with that." The manager stood and walked to a file cabinet to get the form.

Grace twisted in her chair. "I have a good reason for wanting the money right away. Can't we forgo the form and move ahead?"

"I'm afraid not," said the manager as she began to fill out the form. "Making a withdrawal that large would trigger federal government reporting requirements."

Grace's hands shook as she signed the form. What if she couldn't change the date with Jerry? "How long do I have to wait?"

"It shouldn't be more than a couple of days," the manager said as if she didn't even notice Grace was upset. "I'll contact you immediately when the funds are available."

Grace fought back tears. "Thank you. I wish I'd known." As she walked out of the bank, she prayed Jerry would agree to postpone. *Lord, you kept me from kidnappers and druggies last summer. Would you please help me outsmart this blackmailer?*

GRACE WASN'T SURE HOW she was going to make the exchange with Jerry, but she knew the results she wanted. If she could convince Pete and LeRoy that Jerry was going to hurt her, they could take him down, get the photo, and run for it. No money would be exchanged, the men would protect her, and Jerry wouldn't be able to do anything about it because what he had proposed was illegal. What she planned was illegal also, but it was self-preservation, and nobody would actually get hurt. She didn't want to injure Jerry, just get the photo and the negative out of his hands and into hers. No negative, no deal. Planning lessons for her fourth graders often called for logistics, but this plan depended on logistics that were far more dangerous and out of her control. There was no room for error, and she hadn't realized she'd have to wait for the bank to get the money for her. She was thankful when, with only one day to spare, the bank called to tell her she could pick up the cash.

She imagined Pete and LeRoy saw this as an exciting adventure, but Grace had known them long enough to know they were apt to get tangled up in each other and end up on the ground like Laurel and Hardy, and she'd end up helpless. If Jerry had a gun, he might shoot one or all of them. Unthinkable.

Grace called them one last time to clarify every detail. She carefully explained to Pete and LeRoy how and why they should subdue Jerry until she could retrieve the goods, and then they could let him go.

"What are the goods?" Pete asked.

"Nothing for you to worry about." she assured him.

"Will it be something heavy that we need to carry for you?"

"Thank you, no," she insisted. "It's just an embarrassing photo and negative I bought from him." She felt guilty about not telling them Jerry might have a gun, but she didn't want them to back out on her.

PETE WAS SATISFIED that he understood the plan. Now he needed to figure out with LeRoy how they would pull it off.

Grace had told them she wanted to meet on a secluded dirt road outside of Baker, and Pete – being familiar with the area – knew just the place. In her last conversation, Grace asked how they planned to subdue Jerry.

"We been talkin' about that, and we're not sure what subdue means," he had said, worried he and LeRoy might blow the job. "Should we hit him over the head with a wrench or sit on him?"

Pete heard what sounded like a muffled laugh. "No wrenches, please. All I want you to do is when you see him get out of his car with something in his hands and I get out of my car, you drive up, grab Jerry, and hold him tight so he can't get away. But don't hurt him. Just hold him and make it impossible for him to run away or grab me until I can get the envelope he'll be carrying and get away. Do you understand?"

"Got it!" Pete had felt more confident after that conversation because he understood what was expected of him and LeRoy. "We'll make sure he can't run off or hurt you," he had assured her. Pete had an idea of his own that he thought would make Grace proud, but he was going to save it for the showdown.

JERRY AND HIS GIRLFRIEND, Madeline, also had plans of their own. They discussed them as they sat at a local diner, waiting for their sandwiches.

"You hide in the car on the floor in the backseat," Jerry instructed. "If things go sideways, you can help me out. At the end of the day, we'll be rich, and Grace can have her stupid photo."

Madeline lifted her perfectly drawn eyebrows. "Should I carry a gun?"

Jerry nodded and leaned in to whisper. "Sure, but don't fire it. I can't afford another charge, or I'll go to prison this time for sure. But if you have to, you can point it at her until we get the money."

CHAPTER 22

On the day of the exchange, Grace put on Calvin Klein jeans, a T-shirt, and tennis shoes. She wanted to be ready to run if she had to. She ruled out the gold tennies she wore to teach P.E. and put on the Nikes she wore to work out. *In my wildest dreams, I never thought I'd have to deal with blackmailers. What else can I do?*

She definitely could afford the money, but she did not want to put it in Jerry's hands if she could help it. After all, he was a slimy character who had accused her of stealing drugs from him last summer.

Before Grace left the house, she called Pete to tell him she would be leaving right away. The weather was typical for Highland in winter – sunny with the temperature nearing seventy degrees. There wasn't a cloud in the sky, and it would be clear as a bell in the desert.

As planned she arrived ahead of schedule on the deserted dusty road Pete and Leroy had scoped out for their meeting. She smiled with surprise when she saw the two men approach. In spite of their ill-fitting FBI suits, they had shaved and cleaned up. It looked like they might have cut each other's hair, but it was a great improvement over their greasy caps, which they had thankfully left behind.

"You guys look so professional. Thank you so much for doing this for me. Just be careful, and let's see if we can do this without anyone getting hurt."

"I thought about bringing a gun, but I don't have one," Pete said. "My brothers have some paint guns, but . . ."

"No," Grace declared. "Absolutely not. Let's not make this worse than it is." Grace was getting antsy, and she wanted to get it over with. "Let's get in our positions and wait. You guys get out of sight."

An old abandoned shed stood about forty yards away. Pete started up the truck and drove around the shed where it couldn't be seen from the dirt road. Pete and LeRoy were instructed to create a distraction if they saw Jerry get too close to Grace. Surprisingly, she didn't have to explain distraction to them – or at least she didn't think so.

Her last sight of them before they ducked out of sight showed Pete with a toothpick in the corner of his mouth in the absence of a cigarette, and LeRoy with a mouthful of gum, chewing energentically.

The two men were hidden, and Grace was waiting in her car when Jerry pulled up in his black Chevrolet. She planned to draw Jerry away from his car, which faced her. He would have his back to the shed if Pete and LeRoy had to rush him. She was relieved when he parked right where she had hoped he would.

Grace got out of her car, left the engine running and door open, and waited. She dropped the bag of money in the dirt beside her as Jerry got out of his vehicle. He exited the car slowly and walked to the front, facing Grace. It was exactly the way she had envisioned it. A fifty-foot expanse lay between them.

Grace had nearly forgotten how absolutely unattractive Jerry was, but she was quickly reminded. He had thin, dusty brown hair that looked as though it had never been combed. His skin was pasty, and his scrawny arms hung out of his T-shirt like shapeless noodles. He wore faded jeans that hung low on his hips, and his beat-up loafers did not look like running shoes, Grace noted. "Come and get it, Jerry," she called.

He hesitated, then reached back into the car and pulled out a manila envelope. He walked slowly toward Grace. She wanted to get him as far away from his own car as possible. About twenty feet from her, he stopped.

"How we gonna do this?" he asked.

"I want to see that you have the photo and the negative. Open the envelope, and lay them out on the ground before you come any closer."

"They'll get dirty."

"I don't care. I'll shred them when I get home anyway."

From the corner of her eye, Grace saw LeRoy sneak out from behind the shed, half-walking and half-crawling toward the back of Jerry's car. Though Grace could see him, Jerry could not. As Grace held Jerry's attention, LeRoy hooked a tow chain to the back of Jerry's car then scampered back to the hidden tow truck. Grace nearly allowed a laugh to escape when she saw him doing a modified crab walk, no doubt to keep from getting dust all over the knees of his FBI suit.

As Jerry knelt down and placed the photo and negative on the ground, Grace stepped away from the moneybag and took a few steps toward him.

"I want to see them before you're getting any money," she insisted. When she got close enough to see the photo, Jerry's car started moving backwards away from him, slowly and quietly at first, then accelerating. A scream erupted from inside Jerry's car, and he whipped around and looked back to see his car rolling away.

"Hey!" he yelled, looking confused and undecided about whether to run after his car or Grace.

While Jerry's head snapped back and forth, Grace lunged forward and snatched up the photo, the negative, and the envelope, and quickly turned toward her car. Another scream came from Jerry's vehicle.

"What the . . . !"

Grace didn't waste any time. The minute she saw Jerry turn to race after his car, she dashed toward her own as fast as her legs would carry her, scooping up the bag of money on the way. She knew it was a matter of seconds until Jerry gave up on his car and turned to pursue her instead. As she threw the bag, the photo, and the negative in through the back window she had left open, she could hear Jerry closing in on her. She jumped in the driver's seat and gave it the gas as he came so close she almost hit him when she pulled away. Glancing in her rearview mirror, she could see him shaking his fist and screaming in the cloud of dust she left behind.

She might have been more frightened if she had known Madeline was in Jerry's car with a gun.

PETE AND LEROY STARTED pulling Jerry's car faster and faster toward the shed. They couldn't see Jerry, but Pete was certain he would be running in their direction once Grace had made her getaway. He just wished he knew who was in that car screaming like a banshee.

A fender ripped off as they yanked the vehicle around the side of the building. Ear-piercing screams continued to emanate from inside the car. When they put enough distance between them and Jerry, who was now in foot pursuit, LeRoy jumped out, released the hook, and he and Pete sped off in the opposite direction.

Pete imagined Grace had safely hit the freeway bound for Barstow by now. He and LeRoy knew the back roads well and were out of sight in a cloud of dust in no time. Pete was glad their plan had worked so well, but he was a bit disappointed Jerry didn't follow them, which would have been icing on the cake, like a car chase in the movies. He didn't consider that the tow truck probably would have fallen apart and left them afoot to face Jerry.

JERRY GATHERED UP HIS fender and threw it in the trunk. He was about to jump in the front seat when Madeline screamed one last time. He opened the back door, grabbed her arm, and pulled her out.

"You're useless!" he spit out. "I don't even know why I brought you along. You were supposed to cover for me, but instead you're back there screaming your fool head off."

Madeline's ample chest was heaving, and her face was red. "What was I supposed to do?" she huffed. "You gave me a gun and told me not to shoot it. How did I know some guys were going to pull the car down the road backwards? Seems like the last time you got me to take part in your plan, we both ended up in jail. This didn't turn out any better."

"At least we didn't go to jail," he replied.

"When I hit her across the forehead with the broomstick at the casino, I should have killed her then," Madeline hissed.

"That Grace is bad news," Jerry snarled. "I knew that from the time I first met her. She's too darned smart."

"Well, she's a school teacher, ya know," Madeline said, her voice dripping with disdain.

"School teachers shouldn't be messing around with criminals."

"Very funny, Jerry. You got beat at your own game."

He frowned and looked off in the direction where the tow truck disappeared. "I wonder who those guys were anyway. Looked like they were driving an old broken down tow truck."

"I didn't get a good look," Madeline said, "but I did get a peek at them from the back seat, and I could've sworn I saw a guy in a suit blowing bubbles – you know, with bubblegum."

"Oh, sure." Jerry kicked the dirt. Useless. That's all Madeline was. Useless.

GRACE COULD HARDLY breathe until she put ten miles between herself and the dusty road. When she was sure nobody followed her, she started to laugh. She and the boys had pulled off a successful caper. A schoolteacher and two tow truck drivers; what an unlikely team! The three of them would meet in Barstow at Buford's Bar, but Grace knew she'd get there ahead of them.

Buford's wasn't the kind of place Grace frequented, but she promised to meet Pete and LeRoy there and pay them for their services. Feeling somewhere between euphoria and terror, she hoped the tow truck didn't fall apart before they got there. Grace found the bar easily and noticed her hands were still shaking.

Inside, the darkness made it impossible to see, and her eyes did not adjust quickly. So she stood inside the door for a few seconds before making her way to a booth, planning to sit quietly until they arrived.

"Can I help ya, lady?" the bartender called from across the room where he was washing glasses behind the bar.

"I'd love a glass of ice water, please."

"Okay, lady. Are ya sure you don't want a beer?"

She shook her head. "No, thank you. I'm just waiting for some friends."

"Who's meeting you? I know most everybody who comes in here."

"Two men named Pete and LeRoy," she answered.

The bartender did a double take, "Huh? What business would a nice lady like you have with those two clowns?"

"They happen to be my employees and friends," she explained, her voice cool as she hoped to forego any further conversation. "And I'm looking forward to meeting them here."

"Well, you'd better keep your purse zipped up tight or they'll steal you blind."

Grace chuckled in spite of her annoyance at the man for continuing to talk to her. "Don't worry about me. I actually came to pay them for a job well done." She felt defensive and knew she shouldn't be sharing information with the know-it-all bartender.

"What did you have them do . . . steal a car?" He laughed.

Grace could hardly keep a straight face. *If he only knew. They didn't really steal a car they just dragged it a little ways and cut it loose. No harm, no foul.*

"No, they pulled through just when I needed them." She thought that quite clever and once again wished the man would stop talking.

The bartender delivered the water, scratching his head before he started back to the bar. Then he turned to and spoke to Grace again. "Ya know, somethin's happened to those two boys lately. You aren't the one who got them wearing suits and goin' to church, are ya?"

Grace raised her eyebrows. "Hmmm, I'd like to think so, but I think it may have been a little Angel." Grace loved the thought and grinned.

The bartender squinted and stepped away looking puzzled.

Grace drank her ice water and waited patiently. She felt good. They had pulled it off.

When Pete and LeRoy finally walked in wearing suits that almost fit, slapping each other on the back, the bartender shook his head. Grace got up from her booth and gave both of them a thankful hug. All three of them were smiling like cousins meeting for a family reunion.

She noticed Pete was eyeing the bar longingly. "Uh, Mrs. Partain . . ."

"Call me Grace, please."

"Grace, would it be okay if we had a beer? I mean, would ya mind?"

"Pete, I'll even have one with you, and the round's on me."

The men's eyes widened as they looked at each other in surprise, and then grinned from ear to ear. When they were served, they all chuckled as they celebrated pulling off their plan. But in spite of their excitement, they kept their voices low and secretive.

"I wish we coulda seen the look on that guy's face when he saw his car goin' away backwards," LeRoy said after a long swig of the cold beer.

"I don't know who was doing all the screaming from the inside," Grace said, still puzzled. "That just added to Jerry's confusion, I think. It gave me just enough time to grab what I needed and run."

"It was almost too easy. I was hopin' for a little more action," Pete said.

Grace giggled. "Quite enough action for me, thank you very much. I didn't know I could run that fast. What happened after I left?"

"We kinda accidentally ripped his fender off pulling his car around the shed." LeRoy was more animated than usual. "When we had enough distance 'tween him and us, we unhooked 'er and skeedaddled."

The men seemed proud of their perfect timing, and Grace couldn't have been prouder of her own speedy getaway with the bag of money. They were like three kids who just robbed a candy store – and got away with it. When they finished chatting, Grace thought the boys might want to carry on their celebration without her, so she invited them to come out to her car so they could finish their transaction.

The bag of money sat on the floorboard in the backseat. Grace reached in, fished around until she came out with two packets of bills, and handed each of them ten thousand dollars.

"Never forget the 'Terrible Trio and the Baker Caper.'" Grace didn't usually make jokes, but she thought that was pretty funny.

The men stood with their mouths agape, staring at the cash in their hands. They had never seen so much money or anything close to it.

"Ohhhh. Jiggers. This is crazy! How do we . . .?" LeRoy stammered.

"Promise me you'll get that money safely to the bank, and each of you start an account for yourselves. Meanwhile shop around for a good used tow truck, something a little more reliable than the one you have."

Pete's brow furrowed. "What? Wait a minute, Mrs . . . Grace. I don't think I can find a good used tow truck for twenty thousand dollars."

"I don't mean for you to," she explained. "I want each of you to have ten thousand dollars to start a new life. But you did something wonderful for me, and I want to buy you a better truck. A *much* better one so you can build your business."

The men looked at each other, obviously dumbfounded.

"Seriously?" Pete said at last, turning back to Grace. "That's a lot of money. Tow trucks ain't cheap."

She smiled. "Well, try to keep it under fifty thousand."

The men's eyeballs looked like they would pop out of their sockets. "*Fifty thousand*! Are you kidding?" Pete was nearly hyperventilating as he spoke. 'You've already given us twenty thousand, and with buying us a truck, you'll just about use your whole bag of money."

She shook her head. "That's not an issue. I wasn't worried about giving *all* the money to that guy, after all. But I was worried about what he wanted to do to my reputation. He wanted to make people think I killed my husband."

Pete nodded. "I know, but we didn't do twenty thousand dollars worth of work."

"Don't worry about that. You guys didn't have the advantages I've had. I've inherited a lot of money, and I want to help you two get a new start. Somehow you found my driver's license and returned it, you stopped to help Sadie when she broke down on the freeway, you provided a place for her to deliver Angel, and you came to Phil's memorial service and to Angel's dedication. You've almost become a part of the family, and according to the bartender, you've even started going to church. I'm so proud of you both. Just let me know when you've found the vehicle you want, and I'll come and help you negotiate and pay for it." Grace felt like she might be changing two lives for the better.

LeRoy wiped away tears with his sleeve and hugged Grace over and over. Pete hung his head and didn't seem to know what to say, but Grace could tell he was fighting tears.

"Now I'm serious about you getting this money safely in the bank," she cautioned.

"Yeah, Pete," LeRoy said, "'member the night someone hit you over the head in the parkin' lot? If anyone sees us with this money, they might try to take it."

"That's exactly what I'm talking about," Grace said. "I know you want to celebrate, but I'd encourage you to go straight to the bank and not back in the bar for right now."

"Thanks, Grace," Pete said, still blinking back tears. "I think you're tellin' us right." He stepped forward and hugged her lightly. His round stomach bumped against Grace and reminded her of her pregnancy for a moment.

She pushed away the sad memory. "I just want to bless you two. You did something good!"

"Did ya hear that, Pete? We done somethin' really good."

Grace sang all the way home. Hopefully the whole Las Vegas escapade was behind her now. Her teacher friends would never believe what she had been through in the past seven months. She couldn't believe it herself. *Lord, you've seen me through. Is it okay if I thank you for saving me from drug pushers and blackmailers? Is that a category you deal with? After all my whining, I hope you're still listening to me.*

When she arrived home, she burned the photo, the negative, and the manila envelope in the sink.

JERRY AND MADELINE had no place to go, and they continued to argue over whose fault it was their scheme failed. As they zig-zagged down the dirt road toward the freeway, their fender hanging out of the trunk, a siren caught their attention, followed shortly by red lights directly behind them. Jerry took a deep breath and brought the car to a stop. He hoped they could get out of this with no trouble. Then a frightening thought hit him. "Ditch the gun, Madeline," he ordered, but it was too late.

Officer Mike Purcell appeared on the passenger side and directed them to stay in the vehicle. "I'll need to see your licenses, please."

From the corner of his eye, Jerry noticed Madeline trying to shove the pistol under the seat when she reached for her purse, but Purcell apparently saw it too. "Keep your hands out in front of you and exit the car." He cuffed Madeline then reached into the car and grabbed the gun.

"Is this yours, Madeline?" he asked, reading her name off her license.

"No!" She shook her head. "Absolutely not."

"Well, then, if it's not yours, it must be his."

Purcell turned to Jerry, whose shoulders slumped in recognition. He and this cop had met before, and that wasn't good.

"And if it's his," the officer continued, "this is a parole violation, and you're going back to jail, aren't you, Jerry?"

"That's nuts!" Jerry protested. "I did my time."

"And you'll do more for possession of a firearm. You know how this goes, Jerry."

Jerry grimaced. "This just isn't my day."

"So what happened to your fender?" Purcell asked. "That's what caught my attention, you know."

"Two clowns in a tow truck pulled it off," Jerry mumbled.

"Hmm." Childers raised his eyebrows. "Very interesting. I just happen to know a couple of clowns in a tow truck. I wonder if it's the same ones. I've been wondering what they might be up to these days." He chuckled as he finished cuffing Jerry and putting him in the backseat with Madeline. Jerry couldn't imagine what he was laughing at, since nothing seemed humorous to him.

CHAPTER 23

Grace had seen an ad about a missionary group called MTI (Mission Training Internation), and she determined to look into the possibility of getting involved with them. Money was no object, and this would be just what she needed. After applying and being accepted, she shared the details with Nancy and John and asked for their blessing.

"I'm going for a short-term with a team and will be welcomed as a teacher of English, but the best part is I can visit Angel, Sadie, and Blaine and see if I like India."

"India?" Nancy squealed. "That's great."

The pastor smiled. "So you know you'll be in Mumbai?"

"Yes, and the papers were much simpler to fill out than I expected. You helped by vouching for me in regards to my church involvement and fellowship. Thank you, John."

He nodded. "No problem. It seemed like a perfect change of pace for you. I just didn't realize you'd be going to India."

Grace smiled at Nancy and then looked back at John. "You and Nancy have been such an encouragement to me. I don't know what I'd have done without you."

"We're thrilled to see you take an interest in something new and inspirational." Nancy always had the most encouraging words. "You'll be able to use your skills and talents to work with young women. It'll be perfect. Remember, it wasn't all us who saw you through; it was Jesus."

"Yes, I haven't forgotten." Grace nodded and smiled. "He's gotten me through more than you know."

The conversation continued, and they shared their excitement at the opportunity.

When Grace returned home, she toyed with the idea of not letting the Markems know ahead of time and surprising them, but if they happened to be gone for some reason that would be terrible. So she called.

"Hello, Sadie. It's Grace."

She could hear the mixture of excitement and concern in the younger woman's voice. "Hey, Grace! Are you okay? Is everything alright?"

"Yes. I'm fine. I just wondered if you have enough room in India for me."

"What?" Grace could almost see Sadie wiping the sleepy dust out of her eyes to see if it would help her hear more clearly.

Grace smiled. "I'm coming to India on a short mission trip. I want to see you if I can." Sadie squealed so loud, Grace had to hold the phone away from her ear for a few seconds.

"That's fantastic," Sadie exclaimed. "Angel's in bed right now, so I can't put her on, but she'll be so happy to see you, and so will we. I can't wait! It's perfect timing. You'll cure my homesickness for America. You're exactly what I need."

Grace gave her the dates and arrival time so they could keep their conversation brief. She could hear Blaine in the background asking Sadie what she was doing up in the middle of the night and who called. Grace smiled as she heard Sadie give her husband a brief explanation; hoots of joy followed.

The date was set, and as a late-comer to the team, Grace had only one week to get ready. She quickly made her packing list and threw herself into the necessary preparations.

In the meantime the investigator contacted her again, inquiring about the Hargraves, but she honestly had no idea where they had gone. She knew they had not been totally satisfied with the way the business was divided on Grace's behalf and made it obvious they didn't care to communicate with her. She never wanted or expected those results, but life happens and nothing she could do would change it. Maybe time would remedy the situation. Sheldon had left the office in the care of some seasoned sales agents and disappeared. It was very strange, but Grace thought they probably took that huge commission from the Wilburn deal and were traveling around the world. They deserved time away, and since they had come to a financial agreement with Grace, they had not been on the best of terms.

She dismissed her concern. She had enough of her own business to take care of before she departed. Inoculations, travel itinerary, flight tickets, and packing for a four-week stay filled every moment. She was glad she had a current passport because she had heard horror stories about last-minute passport procurement.

IN THREE DAYS GRACE got a call from Nancy. "So how are you doing? Do you need my help with anything?"

Nancy had always been a help to Grace: from the day of their wedding when she made sure the flowers were in place at the last minute, to holding her in her arms when she finally had to face Phil's death, to the loss of her baby. Grace knew Nancy's unconditional love came from her connection with Christ, and it was always available.

"Thanks, but I'm in the last of it. I think I've got everything done except last-minute packing. The house is clean, the clothes are all washed and ironed. I just need to put them in the bags and get some magazines in my carry-on."

"It's going to be a long flight. But you know that."

"Yes, I read a list of things you should know for a long flight, and I'm trying to do them all. I have one of those neck pillows, and I'm going to wear a sweatsuit that's loose and comfortable, but presentable."

She heard Nancy chuckle. "Nobody cares what you look like."

"I know, but I just want to look nice. You know me. I'm taking sleeping pills they gave me on the ship when Phil went missing, and I needed to be knocked out."

"Do you have an eye mask and earplugs?"

"Oh, good idea. I'll dig mine out. I so seldom use them I wouldn't have thought of it. Thanks."

Nancy continued with her practical advice. "On a long flight like that, I know they'll feed you, but if you're like me, I get sick of peanuts and pretzels all day. If you have room in your carry-on, you might consider taking a couple of boiled eggs with salt and a halved avocado with a plastic spoon. Two good sources of protein, and they're really good if you get stuck somewhere or don't get to eat for a long time. I've been doing that for years."

Grace was so appreciative. "I never thought of it, but I could also throw in some almonds and maybe some dark chocolate to treat myself. Truth is I bought first-class tickets, so I think they'll give me lots of treats and delicious full meals."

"Well then I'll just stay out of your way, and I'll see you tomorrow when I pick you up to meet up with your team in Pasadena."

Grace felt well-prepared and had plenty of time to finish her packing when the phone rang again. She almost didn't answer it, but she didn't want to leave any loose ends.

"Grace Partain?" The man's voice sounded very official, not like a sales call. "This is Officer Coolidge calling from Barstow. We have Pete Jensen and LeRoy Ratcliff in our jail here."

Grace's heart missed a beat. *What have they done now to get into trouble? And what do I have to do with it?*

"They say you know them and will vouch for them."

Grace had come to like the guys, but she was not quite sure they had left their old life behind. She knew that wouldn't happen overnight.

"Yes, I know them. What's happened?"

"A large sum of money was stolen from one of our local businesses. And suddenly that amount of money showed up with Pete and LeRoy at the bank. They swear you paid them for working for you. But this large amount of money seemed suspicious."

Grace wasn't about to tell the officer what she paid them to do for her. That might open a can of worms. Even saying she needed them to tow a car would open the question of whose car. If she said they were protecting her, he might ask who they were protecting her from. She hadn't lied to anyone since she had committed her life to Jesus, and this wouldn't be a time to start.

"This is going to sound ridiculous, but it's the truth. My daughter's car – well she's actually my friend, but she's like a daughter – broke down on the freeway on the way to Las Vegas a few months ago. Pete and LeRoy were the first ones to come along and offer help. While they were helping her with her car trouble, she went into labor, and they made their tow truck seat into a delivery room and helped her give birth and get to a medical center. I felt I owed those boys quite a lot, so I gave each of them ten thousand dollars."

"Really? Ten thousand dollars?"

"I know it sounds crazy, but my husband died recently, and I inherited a business and plenty of money. These guys have almost become a part of our family, and I wanted to help them out."

"You swear this is the truth?"

"Yes, absolutely. What else do I need to do?"

"You need to show up and bail them out, but we need to verify that you're who you say you are, so you need to bring your driver's license. If you can prove who you are, we can let them out on their own recognizance. But you do realize these guys have a bit of a rap sheet that goes back at least twelve years and includes car theft, petty theft, and indecent exposure, right?"

Grace smiled. "I know they aren't angels, but I think they've changed."

"Yeah, I've heard that before."

"There is a problem, though. I have to leave on a month-long trip in the early morning, and it's already five o'clock."

"I'm sorry about the inconvenience, but if you don't want them to sit in jail for a month, I hope you can make it."

Grace sighed. There went her feeling of confidence about being ready to go and packing in leisure.

"I can do it. I'll be there as quickly as I can."

She put down the phone, looked at herself in the mirror, and made a face that said "phooey." Then she punched in the Troude number.

"Nancy, you offered your help, and have I got a deal for you!"

"Huh? I don't understand."

"I'll explain more later, but for now would you ride with me out to Barstow to bail out Pete and LeRoy?"

"Bail out?"

Grace tried to curb her impatience. "Will you ride with me? I promise I'll make it worth your while just by telling you a story you won't believe."

"Sounds juicy. Those guys must've really gotten themselves into big trouble this time."

"Actually, they didn't," she said, "and I'm just going there to vouch for them and prove their innocence."

"Are you sure you want to do that?"

"Absolutely. Not on this particular evening when I still have packing to do, but believe me, I must."

"Okay, then pick me up, and I'll make sure John has his dinner set out for him."

"Come as you are. I'm going just like I am. I may comb my hair, but that's about it."

They said goodbye, and then, as an afterthought, Grace picked up the receipt from the bank that proved her withdrawal.

THE TRAFFIC BETWEEN Highland and Barstow was congested almost all the way. Staying in the middle lane, Grace told Nancy the whole story about her trip last summer to Las Vegas, including how she ended up working in a casino for a few days for a criminal named Jerry. Then she told about his attempt to blackmail her and how Pete and LeRoy helped her get the photo and keep the money.

They both laughed to tears when she told about LeRoy crawling in his FBI suit to hook a chain to Jerry's car and then dragging it backwards.

"For some reason," Nancy said once she'd caught her breath, "I can't picture you running with a sack of money and tearing off in your car. Sounds like a movie plot!"

Grace nodded. "You're right. So I paid Pete and LeRoy ten thousand dollars each and promised to buy them a new tow truck – a good used one. I know I didn't have to, but I don't need the money, and I wanted to help them out. They haven't had the advantages I have, and believe me, they were so sweet and appreciative."

Nancy shook her head. "I can't believe it. You . . . Grace Partain . . . schoolteacher who leads the calmest life in the world. Probably the riskiest thing you ever did was renege on a play with your bridge friends. I can't believe it." She laughed again.

Grace laughed, too. "It sounds crazy when I tell the story. But Angel and you and John also had something to do with this whole thing."

"How's that?"

"You already knew they were the ones whose tow truck served as a delivery room for Angel. Then they came to her dedication and had dinner with all of us. You and John and the kids treated them with love even though they showed up in a zebra striped hotrod, suits that made them look like clowns, and wearing their greasy caps. They'd never been in a church, and I'm sure they'd never eaten in such a nice restaurant. They were like two kids in a candy store, and I've become quite fond of these two comical characters. I even found out from the bartender that they've been going to church, and I'm sure they've taken quite a ribbing about it from their hoodlum friends."

"Bar? When were you hanging out in a bar recently? Boy, you are full of surprises."

"That's where we met after the 'Baker Caper.' Yes, I even had a beer with them. Well, part of a beer."

"Are you lifting them up, or are they dragging you down?" Nancy teased. More laughter.

"I don't think I'll go to hell for drinking a beer, but I think they were surprised."

Nancy continued the conversation. "I'll never forget when LeRoy stuck his greasy finger out and Angel took hold of it. His eyes nearly jumped out of his head, and he got the biggest grin on his face. It must be how God looks at us – with a look of love and joy, no matter what we look like on the outside or how greasy we might be. We're precious to Him, and He looks at our hearts."

"Then you get what I'm talking about."

"Love thy neighbor," Nancy said, "even if they live in Barstow." They both laughed again.

"So this'll be another first for me," Grace admitted. "I've never been to a jail. But I count it an honor to help these guys out and help them change their reputation in Barstow."

"We better not hang around long, though, because you've got to get home and finish packing, so you can leave in the morning."

"Yes, but I'm glad you're with me to see them in this environment. I think you'll be surprised how much they've changed."

CHAPTER 24

"I'm so excited about Grace coming to Mumbai. I know she'll love it even though she's only here for a short time," Sadie said as she bustled about putting the house in order. "She'll be so surprised to see how much Angel has grown."

"We'll have to take her out to the beach for awhile," Blaine suggested. "And I want to take her for a tour around the production company so she can see what I've been doing."

Sadie could tell Blaine was excited, too. "I guess she's probably been pretty bored since we've been gone. I wonder if she's ever heard anything more about Phil's murderer. What a mystery."

GRACE AND NANCY ENTERED the jail uncertainly. The desk sergeant greeted them and asked why they were there.

"I understand my friends Pete Jensen and LeRoy Ratcliff have been arrested, and I'm here to prove their innocence and see them set free. I'm Grace Partain. Here's my driver's license and my passport."

The sergeant glanced at the documents before looking back at them. "Thank you for coming, but they're suspected of theft. In fact, they both opened new bank accounts and deposited ten thousand dollars each."

"Yes, well, that's exactly what I paid them . . . in cash. Here's the receipt I got when I pulled the money out of my account. I warned them not to go back to the bar but to take the money straight to the bank where it would be safe. I'm glad to hear they took my advice."

"When did you do that?"

"A week ago."

"Well, they just deposited the money yesterday."

Grace shook her head. "I don't know why it took them a week to do it, but that's okay. I'm also going to purchase a new tow truck for them – well, a new used one – so when you see them driving it, please don't put them in jail and accuse them of stealing it."

The officer frowned. "Why would you do a thing like that for these two thugs?"

"Because those two *men* deserve a break, and I believe in second chances . . . and so does God. They helped my daughter – friend – when she needed help, and we've seen another side of them. Can we move ahead with getting them out of here? I need to get back to Highland, and the traffic is awful."

"Sure, Ma'am. We don't usually get cases like this, so I really appreciate you coming, and I'm sure they will, too." He got up and headed back to the cells.

Some time passed, and Grace assumed they were collecting their belongings and being released. For some reason, she expected them to come out in their FBI suits, but they emerged wearing their old dirty overalls with T-shirts and dusty boots, much like Sadie must have seen them when they met her by the freeway.

"Oh, my, they certainly have changed," Nancy whispered.

Grace ignored her, pleased to see the men were none the worse for wear—just wearing worse.

"Boy, we're glad to see you, Grace." LeRoy walked right up and gave her a hug. She was reminded of the first time she saw these guys at the funeral and was taken aback by their appearance. Now she felt good to be hugged by a skinny guy in overalls who looked like he'd been working as a mechanic all day. It reminded her of the contrast between LeRoy's greasy fingers and Angel's yellow dress.

"Hey, you're the preacher-man's wife, huh?" Pete said, as he walked up to Nancy and stuck out his grease-stained hand.

She didn't hesitate to put her hand in his and shake it. "Yes, Pete. I remember you from the dedication day at our church."

"That was fun." LeRoy offered his blackened hand as well, and Nancy shook it warmly.

"I'm so glad you enjoyed yourself," Nancy said, "and I remember how little Angel took to you."

LeRoy grinned. "How's that little cutie? I bet she's growed a lot."

"Sadie, Blaine, and Angel are living in India for six months," Grace explained. "I'm going there tomorrow."

LeRoy looked confused. "India? Is that where Indians come from?"

Grace smiled. "Yes, but not American Indians, *India* Indians." Grace had already been through this with Pete, so she stifled a giggle and noticed that Nancy covered her mouth with her hand as well, no doubt to cover her grin.

"Huh? I never heard of that." LeRoy scratched his head.

"Oh, yeah," Pete added as though this was common knowledge to him. "It's another country clear on the other side of the world."

Grace was captivated by their mixture of innocence and ignorance; they really did need an advocate or a guardian angel to watch over them.

"We didn't tell the cops nothin' about the thing with Jerry," Pete said. "We just told 'em we done some work for you. Is that okay?"

"That's perfect. Thank you." Grace smiled. "We don't need for anyone to know the rest of the story. That'll be our secret. Nobody got hurt, and justice was served."

"Undercover work," Pete said.

LeRoy brightened then and looked straight at Nancy as he spoke. "Oh, ya know what? Me and Pete have been goin' to church. We're still wearin' our FBI suits, but Grace told us to buy some new ones. We just haven't figured out how to do that yet, but we will. She said maybe Macy's, but that's pretty high falootin'. Next time you see us, you'll be surprised."

"You always surprise me, and I'm so happy to hear you're going to church," Nancy responded.

"Yeah, there's this real perty . . ."

"LeRoy, forget it," Pete said, jumping in before he could finish. "She don't have no interest in no tow truck jockey."

"She will when we get our new truck . . . and some new church suits."

Grace hated to cut the conversation short, but she worried about the traffic and wanted to get home and finish packing. "I have to go, but I'll be back in a month, and you make sure you have a new truck lined up for me to purchase for you. How does that sound?"

Both men beamed as Pete answered. "Sounds great."

Hugs all around, and Grace and Nancy were back on the road. As they pulled out on the freeway, Nancy chuckled. "Well, you were right. They went from poor-fitting suits to greasy overalls. But there's a real difference in the way they care about you. You've become their fairy godmother."

"I just love them," Grace said, meaning every word, "and I pray they'll get more involved in their church and become upstanding citizens. Everyone deserves a second chance. I want to be part of that. Since I don't have Phil, I feel good about doing something good for others. I don't want to be a fairy godmother. I want to be a *merry* godmother. Now that's silly."

"This is kind of funny, Grace. You're going clear around the world to teach girls English as a missionary, but you just drove an hour to be a missionary in San Bernardino County. Actually, that's what Christians are supposed to do. Love your neighbor whether they live next door, across the county, or around the world."

"I never thought about it that way," Grace admitted, "but when I get back from India, I'd love to speak to the women's group at the church about my experience. And I love that theme if you don't mind me using it . . . 'Who's My Neighbor?' I like that."

"By all means. We all should be missionaries and purveyors of God's love, no matter where we are."

PETE AND LEROY WERE afraid to spend any of the money. They could hardly believe it was truly theirs. They'd never had money to spend, budget, or save.

"That's it. I'm gonna buy me some new shirts and jeans. I think that'd be a really good thing to do." Pete thought about Grace and how she had gone out of her way to come and rescue them. "If we're gonna be drivin' a new truck, we ought to look respectable. I've been wearing these old overalls for years. We should get some new boots, too."

"Hey, Pete, how 'bout we get some shirts with our names on 'em, like real business people?"

"You finally came up with a good idea, LeRoy. They'll say Pete and LeRoy's Towing Company."

"Why not LeRoy & Pete's Towing Company?" LeRoy countered.

"How about Jensen and Ratcliff Towing Company?"

"How about Jensen, Ratcliff, and sons?"

"Now that's stupid, LeRoy. We don't have no sons."

"Well we might someday."

"By then the shirts'll be worn clean out, and we'll have to buy new ones anyhow."

"Yeah, you're right," LeRoy admitted. "This is harder than I thought. We can ask Grace. She's like our business manager or silent partner or somethin'."

"She's gonna be gone for a while," Pete cautioned, "so we'll have to figure it out our ownselves. We gotta find out where to buy some Sunday-go-to-meetin' suits."

"Yeah, there's that cute gal in church. I think she likes me." LeRoy's cheeks turned pink.

Pete was amused. "What would make you think that?"

"Last week she set in fronta me 'n' she turned around and smiled at me. She even told me her name . . . Tammy."

"Stupid, the preacher said for everyone to take a minute and greet someone around them. She was just followin' directions." Pete resisted smacking LeRoy with his new cap because he didn't want to dirty it on LeRoy's greasy hair.

"Yeah, but I could tell she was wantin' to shake my hand."

"So why didn't you stick it out there?"

LeRoy looked down at his grease-stained hand. "It was dirty."

AS GRACE WALKED OUT of the terminal, Sadie flew into her arms, almost knocking her down. Blaine held Angel in his arms and lagged behind, no doubt to let the two women have their moment. Grace appreciated it but couldn't wait to get hold of the baby.

"Let me see that little Angel." Grace came closer but carefully and slowly as not to scare the baby. She extended her arms, and Angel came right to her. Nuzzling the child she wept tears of joy. With her other arm she gave Blaine a half-hug and stood on tip-toes to give him a kiss on the cheek.

"I'm so glad to see you. It hasn't been the same since you left."

An understatement. She wasn't sure she wanted to tell them about the adventures with Pete and LeRoy. Quite a lot of questionable behavior might make them wonder what had happened to their peaceful landlady and friend. Sadie knew Jerry from her job in the casino where she and Grace met, but that story could wait until later. Grace wanted to hear more about their stay in India, Angel's progress, Sadie's life as a housewife, and Blaine's internship. She would have only two days with them before her assignment in a school a few miles away. "So . . . tell me everything you've learned about India and how your stay has been."

Blaine waved down a *Tuk Tuk (*a three-wheeled vehicle with the motor of a small motorcycle that somehow has the emissions of an 18-wheeler.) and put the bags in the rack. The women piled in the backseat with Grace still carrying Angel. Blaine jumped in the front by the driver.

The ride made Grace's hair stand on end. She had never seen so much traffic going every direction at once with no lanes and no rules. Bicycles, buses, people, and Tuk Tuks filled every space.

"This is like Mr. Toad's Wild Ride!" Grace laughed as she clutched Angel to her chest and hung on for dear life with her spare hand.

A KNOCK AT THE DOOR made John jump. He expected to hear Nancy come in from the garage hours ago, but when she didn't he had become anxious and wondered what might have happened. He went to the door, where two officers introduced themselves and handed him their cards.

"Mr. Troude," the one whose card identified him as Officer Bennet said, "is there someone here with you?"

"No, why?"

"Is Nancy Troude related to you?"

His heart jumped into racing mode. "Yes, she's my wife. Has something happened?"

"I regret to inform you there's been an accident on the I-10 freeway this morning, and Mrs. Troude has been killed. Another driver going the wrong way on the freeway hit her head-on."

He wasn't sure when the ringing started in his ears, but it was getting louder by the moment. "It can't be her. My wife took a friend to Pasadena early this morning to meet a missionary group headed for India."

The officer didn't seem to hear his denial. "I'm so sorry for your loss. I don't believe she suffered, as she had expired before I arrived on scene. She was probably killed on impact. I'm so sorry."

John's knees buckled. His world collapsed while he tried to breathe. The officers reached out to steady him.

"Mr. Troude? Are you okay?" He accepted the support of the officers and took three slow, deep breaths.

"The Lord giveth and the Lord taketh away. Blessed be the name of the Lord." Was that him mumbling those words he had said so many times to others? They seemed to come from far away. He broke down sobbing then and wished he had never answered the door. If he could turn back the clock five minutes, maybe it would not be true.

He realized then that the two officers were waiting for him to regain control. "Tell me what I need to do," John muttered.

The patrolman told him where to go to identify Nancy's body and suggested he get someone to drive him.

When they left, John fell to his knees. He prayed passionately for God to help him have the strength to get through this. He could not bear to think of Nancy sitting dead in her car. He thought of her beautiful life cut short. And yet was it short, or was it exactly what God had planned? He thought of Phil and others whose lives were a lot shorter than Nancy's. He thought of Grace and how saddened she would be to hear Nancy died on her trip home from taking her to Pasadena. How would he tell his children? How would he tell his congregation? Grace would be gone for a month. *Should I contact*

Grace and interrupt her mission trip? Where should I start? And then, of course, he knew exactly where to start. He called his kids.

CHAPTER 25

Sheldon and Marilyn arrived home at midnight. Everything remained as they left it, except for dozens of messages on the answering machine. Without dealing with the messages, they both slumped into their overstuffed sofa.

Sheldon spoke first. "It was great cruising the Mediterranean Sea, and I loved the land tour of Europe, but let's stay home for a while. I've got to get back to work and see how business went in my absence." He didn't even mention how exhausted he was nor did he address that same exhaustion he saw etched on his wife's face.

"You're right," Marilyn agreed. "I hope I still have some customers at the salon. I'll call in tomorrow and get back on the schedule."

"It'll be different to work without Phil as the motivator always pushing to make more money."

"Yeah, well, no more pushing, so maybe you'll be able to make it to some of my softball games. I need to call the coach and see if the season games have started yet and ask if anyone has taken my position as catcher. The coach won't be happy that I missed spring training, and I bet some of those messages are from him."

Her comments spurred Sheldon to start listening to the messages and taking notes.

"I'm glad Phil brought on a couple of great sales people before we left on the Alaska trip," he said between messages, "because they've closed some fair-sized deals in our absence, and Phil would be proud of them."

"Now that we're home, can you stop talking about Phil every minute? He's gone, and we're here." Marilyn put her arms around Sheldon and came in close for a kiss.

"Phil and I were joined at the hip for the last twenty-five years – playing football, selling real estate." He paused and grinned. "Getting in trouble with our wives for working too late." He pinched Marilyn on the rear, and they laughed. "I'll try not to mention Phil every minute, but when you lose someone so much like a brother, you miss him."

"That's understandable, but you're the boss now, so go sell something tomorrow! Meanwhile, let's get to bed. It's late, and I'm exhausted."

"SO IS THERE A CHURCH we can attend?" Grace asked Sadie after dinner the first night.

"Christianity isn't accepted here," Sadie explained. "One missionary showed the 'Left Behind' movie, and the next day the extremists burned his house down. And if a Hindu converts to Christianity, their family usually kicks them out and disowns them." As they talked, Sadie prepared a tray with tea and dessert, and then they went into the living room.

"Wow, I had no idea," Grace admitted. "I mean, I knew there was some persecution in various countries, including India, I suppose. Ashish told us about that, but I had no idea it was so bad. I guess I'd better be careful about sharing Jesus with these girls. I thought missionaries were free to do that . . . share the Bible and tell about Jesus."

Blaine chimed in. "It's my understanding that our missionaries come to teach English or work in hospitals or various institutions.

The idea is to come to help with skills that show caring and love. A helping hand extended in love can go a long way to break down the cultural barriers and misunderstandings. Hopefully the end result is forming relationships and opening doors."

"Well, that makes sense," Grace admitted. "One of the organizations I found in my research was aptly named Open Door. I just hope I'm worthy of the calling and can be a positive influence on these girls."

"Don't sell yourself short," Sadie said. "I remember the first day I met you in the casino, and I knew you were someone special."

That triggered Grace's memory about the run-in with Jerry, or the "escapades of the Terrible Trio," namely Pete, LeRoy, and herself. "That reminds me, I haven't told you about the 'Terrible Trio and our Baker Caper yet.'"

Sadie's eyes widened. "What in the world are you talking about?"

It wasn't long before Grace had them rolling with laughter as she told about LeRoy half-crawling in his ill-fitting FBI suit to place a hook on Jerry's bumper. As she laughed and gasped for air, she told about Pete pulling it away backwards, Jerry running like a wild man after the car, while a woman screamed like a crazed lunatic from inside the car, and Grace sprinted for her own car with the photo, negative, and a bag of money. "I laughed all the way to Buford's Bar to meet the boys. I wanted to call you but decided to wait until I could tell you face-to-face, and we could laugh together."

Sadie, her cheeks pink from laughing, said, "That's hilarious! How did you ever get LeRoy and Pete to help you?"

"I told them they could wear their FBI suits and be my bodyguards. They were like two kids playing cops and robbers, and they didn't even know what we were trying to accomplish. They were the ones who got the idea to distract Jerry by pulling his car away. That brilliant move made the whole caper work. I did ask them not to smoke or spit when they were on duty." They all laughed again.

"Did they ask you for money?" Blaine asked.

"No, but I had promised to pay them for their services beforehand. They just didn't know how much."

Sadie got up to put Angel to bed while Grace told Blaine what a great job Bernard had done with the landscaping and yard service.

When Sadie returned, she wanted to know more about LeRoy and Pete. "So were they satisfied?"

"Oh, yes. I gave each of them ten thousand dollars and suggested they each start their own bank account."

"Wow! What did they say?" Blaine asked.

"They were pretty much speechless. I don't know what it is about those guys, but I just feel like they could use some help. I told them I'd buy them a new tow truck when I get back."

"Will that make you business partners?" Sadie teased.

"Well, that wasn't my intention," Grace said. "It's not a loan . . . but even the bartender in Barstow said he'd noticed they were cleaning up their act and going to church."

Sadie smiled and shook her head so her ponytail swished from side to side. "Wow! Church. That's wonderful!"

"Yes, they told me again when I bailed them out of jail, but that's another story for tomorrow."

GRACE'S FIRST DAY ON the job was nothing like she expected. She thought she'd be in the slums with frightening surroundings. Instead, she found herself in a small classroom with a whiteboard, markers, some workbooks, and sixteen girls ranging in age from eleven to fifteen, all eager to learn. They oohed and aahed over Grace's blonde hair and bright clothing.

Grace, who usually wore suits to school, had gone more casual according to the advice Sadie had given her for the trip. She took a colorful scarf, a white sleeveless cotton blouse, and loose white linen pants. The scarf would cover her head and shoulders. Sadie had told her to cover her head, shoulders, and cleavage. None of the local women wore shorts. Long loose dresses were also another choice Grace had collected, even though it wasn't her style. She felt more comfortable than she expected.

The team stayed at a dormitory-type building with women in one room and men in another. Each person had a storage cabinet but not much privacy.

Grace visited Sadie and her family often. As the two women chatted over tea one day, Grace told Sadie, "The girls are all so sweet, and they look at me like I'm someone special."

"It's Jesus in you that makes you special," Sadie said. "I'm so glad you came. How is it living with the other missionaries nearer the school?"

"We made the long flight together, and at school we cross paths occasionally, so I feel safer with them than I would in an apartment by myself."

Sadie smiled. "It was very nice of Ashish's family to try to find you a place, but they understood your apprehension."

"They were wonderful about it," Grace agreed. "I enjoyed meeting them and hope to see them again before I leave. They invited all of us to dinner if you want to come."

"We'd love that. They seemed really nice, and I think Ashish would thank us." Sadie refilled Grace's tea.

"I wanted to tell you more about the school. The director is originally from Pasadena, and he's quite nice. His name is Glen Sanford. I think we may be about the same age. He comes in and out of the classrooms offering support."

"Is he a teacher, too?"

"No . . . well, I guess he used to be, but in California his position as school principal kept him busy until recently. His parents died and left quite an inheritance that made it possible for him to retire early from his job and go on the mission field."

"Sounds like he's putting his experience to good work." Blaine got up from the sofa. "You women can keep up your chatter, but I'm going to bed. And by the way, if your group hasn't already planned a closed worship service, you're welcome to come back here and worship with Sadie and me and a few other Christians who come to the house. Then you can meet some of our friends."

"Sounds good. I'll see what they have planned."

"WHEN WE GO LOOKIN'" for a new truck, I'm wearin' my new jeans and stuff," LeRoy said as he spit a stream of tobacco into the dirt and Pete lit a cigarette.

"I don't think Grace approves of us spittin' and smokin.' I feel kinda guilty spending her money on smokes. Sadie said something about it the day we all went to lunch."

LeRoy shook his head. "I been chewin' so long, I don't know iffin I could go without."

"Could you do it for fifty thousand dollars? Could you do it for a new truck?" Pete challenged LeRoy's thinking.

LeRoy seemed to think for a minute and then nodded. "Iffin Grace wanted me to, I'd dern sure try."

The next day they agreed to go tow truck shopping in Las Vegas in their new jeans and polo shirts with their own names embroidered on them – just "Pete" and "LeRoy." They didn't want to get too complicated yet.

"When we get the truck, we'll decide on the name and paint it on the doors," Pete said. "Then we'll have some more shirts made with the name on 'em. By then these will be good and dirty and half wore out."

Pete's mom sneaked his clothes out of his room every once in a while and ran them through the washer. He knew it and liked it, but he pretended not to notice. Sometimes he would even add some of LeRoy's clothes to the pile. Pete suspected his mom knew, but she too pretended not to notice. She just washed them, hung them out, and returned them to Pete's room.

Pete's father was drunk most of the time, so he didn't notice much of anything. He hardly left the house except to buy booze and couldn't hold down a job for any length of time.

"When we find a truck and come rollin' in to that church yard, I bet Tammy's gonna notice. We need to get new suits while we're in Las Vegas, too. We're gonna be stylin' something fierce. How did we get so lucky?"

"I'm thinkin' it's what I've heard the preacher call a "God thing." If we hadn't stopped to pick up Sadie when her car was broke down, or if she hadn't decided to deliver her baby in our truck, or if we hadn't found Grace's driver's license—I hope she never finds out why we had it—and if God hadn't made all that happen, we wouldn't have met Grace or got to help her outsmart the casino guy, and we wouldn't be lookin' for a new truck that we couldn't have ever afforded . . . and we wouldn't be goin' to church or wearin' new clothes." Pete knew their old tow truck was barely hanging on by a spark plug.

"Wow, Pete, you really said that clear like it made sense," LeRoy said, his eyes wide. "It hurts my brain to think of all of that there in one think."

SHELDON WENT BACK TO work and picked up right where he left off, head down right off the starting blocks.

It didn't take long for Marilyn to fill her appointment book with clients. Sheldon had made a point to be home by six o'clock every night, although Marilyn wasn't always home until later. She often changed clothes at work and went right to ball practice. It didn't make sense to him to come home at six if she wasn't there fixing dinner.

"Marilyn, you haven't seemed yourself ever since we got home. Is something bothering you?" Sheldon asked.

"I'm fine. Just trying to get back into the swing of things."

"Yeah, well, I'm trying to get home earlier, and you usually aren't here. What's the point?"

Marilyn frowned. "What's the point? The point is, you could start dinner when you get home. I've never been the little housewife that has dinner steaming hot when you walk through the door. I did that for a few years, and it usually sat until it was stone cold or stuck to the pan, and I gave up. Now it's your turn to lift a finger."

Sheldon was incredulous. "*Oh, my gosh, Marilyn! Lift a finger*? Who brings in the money and works seven days a week? I can't believe you. You wanted to travel; we traveled. You wanted a new house; we got a new house. What else do you want?" He could almost feel steam coming off the back of his neck.

Marilyn put her hands on her hips. "I've made money, too, you know. It wasn't all you and Phil."

"I thought we weren't going to bring Phil into this anymore. And now you're doing it."

Marilyn sat down and put her head back. "I'm just tired . . . maybe jet lag. Give me time to make a better schedule. Maybe I could order some of that food that comes ready-made that gets delivered to the house. We can afford it now. I'll do better, I promise."

Sheldon went to the wine cooler and pulled out a bottle, examining it carefully. "What's this bottle of wine? I don't recognize it? It's not the kind we usually buy."

"Uh, I don't know. Why don't we drink it and get it out of here?"

"Huh uh, it doesn't look familiar. I'm gonna wait until we have visitors and feed it to them. Or give it to someone in the office for a prize for the next one who closes a sale."

"No!" Marilyn said sharply.

Sheldon frowned. "What's wrong with you? What difference does it make? We can buy more of the kind we like."

"Well, if you must know, that's the bottle of wine I bought on the ship. I brought it home in my suitcase."

Sheldon was confused. "Did it mean something to you? Why are you being so weird?"

Instead of answering, Marilyn grabbed the bottle of wine and stormed out of the room.

CHAPTER 26

Sadie and Blaine welcomed Grace for dinner often so she would feel completely safe and at home during her stay in India. Besides, they were so glad to have her with them. Angel seemed especially pleased to have her there, and Sadie worried the baby would be sad when Grace's visit came to an end. Some nights they stayed up visiting so late Grace slept on the sofa in their apartment.

One evening, as they were enjoying dessert after dinner, Sadie asked, "So what did the cruise line ever find out about Phil's death?" Sadie and Blaine had agreed they wouldn't mention it until Grace brought it up, but she didn't. Sadie decided she couldn't ignore it any longer because then it seemed as if they didn't care, and they did.

Sadie's heart ached at the pain she saw on Grace's face as her friend anwered. "I've given up on it. Evidently the FBI should have been notified sooner when foul play became apparent. An agent should have been waiting for me at the dock, but I didn't know that. It's almost like the cruise line washed their hands of it and were satisfied to believe Phil got swept out to sea or jumped overboard. It wasn't until they discovered his body . . . " Grace swallowed hard and continued, ". . . that they really dug in and started working the case. The FBI didn't have much to go on. I had a few phone calls from them regarding the Hargraves, but at the time they were out of town. When I get home I'll check in with Sheldon and the FBI and see if anyone knows anything."

GRACE ENJOYED HER ASSIGNMENT more each day. The girls had really taken to her and occasionally gathered around for a group hug.

Glen stopped in more regularly and took a genuine interest in her teaching style. "Say, Grace, when you finish up with the morning lessons, would you like to go for lunch at one of the local places that serves wonderful food? We could talk about the students' progress and the next couple of weeks' curriculum."

Grace's heart warmed at the invitation. "Why, thank you very much, Glen. I'd like that." She felt comfortable with his invitation and noticed for the first time how handsome and clean-shaven he was. He had a full head of hair that greyed at the temples, making him look quite distinguished. His clothes were always ironed and fresh, and she could tell he took time to look his best. She thought his eyes were hazel, but she hadn't been close enough to tell for sure.

As it turned out they didn't talk about the students or the curriculum during lunch. Instead Glen kept Grace busy answering questions about her life. Surprised and flattered she shared more than she expected. He did the same, telling her he'd been married quite young, but it didn't work out. His wife divorced him, but he had two grown daughters he had raised by himself until they went off to college.

"I've always had a heart for missions," he explained, "but I didn't think I'd find a mate who would be willing to go to India, so I didn't try."

Grace wondered if he meant for her to respond to his comment. After an awkward silence, she noticed they both were looking down at their empty plates.

At last Glen cleared his throat and asked, "So what are your plans after this stint in India?"

Grace swallowed and twisted her napkin. "I don't really know. I've been in limbo ever since my husband's disappearance . . . death.

Not knowing what really happened has been most disconcerting. I haven't known what to do with myself."

Glen reached across the table and put his hand over hers. "Could I talk you into coming back for a longer stay?"

Grace sat up straight. She hadn't expected anything like that, and she wasn't ready to respond. After a split-second hesitation, she pulled her hand away. "Glen, I'm not sure what you're thinking, but it's only been a few months since I lost my husband, and I'm not sure I'm ready to make any commitments about anything. My pastor suggested I create a new life by doing something new, and this is my first try."

Glen's cheeks reddened, and he nodded. "I understand. I'm sorry if I acted too soon, but you'll only be here another couple of weeks, and I don't want to miss the window of opportunity, if there *is* a window." Grace saw him take a deep breath before saying, "The minute I met you, I felt an attraction."

TWO WEEKS PASSED QUICKLY, and the India commitment was over. Grace couldn't figure out why Nancy didn't show up to drive her home. Bewildered she walked outside the baggage area and looked around. A limo driver held up a cardboard sign with the name "Grace Partain" on it.

Hesitantly and a bit confused, she approached the driver. "I'm Grace Partain, but I have a friend coming."

"Yes, Ma'am, your friend couldn't make it. If you need to see my credentials or anything, here they are." He showed her some papers and his card that said Alfonso, Angel Limo Service. Grace smiled at the name.

Grace thought it strange that Nancy wasn't there to pick her up, but she handed over her carry-on, satisfied that something very important must have happened. Maybe they had planned a homecoming party for her, she mused.

When Grace arrived home, she felt exhausted from the long trip but somewhat renewed in her heart. Seeing Angel, Sadie, and Blaine had been full of fun and cuddles. Teaching the Indian girls had been so rewarding; she hated to leave them. Meeting Glen brought a surprise she never imagined. He had touched her heart in the two weeks they still had after their first lunch date, and he kept asking her passionately if she would consider coming back to develop their relationship.

It felt good to be home, even though nobody greeted her. She noticed her voice mail was full again, so she dropped her purse on the counter and took the bags as far as the den. Then she returned to the kitchen, grabbed a notepad, and started to listen to each message, taking notes and numbers of those she needed to call back.

The first was from the FBI, which immediately caught her full attention. "FBI Agent Watkins. We've been trying to reach you for three weeks. We're finally able to release your husband's remains, belongings, and ring. We also have a lead on the killer and look forward to hearing from you to discuss it." He left a number and signed off.

After a brief pause to calm her heart, she moved on to message number two. "Hi Grace, Sheldon here. Just wanted you to know we're finally home after gadding about Europe and the Mediterranean. I'm back at the office playing catch up, and Marilyn already has a full booking at the salon. If you want to get your hair done, you'd better call ahead for an appointment. She's swamped." He chuckled a bit before clearing his throat and moving on. "I'm sorry you and I had a riff before we left. I don't want our friendship to end that way, so let's get together and talk. Okay, I know this is a long message. Call me when you get time."

Message number three brought a smile to her lips. "Hey Grace, it's Pete. Me and LeRoy was in San Bernardino today and we found a cherry truck and it's almost new. Can't wait for you to see it. Call us when you get home so we can go get it. No hurry. I mean . . . we can wait, but . . . well, the sales guy wants us to hurry up. We'll be glad to see you. Call us . . . okay? Bye."

The gardener was next. "Hello, Mrs. Partain. This is Bernard, Blaine's friend. I've been doing his lawn service, but I've run into a problem. The other day I played flag football with some of the guys at the dorm, and I broke my foot. I don't know what to do. I don't really know how to get in touch with Blaine, and he couldn't do anything about it anyway. Call me when you get home, please. Meanwhile, I'll see if I can get one of the other guys to fill in. Sorry to burden you with this, but I know you'll be home soon. Bye."

She pushed the button for the next message. "Hi Grace, it's Fran. I'm so sorry I couldn't come to the airport today. I told John I could do it, but then Alfie had other plans for me, and I had to go to his business conference with him in Santa Barbara. I sent the Angel Limo service for you. I've used them many times before, and I knew he'd get you home safely. Welcome home! I'll call you when we get back. I'd love to hear about your trip to India."

Grace thought it was odd that John had asked Fran, rather than Nancy, to pick her up. Obviously something had come up. The next message nearly brought Grace to her knees. "Grace, it's John. I wanted to call you in India, but I just couldn't bring myself to spoil your time there. You couldn't have changed anything here anyway." After a slight pause, he went on. "Nancy was involved in a terrible accident on the way home from taking you to Pasadena and was killed. Another driver hit her head-on and she died instantly. I'm so sorry to tell you this way, but we're planning a memorial for Friday, and I know you'll hardly have time to unpack or get over jet lag by then, but I wanted you to know. I asked Fran to pick you up at the airport, and I hope that worked out okay. Call me when you get home."

If there were more messages, they would have to wait. Grace let herself fall onto the sofa, put her head in her hands, and sob openly. She hadn't even unpacked, and the weight of the calls overwhelmed her. She hadn't had much sleep for two days because of leaving Glen behind, saying goodbye to Sadie and her little family, packing, and traveling around the clock. No way could she return calls in her condition, expecially John's. Nancy's death, Phil's remains, a lead on the murderer, Sheldon wanting to make up, Blaine's business failing, John being left alone, Pete and LeRoy in a hurry to get a new truck . . . It was all too much. Overcome by grief, exhaustion, fear, and lack of sleep, she cried until she fell asleep.

WHEN GRACE WOKE, HER eyes were swollen, her clothes were rumpled, and her stomach muscles were sore from the deep sobs. She pulled herself to a sitting position, and all the sadness from the night before came flooding back in. *How will I face this day? Where do I start?* The tears slipped down her cheeks, and she lay back down. *Help me think, Lord. Help me put my feet on the ground.*

Fighting the urge to go back to sleep, she forced herself to stand up, then putting one foot in front of the other, she pulled her suitcases into the bedroom. Her body moved slowly, but her mind revved up to high-speed thinking about all that stood ahead. She left the suitcases unpacked in her bedroom and went to the kitchen to make a cup of coffee. Then she pulled a stool up to the kitchen counter and perched atop it.

Grace listened to every voice message again and numbered them in order of importance on the list she'd already made. She knew she was stalling, but she needed to gain control of the items on her list somehow. With a deep breath, she picked up the receiver and punched in the first number.

"Hello."

"Hello, John. It's Grace. . . . Oh, John, I'm so sorry. I didn't know. I wish you'd called me."

"I'm sorry, Grace, but I knew there wasn't anything you could do, and I didn't want to spoil your time with Sadie and her family. It's been awful. I don't know what I'd do without my faith. And the church family has been so supportive and thoughtful. They've been wonderful; they stop by, bring food, sit with me just to listen and pray . . . and cry."

Grace swallowed the lump in her throat. "What can I do?"

"Just keep me in your prayers. As you know from my message, there'll be a memorial service on Friday. I put it off until I knew you'd be home. Would you be willing to speak?"

After only a very brief hesitation, she said, "Of course. You know how much I loved Nancy. In fact, I feel responsible. If she hadn't taken me to Pasadena, she'd still be here."

"No, Grace. You had nothing to do with this. I hate it when people say, 'it was her time,' but it was her time. Wrong place, wrong time? I don't know. Only God knows. But it had nothing to do with you. Nancy loved you and counted it a blessing to drive you that day."

For a moment Grace couldn't speak, as hot tears burned her eyes and trickled down her cheeks. She had the feeling John too was crying when he went silent. She forced herself to speak, hoping her voice wasn't as shaky as she felt inside. "So I have a couple of days to prepare, and I so want to honor Nancy. I hope I can find words that will capture her wonderful heart for the Lord and everyone she knew."

John's voice broke as he replied. "Thank you, Grace. I have a lot of arrangements to see to. I'll call you again before the service."

Grace hung up the phone and took a deep breath. She ripped off a blank sheet and wrote "Nancy" at the top. Before she made the next call, she listed key words for four stories about Nancy's generosity. She wrote "flowers" because of the funny story about how she took care of the flowers when she and Phil got married. She wrote "friendship," "Angel," and "Barstow jail," and wondered how she could craft that story appropriately.

She sighed. Okay, she had found something constructive she could do to honor Nancy, but the list of callers remained.

She picked up the phone and punched the numbers. "Hello, this is Grace Partain," she announced after a woman's voice answered the call, "and I'm returning a call from Agent Watkins. Is he available?"

"Just a moment . . . I'll connect you."

Grace waited until she heard, "You've reached Agent Watkins' voicemail. Leave your name, case number, phone number, and I'll get back to you."

Grace didn't know her case number, but she left a brief message and sighed in relief. Dealing with Phil's remains terrified her.

Fran had been kind enough to send a limo to pick her up at the airport, but she said she'd call when she got back from Santa Barbara, so Grace checked her off.

She punched in the number of Phil's office, and a female answered. "Hargrave's Highland Home Office, serving you. This is Caroline. How may I help you?"

Grace winced when she heard the business had been renamed. "This is Grace Partain. I'm returning a call from Sheldon."

"Just a moment. He's in his office. I'll connect you."

"Hi, Grace," came the greeting when the call was connected.

"Hello, Sheldon. I just got your message. I've been in India on a month-long mission trip."

"Wow, I had no idea. What did you do there?"

"I taught a bunch of sweet young Indian girls English as a second language. It was so rewarding, and I got to visit Sadie and her family for a few days."

"Oh, yeah, I forgot they were there. We were traveling for so long we kind of lost touch."

"Blaine has three more months in his internship," Grace explained, "and then they'll be home. He has another year of school here, I think."

"Good for him. So . . . have you heard anything else about Phil's death?"

"I don't know how much you know, but they found his body in a crate in Wrangell. They've been trying to match DNA with possible suspects, and I'm supposed to deal with his personal belongings and remains. I dread it."

"I'm so sorry. Listen, Grace, I'm really sorry we had such harsh words over dividing the business. I hope you can forgive me. Phil would've been very unhappy with the way I handled things when you were in a really rough spot emotionally."

Grace found herself smiling, if only slightly, for the first time since coming home and listening to her messages. "Sheldon, you're forgiven. We were all in a rough spot. Emotions were off the charts, but we got through it, and it's over."

"You're right," Sheldon admitted. "I'm happy with the final deal, and I hope you are, too. Phil had it set up so you got half of the business at his death and a percentage of every sale for the rest of your life. But then, you already know that."

"Yes, I do, and I'm more than happy with it. I know I'll never have to worry about money." Changing the subject she asked, "How's Marilyn?"

"Working herself into a tizzy," Sheldon said, "and playing softball at night. I thought traveling would help her gear down for this emotional time of her life. I'm no expert, but I feel sure she's going through menopause. Some days it's like dealing with a porcupine or a badger."

In spite of herself, Grace laughed. "I know the feeling. It's good she's still working and getting exercise, but she also needs rest and relaxation."

"Absolutely. And we relaxed and traveled for over two months. You'd think that would do it, but . . ."

"I know it's not easy," Grace cautioned, "but be patient. Sooner or later there'll be a light at the end of the tunnel. But it might be quite a long time."

Sheldon paused, then said, "I'm glad we had this conversation. And, Grace . . . if there is ever anything you need, please let me know, and I'll be there. Deal?"

"Deal. Thank you so much, Sheldon. I'll drop by the office when I get time. Seems things kind of piled up here while I was gone. I'll have to do some catching up."

"I understand. Let me know, and I'll treat you to lunch. We can talk about old times."

"Now that you mention it, maybe I could use your help with . . ." Her voice trailed off, then she took a deep breath and forged ahead. "I already told you about this, but they're releasing Phil's remains to me. I don't know how that's going to go, but I'm so frightened."

"Do you want me to go with you?"

"I don't know, but I know I don't want to go alone. I had thought our pastor would go with me, but with his wife being killed in a car accident, he has his own grief to deal with."

"Yeah, I read about his wife. That was terrible. Just let me know if you want me to go along with you. I'll be glad to."

"Okay, thank you." The conversation wasn't as bad as she had feared, and by the time she hung up, she felt better about her relationship with Sheldon.

Grace hadn't eaten since she got off the plane, and she felt weak. The refrigerator was empty except for condiments, but she found a loaf of whole wheat bread in the freezer and peanut butter on the shelf. Toast and peanut butter accompanied by another cup of coffee gave her the energy she needed to continue the phone calls.

Pete's next, and he always makes me laugh. Knowing his call wouldn't be so stressful she punched in the number.

"Hello." It was a woman's voice.

"Hello, this is Grace Partain. I'm calling for Pete Jensen."

"Oh, Grace! I'm Pete's mom, Irene. It's nice to talk to you."

"Thank you. I feel like we should've met a long time ago."

"Absolutely. I can't tell you what you've done for my son and his partner LeRoy. You've changed their lives."

"Thank you," Grace responded, "but I think maybe it's God who's changing their lives."

"Could be. They've been going to church, as you probably know, and they're excited about getting a new truck. They even bought themselves some new clothes. I was so surprised when Pete brought home some pants and blouses from Target for me. New things. I haven't had any new clothes for years."

Grace smiled. "I'm so happy to hear that. I'm not sure if you know, but we met because they stopped to help my friend when her car broke down, and she ended up having her baby in the front seat of their tow truck."

"I heard about that." She sighed. "I'm afraid our boys haven't had the best lives. Pete's daddy . . . well, let's just say he wasn't any help to Pete. He and LeRoy barely made it through high school, and they were on suspension more than in class. I tried . . . I did the best I could by taking in wash, mending, and ironing. I didn't do much else."

Grace's heart went out to this woman she'd spoken to for the first time. "If my help has changed a life, then I'm happy to do it. A murderer took my husband's life, but I'm left with plenty of resources. If I've used it wisely and two men's lives are changed, I thank God for the opportunity. It wasn't an accident they helped my friend Sadie. It was all part of God's plan."

"That's what Pete's saying now. He even invited me to come to church."

"That's great. So how do I get in touch with him? One of my friends got killed in a car accident, and I might have to reschedule our truck-buying trip. I planned to help them, and I still will, but we might have to postpone it for a little while."

"I understand. He'll be home soon, and I'll have him call you. Would that be okay?"

"Sure, but please stress to him that I'm not backing out of the deal. I just have some business to take care of first."

"I will. I hope we can meet sometime."

"That would be nice." Grace hung up and looked at her list again.

BEFORE TACKLING HER next phone call, she walked out on the patio and looked at her backyard. Obviously Bernard hadn't been there in a while. She'd call him next, but she couldn't imagine how she'd help him catch up on the lawn business. She hoped and prayed he had found someone to fill in while he healed. She punched in his number.

"Hello."

"Bernard?"

"Yes, this is Bernard."

"This is Grace Partain. I was sorry to hear about your broken foot. How are you doing?"

"I'm in a walking cast for a while, but I did find a girl who said she'd cover for me on the lawn work."

"A girl? Well, good for her."

"I guess she has another friend who'll help her, too. I'm going to loan them my pickup, so they can pull the little trailer with the mower and tools. I think it'll work out until I can get back to work."

"What will you drive?"

"Oh, I should have said, we're trading vehicles for a while. That suits me because she drives a Corvette. Cool, huh? Such a deal."

Grace chuckled. "How long do you think you'll be off work?"

"Probably for another four weeks. They said they could do it for a month, and I'm giving them the names and addresses of the customers today."

"Blaine hasn't lost any customers, has he?"

"No, I called them all and told them help was on the way. We're all good. Sorry to worry you, but I thought if a couple of girls showed up at your house, you'd wonder what the heck was going on."

Grace chuckled again. "Okay, then. You've got everything under control. Blaine'll be surprised two girls could cover for him – maybe even one."

Grace had completed the list. She wondered if she should try Agent Watkins again or just wait. She hadn't unpacked anything yet, and she would have plenty of clothes to wash and put away. She hadn't had time to think about Glen and their time together in India. She promised she would write, but a big decision stymied her. Carrying on a relationship around the world didn't make sense, but did it make sense to go back to India when they only had a month to get acquainted and only two weeks when they realized it might be more than that? With all the pressure on her now, it scared her to think about packing up and leaving again.

She had spent two hours unpacking, putting things away, and washing when the phone rang. Every call made her nervous all over again.

"Hello, this is Grace."

"This is Agent Watkins here. Sorry I missed your call. First let me say I'm so sorry for your loss. When we get finished speaking, one of our agents will talk to you about claiming the remains and how to proceed."

"Thank you. I appreciate that." She had been too distracted by everything else to imagine how this would work.

"But the other reason for my call is to ask a few more questions. I hope you don't mind."

"If it'll help, go ahead." Grace hoped he would be brief.

"How close were you and the Hargraves?"

Grace lifted her eyebrows. "Very close. Phil and Sheldon Hargrave played football together in high school, and they were like brothers. Shortly after high school Phil took the real estate test and not long after, he talked Sheldon into taking the test also. He did, and they went into business together. Like I said, they were like brothers."

"How about Mrs. Hargrave?"

"Marilyn? She and I are quite different. We've been friends because of our husbands, but we don't socialize outside of the real estate conferences and events."

"But you were cruising together?"

She had hoped this topic wouldn't come up, but it had, so she might as well jump in with both feet. "Yes, well, last summer I did a very stupid thing and kind of ran away from home. Phil thought I'd been kidnapped, and he and Sheldon had to get together a lot of money for ransom. It's all very confusing, but there were no kidnappers, the money went back into the business, Phil forgave me, and he decided we all needed a vacation. So he footed the bill for the four of us to take a cruise." Her voice cracked. "It was supposed to be a celebration."

"So did that change your relationship with the Hargraves?"

"I don't think so. I just talked to Sheldon today. Marilyn and I talked about what to wear and all that before the trip. We haven't seen each other since because they've been traveling, and my life has been crazy."

"How about during the trip?"

"Well . . . we had one little issue, but it didn't amount to much."

"What was that?"

"The second night Sheldon got his nose bent out of shape a little because we'd made a couple of new friends and asked them to join us for dinner."

"So, then what?"

"They got in a bit of a huff and didn't eat with us. It was just childish jealousy. Nothing really serious."

The detective's voice took on a more serious note. "We took DNA samples from the Hargraves," he said, "and although a lot of time had elapsed before the body was discovered, there's a match."

"To the Hargraves? No! It can't be. Sheldon would never hurt Phil." She threw down the phone in disgust and didn't pick it up until she was sure the connection was broken.

I can't believe it. I won't believe it. It simply can't be true.

CHAPTER 27

"Hey, Mom." Pete greeted his mother as he pulled a soda out of the fridge.

She looked up from the sink where she was peeling potatoes.

"Mrs. Partain called, and she's hoping you'll call her back."

"No way. I hope she ain't decided to back out of the truck deal." Pete flopped down in the kitchen chair looking dejected.

"Not at all. She said to make sure you knew that. A good friend of hers was killed in a car accident, and she had to take care of some things. She didn't say what."

"Did she say who the friend was?" He immediately thought of Sadie.

"Nope, but she wanted you to call her back."

Pete jumped up and went straight to the wall phone to punch in the number Grace had left.

"Hello, this is Grace." He could tell by her voice she had been crying.

"LeRoy and me are sorry about your friend dying. Who was it?" He didn't know what else to say.

"Remember Nancy? The pastor's wife you met her at the dedication. She came with me to bail you out."

"Oh, no. That's bad. Dang! She was a good lady. She treated us real nice. I'm sorry."

"Yes, she treated everyone nice . . . all the time."

A silence hung on the line for a few awkward seconds until Pete spoke. "So . . . can we come to the funeral?"

"Of course. It's Friday. That's why I had to postpone our trip to Las Vegas to look at the truck."

"This is even better. Me and LeRoy found an almost new tow truck with all the accessories and equipment. And I probably shouldn't talk about money, but it was only thirty-five thousand dollars. Better yet, it's in San Bernardino, so we don't need to go to Las Vegas! Cool, huh?"

"Sounds great. Come to the church on Friday. You remember where we held the dedication? The funeral is at eleven. After the reception, we'll go look. It'll take my mind off of everything else."

Pete grinned. "You're gonna be surprised."

"Why? Are you bringing your friend's zebra car again?"

"Nope, I'm not tellin'. You'll see."

GRACE HUNG UP THE PHONE, smiling at the vision of Pete and LeRoy driving up in the zebra car. If that wasn't enough, she couldn't imagine what they had in mind to surprise her this time. But just talking to Pete lifted her spirits. Her heart had been broken so many times lately she had begun to think it would become calloused. It was nice to know there were still a few things in this world that could make her smile.

Before Grace could gather her senses and call Watkins back, she heard what sounded like a pickup truck drive up in front of the house. She peeked out the window and smiled when she saw two scantily clad girls hop out of the truck, unload the mower and weed-whacker, and go right to work. She breathed a sigh of relief, knowing that one of the prickly situations in her life was at least temporarily under control.

The phone rang then, and Grace picked it up.

"It's Fran. We're back from Santa Barbara. I'm so sorry I wasn't there to pick you up. When I heard about Nancy, I volunteered to come get you before I knew Alfie had registered us for his conference. I'm so sorry. I know how close you and Nancy were since . . . Phil's disappearance."

"Thanks for making sure someone picked me up. That's all that matters."

"I hope you had a wonderful time in India."

Grace didn't know where to start. "When I was there, I didn't know about Nancy, and I didn't know about the DNA or anything. What a shock when I got home to all the calls."

"DNA? Does that mean they've found Phil's murderer?"

"I'm not sure. The FBI agent said they have a DNA match from the body, but I just couldn't bear to hear it and dropped the phone. I don't know anything else about it. I have to claim Phil's remains and belongings at the morgue. I'm still not sure about all that, and I'm terrified to call back." She gave in to the tears and sobbed aloud.

After a brief pause, Fran said, "I'm so sorry, Grace. I wish I knew how to help."

"You can," she said, doing her best to regain her composure. "Come to Nancy's funeral on Friday and hold me up."

"I wish I could, but I have school and we're into testing, so I just can't be there. I took off a day to go to the conference with Alfie, so I can't take off another day so soon. I'm truly sorry."

Grace nodded. "I understand."

So now the lawn service was working smoothly, thanks to two girls, and Fran would not be available on Friday. Brushing away tears, she scratched those two items off the list.

GRACE SAT DOWN TO BEGIN writing her speech for the memorial.

I've known Nancy for over twenty years, she wrote, surprised her hand wasn't shaking. *She had a wonderful sense of humor and a sense of what needed to be done in any situation. Pastor Troude counseled my late husband Phil and I before we got married. Before the wedding, the flowers didn't show up on time, so Nancy rushed out to the church flowerbed and picked handfuls of various colored blossoms. As the attendants walked up the aisle, Nancy stuck a bunch of garden flowers, some with roots still hanging out, in their hands. When it came time for me to walk up the aisle, the frazzled florist arrived in the foyer. She handed me the beautiful bouquet I had ordered, and while all eyes were on me, Nancy ran to the front of the church through a side door, placed the baskets of flowers by the podium, and disappeared. Like an angel she interceded.*

I didn't see much of her for twenty years, but just recently Pastor John accompanied my husband to rescue me from an ill-fated trip I took. Since then, Nancy and John have stood by us and ministered to us as we grew in our faith. I loved Nancy, and I will miss her terribly. Thank you.

She decided not to talk about their trip to Barstow to bail out Pete and LeRoy. There were too many parts of the story she didn't feel comfortable about divulging, especially since the men would be in the audience.

GLEN HAD BEEN DOING mission work in India for over a year. His children were off to college, and he tired of dealing with high-school kids and their crazy lives. When his parents died, he realized they had hoarded their money all their lives, and it then passed to him. Now he could take those funds and do something good for someone. Before he truly thought it through, the MTI mission organization came up, and he applied. He was accepted, and his involvement with the group had filled the "empty nester" void in his heart.

Now in India, he felt that same emptiness again – not for his x-wife, parents, or daughters, but for Grace. From the minute she walked into the school, he felt an attraction toward her. Now she resided in California on the other side of the world. He hadn't dated in years because nobody came along that made him take a second look or give a second thought. Now he struggled to keep going. Phone calls never worked well – uncertain and costly. So he poured out his heart in letters.

> Dear Grace,
>
> I missed you the moment you stepped into the airport terminal. Sadie, Blaine, and Angel were very supportive, and we had lunch together. They also felt sad when you left.
>
> Sadie told me you met when you were working together, but she didn't say where or when. She's young enough to be one of your students, so that seemed strange, but I'll let you tell me about that later.
>
> I hope you got home safely and found a peaceful welcome. All I can think about is seeing you again. I will be coming back to California in June. That's only two months away. I hope I can be patient that long. I think Blaine's internship ends then, so we can all come home together.
>
> I thought India called me, but now my heart is yearning to be back in California with you. Maybe we can come back together, but only if it's God's will.
>
> Please write.

Blessings to you, Grace.

Glen

He sent the letter on its way, knowing it would take two weeks to arrive in Highland.

"HELLO." GRACE ANSWERED with trepidation, wondering who might be on the other end of the line.

"Mrs. Partain, this is Agent Watkins again."

"I'm so sorry we were disconnected. I just couldn't listen to the results of the DNA match. I can't believe Sheldon would do anything to hurt Phil."

"Mrs. Partain, it wasn't Sheldon."

"It wasn't?" She let out a huge sigh of relief. "I must have misunderstood. I just knew Sheldon couldn't have done it."

"No, the match is with his wife, Marilyn."

"What? Are you saying you think that Marilyn killed Phil?" Grace could feel the blood leaving her face, and she quickly sat down.

"We haven't found the murder weapon yet, and we may never, but her DNA showed up around his wrists. Can you think of any way she could have had her hands around his wrists the night he went missing?"

Grace tried to remember exactly what had happened that night at dinner. They hadn't touched the last time they were together when the Hargraves walked away from the table.

"No. We went to the show with the Conovers, and the last we saw of the Hargraves they were headed for the buffet. It looked like they'd already been drinking. That's why I didn't make too much of their anger. I just thought it could be the alcohol talking."

"It's been a tough case, but I wanted to let you know we'll be taking Mrs. Hargrave in for more questioning. It isn't looking good for her, but for now she is being considered as our only suspect. You'll need to keep that to yourself until we come to a definite conclusion."

Grace shook her head. "I can't believe it. I mean . . . I just can't believe it."

"I understand. We'll keep you informed as things develop."

"It's been over seven months since the cruise. After all this time, I never expected to find out anything. What's taken so long?"

"To be perfectly honest, cruise lines don't like to have crimes reported in connection to them, so they often try to sweep them under the rug. When they couldn't find a body on the ship, they pretty much washed their hands in it. And when they found the shirt, they figured they'd done all they could. It wasn't until the body was found in Wrangell that the local law enforcement picked up the crime. They did what they could, but after the remains were transferred to the San Bernardino coroner's office, they passed the responsibility along. That's when the FBI finally got deeply involved. We've been slowly but surely putting all the pieces together, which wasn't easy. We had to get the DNA from the ship's investigation, the details from the guys in Wrangell, and a medical examiner to do a work-up. It's been very difficult, but we feel certain we've narrowed it down to the right individual."

She took a deep breath and sighed. "I appreciate how hard it's been, but I still don't believe it. It's all been so confusing and hopeless. Sounds like the body's already been transported to the coroner's office/morgue. I didn't even know that . . . until now."

CHAPTER 28

Grace had to get out of the house. If the phone rang one more time, she didn't think she'd have nerve enough to answer. The girls were finishing up the yardwork as Grace pulled the car out of the garage.

"Hey, girls," she called through her open window. "This looks fabulous."

One of them waved, and the other responded with a smile and a loud "Thank you."

Grace decided Blaine had lucked out with these two girls. Bernard would have to step up his game to do as well.

Grace headed for the church knowing John would be there. As she entered his office, he got to his feet and opened his arms to her. They embraced as tears came to both of them, but neither seemed to know what to say or how to start the conversation.

Grace finally broke the silence as she stood back and looked into his rugged and tear-stained face. "I'm so sorry. I'll miss Nancy so much."

He nodded, as tears glistened in his eyes. "There really aren't any words that make things better although everyone tries. The best I can do is listen and be grateful."

They sat down facing each other, wiping tears with their heads bowed.

"I wrote part of my speech for tomorrow," Grace said when she looked up, "but I know I'll want to add more."

"Yes, I'm struggling with that too. How do you say goodbye to your partner, lover, and sister-in-Christ for forty years? How do you say goodbye when you want people to know that my good-bye is a celebration of Nancy receiving her welcome home from Jesus? Sad for us, but a victorious arrival in His arms for her."

"I know you'll find the right words," Grace said, wishing she could assure herself with as much certainty. "You always do. What else can I do for you?"

"Well, don't bring food." He smiled. "I have enough food to feed me for the next year." They both laughed.

"I'm putting serving-size amounts in plastic containers and stacking them in the freezer," he added. "They'll be great when I feel like eating again."

"Sounds like a wise idea." She took a deep breath. "So I'll be here early tomorrow if you need anything. Oh, and by the way, remember my two friends who showed up to Angel's dedication in a zebra-striped car?" They both laughed spontaneously.

"How could I forget? I nearly fell over when they came up on the stage as part of the family. What innocent spirits. Weren't they the ones you and Nancy went to bail out of the Barstow jail?"

Grace nodded. "They sure are, but I promise I won't mention that in my speech." She laughed. "Anyway, they're coming to the memorial, and in the afternoon I'm going tow truck-shopping with them."

John's thick eyebrows shot up. "Tow truck-shopping? Now that takes it. Are you kidding me?"

"I guess Nancy didn't get a chance to tell you about the great blackmail escapade. Now's not the time, but let me just say I owe those two guys – not only for helping Sadie, but a lot more. I wanted to do something special for them. It turns out that because of us including them in our lives, their lives have changed dramatically."

"How's that?"

"I talked to Pete's mother yesterday, and she couldn't say enough about his turnaround. He and LeRoy are going to church, and they've recently bought her some new clothes and invited her to come to church with them. When I talked to Pete, he mentioned how nice Nancy had been to them also."

John smiled. "That's wonderful. What could be better than changing lives for good?"

"They wanted to come, but let me warn you, we need to brace for some sort of surprise." She grinned and shook her head. "I can't imagine what it is this time – as if a zebra-striped car wasn't enough."

"It's just sweet they wanted to come."

"Yes, indeed. That's the good news, but there's been some bad news also. I got a call from the FBI, and they say Sheldon's wife is the suspected killer." Grace remembered she wasn't supposed to tell that. "I'm not supposed to tell anyone, but I don't believe it anyway. I won't believe it until they can show me more than DNA results. It's just too crazy."

"My lips are sealed. It's confidential when you tell me," John reassured her and gave her a light hug before opening the door for her to leave.

GRACE KNEW PHIL'S REMAINS were at the morgue in San Bernardino. She hated what she had to endure, but she felt driven to see for herself. She wished it would be some stranger and she would wake up from this horrifying nightmare. But she made an appointment to go and make the identification. She also thought about asking someone to go with her, but who? Sheldon had offered, but if Marilyn was a suspect, she didn't want to go near them while the FBI was on the case. She couldn't ask John. He was busy dealing with Nancy's remains.

When Grace walked into the cold dank morgue, the body lay covered with a white sheet. The smell of death permeated the air. She knew the body would be decomposed and horrible. For a long while she just stood looking down at the sheet.

"Would you like a glass of water?" the medical examiner asked as he stood back, observing Grace's demeanor.

"Yes, please." She couldn't stall forever, but her hands were shaking, and fear gripped her. How could she stand to see what she had to see?

The ME handed her a paper cup of water, and she sipped it slowly. When he walked away, she moved to the foot of the table and pulled the sheet up just enough to expose a shriveled foot. It looked slightly familiar, but she wished he had a tattoo or a scar on his toe so she could be sure, something that would be easy to identify without going farther. The sheet slipped from her fingers, and she walked to the side of the table. Carefully, she lifted the material hoping to find his hand. The fingers were odd-colored and cadaver-like.

"Maybe this will make it easier," the examiner said quietly.

He handed her a large plastic bag with the shirt the cruise officials had kept and finally passed on to the FBI. He also gave her the small jewelry box with the diamond ring. Grace thought Phil must have been planning on giving it to her as a surprise. She slipped it on her ring finger and found he had it made to fit snugly and artistically with her original wedding ring. Phil had thought of everything. His pants and underwear were at the bottom of the bag. When she pulled them out, *his* wedding ring fell to the floor, and she hurriedly picked it up before it could roll away.

She clutched the ring to her heart, no longer able to hold back the tears. Who would have imagined anything so horrific? "Yes, these belong to my husband. Let me take one more moment, please."

She moved to the head of the table. Phil had always had such beautiful hair, which he groomed with great care. Grace had to see it one last time.

She pulled the sheet back a bit more to reveal his entire head. She gasped. Someone had combed what was left of his hair, but she scarcely noticed as her eyes zeroed in on his skull, which appeared to be caved in on one spot. His facial skin clung to the cheekbones. Grace found no smooth skin she could kiss one last time. Instead, she ran her hand through his hair and whispered, "Goodbye, my love."

The FBI had finished their investigation regarding the remains, so Grace signed papers to have his body transferred to a local crematorium. His ashes would mean more to her than visualizing his decomposed body.

AS IF IDENTIFYING PHIL'S body wasn't enough, the time quickly came for Nancy's funeral. When Grace arrived at the church, she heard the thundering pipes of a Dodge Challenger. As it pulled into the church parking lot, she took a deep breath and looked around. Two men exited, but she could hardly believe her eyes. They wore navy blue suits perfectly fit, white shirts, ties, fresh haircuts, and shiny black cowboy boots. It was Pete and LeRoy.

"Oh, my goodness!" For some strange reason, Grace felt like her family had arrived. Without Phil, Sadie, Blaine, and Angel, these two guys had become a blessing to her. She walked out to greet them.

"Wow! I feel like I'm seeing two stars from the MakeOver Show," she exclaimed, extending her hands to clasp Pete's and then LeRoy's. "You look fantastic! Your suits are beautiful, and I think I can see myself in your boots they are so shiny."

Both men grinned proudly. "These are our Sunday-go-to-church clothes," Pete said. "Mom went with us to pick 'em out. We got her some new clothes too, so she'll go to church with us maybe perty soon."

"And what about the car?" Grace questioned, hoping it wasn't an illegal procurement.

"LeRoy and I been workin' on this car since high school. Since we quit hangin' out in Buford's Bar, we got busy and fixed it up. It ain't much to look at, but it runs like a top and sounds like thunder."

"It sure does."

Grace gave each of them a hug, placed herself between them and took their arms. She escorted them right to the front pew with her. Her teacher friends would wonder who these young guys were, but Grace didn't care. They wouldn't believe her history with them if she told them. Strangely enough, she didn't know the whole story either. That remained a secret known only by Pete and LeRoy.

As expected, John gave Nancy a royal send-off. He sang her praises as a wife, mother, Christian, and friend. He told about the high points of their marriage and the joy she brought to him and everyone she ever knew. He finished up by telling funny stories about some of her antics that made everyone laugh.

Grace spoke, and so did both of Nancy's grown children who had come across the country to be there. It was a great celebration of life, and everyone went away glad they had known her.

CHAPTER 29

When FBI Agent Watkins and his partner arrived at the salon where Marilyn worked, he imagined two men in suits and ties must be a rarity in her shop. Besides the crisp expensive black suits, they wore sunglasses and shoes shined to perfection. As he approached her station, where she was busily cutting a client's hair, she spotted him and immediately looked annoyed.

"What's this all about?" Her tone implied that she didn't appreciate being interrupted.

Ignoring her question, Watkins said, "You'll need to come with us, Mrs. Hargrave. There are a few questions we need you to answer."

"Answer about what?"

"About the Partain murder."

Marilyn still had the scissors in her hand, and for just a split second Watkins thought she might try to lunge at him. He waited and watched as she slowly laid them down on the tray.

Marilyn turned and spoke to the beautician in the station next to her. "Dorothy, will you finish this haircut for me? I may not be back this afternoon."

Marilyn grabbed her purse and followed the agents to their car. As Watkins' partner held the back door open, she climbed in the black SUV, and he closed the door behind her.

Once at the field agency, Watkins ushered Marilyn into a windowless room with just a table and two chairs. They sat down across the table facing one another.

"Mrs. Hargrave . . ."

"Marilyn."

"Marilyn," he said, getting straight to the point, "we have reason to believe you had something to do with the death of Phil Partain."

She flinched ever so slightly before answering. "That's crazy. He fell overboard."

"Evidently you didn't hear his remains were found in a container behind a shed at the port of Wrangell."

She lifted her perfectly penciled eyebrows. "Really? I didn't know."

"And we suspect you murdered him."

Her dark brown eyes went wide. "Me? How would I kill him? His shirt was found floating in the water." Marilyn pushed the chair back and started to stand up.

"Just sit down. You aren't going anywhere."

Marilyn hesitated a few seconds before retaking her seat.

"The floating shirt was a nice touch," Watkins said, studying her closely, "but he'd been bashed over the head with something hard enough to cave in his skull."

"I don't know anything about that."

"We think you do."

Marilyn tightened her lips and breathed hard. At last she said, "And you think I did that?"

"No, we *know* you did it."

She shook her head defiantly. "How is that possible?"

"Remember taking the DNA test on the ship?"

"Yes. I thought that was stupid to bother us during our vacation. What can that prove?"

"Your DNA was found around Mr. Partain's wrists. Probably from when you were unbuttoning his shirt sleeves or dragged him into the carton."

Marilyn was silent. She did not volunteer anything.

"Why, Marilyn?"

She sat quietly, clinching her jaw.

"Why?" he repeated.

Watkins waited without moving. When she didn't answer, he shouted, "*Why?*"

Marilyn jerked in surprise, looking as if she were about to explode. When she finally opened her mouth to speak, words spewed out as if pouring from a broken irrigation pipe.

"I just got sick and tired of seeing Sheldon take a backseat to Phil. He idolized him even though he always played second fiddle. He thought Phil walked on water and could do no wrong. He and Grace were uppity and arrogant just because they were college educated. I always felt like a country bumpkin when she came around in her knit suits and perfect speech. Then when we were on the ship, they left us behind and made new friends before we even got to dinner. It upset Sheldon so much he got roaring drunk and passed out. Phil was destroying him. I hated Phil for making Sheldon his puppet. And when he talked Sheldon into taking out five hundred thousand dollars from the business account to rescue Grace from kidnappers, I thought we were going to lose everything. When Phil came to our room to talk to Sheldon, I headed him off."

"So by killing Mr. Partain, what did you stand to gain?"

Tears were building in Marilyn's eyes, but she continued without losing control. "Sheldon would take over the business, and we wouldn't be living in the Partain shadow anymore."

"We never found the murder weapon," he informed her, "but there's a forensics team searching your house as we speak."

Her eyes flashed with what appeared to be defiance – and possibly a last glimmer of hope. "Do you have a warrant?"

"Yes, and your husband made arrangements for the housekeeper to let them in."

"Hmmm." Marilyn slumped back in the seat and let her head fall back.

"Now let's get down to business," Watkins said. "The murder weapon . . . what was it?"

No answer. Marilyn doubled up her fists.

"How did you get him off the ship?"

No response except to sit back up and glare at him. "Here's what I think," the agent went on, pleased at how easily she had confessed. "You paid big bucks for some crew members to take the body off the ship. But when the body finally turned up – something you hadn't counted on—we were able to start putting the pieces together."

"Where did they find the body?" Marilyn looked genuinely interested.

"In a large plastic carton behind one of the warehouses. What do you care?"

Marilyn hit her thighs with her fists and hissed between clenched teeth. "They were supposed to bury it so it wouldn't be found for a long time. I thought the search ended weeks ago. I thought the shirt would throw you off the trail. I didn't imagine it would float as long as it did. And I sure didn't know there was a ring in the pocket."

Watkins raised his voice an octave and spoke distinctly, making his words more of a demand than a question. "How did you get him off the ship?"

She sighed, as if resigning herself to the inevitable. "I convinced him Sheldon was too drunk to engage in a sensible conversation. I talked him into cooling down on the Promenade deck, and as he walked ahead of me, I surprised him. After I hit him, he fell, and I pushed him into one of the deck chairs. Then I put a blanket over him until I could get help. I found a couple of deck hands who were willing to help and glad to get some extra cash. They don't get paid that well working on those cruise ships, you know."

Watkins was pleased. He now had all the information he needed to place Marilyn under arrest. But before remanding her to custody, he called Sheldon to ask him to meet them at the house.

BY THE TIME WATKINS, his partner, and Marilyn arrived at the Hargrave home, other agents were busily searching for evidence.

Sheldon was dumbfounded. Watkins entered first and told him Marilyn was suspected of murder.

Stunned, Sheldon looked at his wife. "Marilyn, how could you?"

Apparently still feeling somewhat justified in her actions, she said, "How could I? Phil came to our room when you were passed out drunk. He wanted to talk to you. I tried to make excuses for you, but he kept insisting to come in. He wouldn't take no for an answer, but I convinced him to come out on the Promenade deck for a glass of wine and cool down. I picked up the bottle of wine and two glasses. When we got outside, I hit him over the head with the bottle, but I didn't mean to kill him."

The detective held up the bottle in a large evidence bag. "Does this look familiar?" he asked.

Ignoring the question, she turned back to her husband. "I bought it to try to get you to come back to our cabin. But you were so broken up about your tiff with Phil you wouldn't listen to reason. You passed out before it got opened, so I used it to put you out of your misery."

"My misery?" Sheldon felt his eyes bulge. "What misery?"

She nearly spit the words at him as she answered. "The misery of serving King Philip for twenty years, that's what misery!" Sheldon shook his head, as if to clear the fog of unbelief he felt surrounding him. "That wasn't misery. If it hadn't been for Phil, you wouldn't have lived like a queen in a beautiful home, had a fancy sports car, and whatever else you wanted. Phil represented more than a friend to me. I loved him like a brother, but even brothers have disagreements. We would have made up, Marilyn, but you took that away from us." He leaned forward and nearly screamed at her. "*How could you do this?*"

Marilyn lifted her head. "I'm so sick of hearing how you two were just like brothers."

"Maybe we'll find some of his brother's DNA on this." Once again, the detective raised the bag with the wine bottle and addressed Marilyn. "I guess you brought it off the ship thinking you were in the clear."

GRACE FELT LIKE SHE had just bought a new tow truck for the sons she never had, even though they were probably only ten or fifteen years younger than her. And their reactions made it all worthwhile.

Pete threw out his chest, put his thumbs under his lapel, and strutted around the truck. LeRoy jumped up in the air and clicked the heels of his cowboy boots together. Grace watched their antics and grinned. She hadn't felt such joy since she visited Sadie and her family in India.

"Well, boys," she said, "let's take her for a spin."

Grace had to get a boost from LeRoy to make it up the high step in her dress and heels. The men slid in on each side, and away they went. It wasn't a sports car or a limousine, but it ran smoothly and was in perfect condition—a major step up for Pete and LeRoy. When they pulled into the parking lot so Grace could pick up her car and LeRoy could get the Charger, the men turned to her and gave her a kiss on each cheek. Grace felt her face grow hot. She could tell from their pink cheeks that theirs had, too.

"Enjoy," she said, "and make some good honest money."

"We want you to come out to Barstow and go to church with us," Pete said. "And maybe we can get our moms to go, too."

"That would be nice." With help from LeRoy, Grace slid down from the truck.

Pete seemed embarrassed as he looked down at her. "We can't thank you enough. You're like an angel to us."

She smiled. "You're welcome. Seeing you in your fancy suits, spiffy hair and all, was really sweet. You certainly did surprise me. I know you're going to do well. Now make those new business cards, and have your name painted on the doors. Your truck is going to be the best one on the road."

"We'll keep it shined up and lookin' perty," LeRoy said, giving Grace a big hug, then turned to walk toward the Charger. "I promise, you're gonna be proud of us," he called back.

"I am already," Grace said, and turned to walk toward her Lexus.

IT SEEMED THAT EVERY time Grace answered the phone, it was another catastrophe. This time it was Sheldon calling.

"Grace, did you know the FBI arrested Marilyn?"

"No, but I knew they suspected her. I just couldn't believe it."

"Neither can I," Sheldon said, slurring his words.

Grace could tell he had been drinking. "Sheldon, do you want me to come over? What can I do to help?"

Obviously ignoring her offer, he asked, "Did you know she hit him over the head with a bottle of wine?"

She gasped at the visual his words brought to her mind. "No, I didn't know. Identifying his body was horrible, and I could see his skull was caved in on one side."

"Marilyn can swing a bat like a man," Pete said, his voice cracking as he spoke, "and she can be such a hothead at times. She kicked me out of the house while you were in Las Vegas last summer. When Phil and I borrowed all the money from the business to come and rescue you, she never got over it. She let me come back home, but she was furious with Phil and felt like he'd used me. She was always insecure about being around educated people like you. I guess it was her lousy childhood. But I never would've expected this. I don't know what to say. I'm so sorry."

They both broke down and cried then, and Grace struggled to find a way to put an end to the conversation. As it happened, she didn't have to.

"Where do we go from here, Grace?" Sheldon finally asked, obviously fighting to stop the tears.

She took a deep breath, brushing away her own tears with her free hand. "I'm trying to start a new life for myself without Phil. I never thought I could do that, but I've come to see it's possible. Don't give up; you still have lots of life to live. Call your kids, and get together with them. They need to hear this from you. They'll be your strength. You probably haven't spent time with them for years, and it'll be good for you to pull together. The business can take care of itself; it did fine while you traveled all over the world."

"Yeah, you're right," Sheldon admintted. "I'm so sorry about all of this."

"Me, too." She brushed away yet another tear. "But it's not your fault."

CHAPTER 30

Glen's letter seemed to arrive at exactly the time Grace needed someone to talk to, someone who wasn't involved in all the chaos and drama surrounding her own life at the moment. After reading the letter several times, she decided it was time to answer him. She sat down at the kitchen table and began to write.

Dear Glen,

You'll never believe all that's gone on since I came home. I've hardly had time to think about India.

The guy who was supposed to take over Blaine's business in his absence broke his foot. Two girls have taken over, and they're terrific, even though they dress a little r*isqué*. Ha!

On a much sadder note, my friend Nancy was killed on the way home from taking me to Pasadena, but her husband didn't want to tell me until I came home. He's the pastor who married Phil and me, mentored us, married Sadie and Blaine, and dedicated Angel. I want you to meet him when you come home.

My tow truck friends bought a new truck and they're making great life changes. I'll tell you all about them when you're here. It's a great story.

Phil's remains are being cremated, and they found his murderer. It was his partner's wife, and I still can't believe it.

If that isn't enough, I think I have a hole in my heart. Yes, it's quite serious. There's someone in India who might be the missing piece. I'm not sure yet, but I'm looking forward to finding out.

I know this is brief, but it would take a million words to tell you all the details. That's why I want you here.

Sincerely,

Grace

SHE WAS BOTH AMAZED and pleased at how quickly Glen answered.

Dear Grace,

All I think about is you. I'm so excited about getting back to California. It's only a month away. I hope you're thinking about coming back to India with me after summer. The girls at the school in Mumbai miss you.

Sadie and Blaine are doing well, and Angel is such a blessing. She's starting to crawl everywhere and can pull herself to a standing position. I think they're looking forward to coming home also.

I know it isn't much, but when I get there, I want to sit someplace quiet with you and hear about everything in your life. There's so much I want to know.

Love,

Glen

GAZING OUT THE SCREEN door, Pete found himself thinking about his dad, even though he had few if any fond memories of him. Not only had he ignored his family, but he never took any interest in their home. Old broken-down cars dotted the place. Not a blade of grass or anything of beauty could be found anywhere.

When Pete's mother found her husband face down in the dirt behind the house, dead as a doornail, no one seemed surprised. He had lain there drunk more times than any of them could count.

Pete didn't know quite how to deal with his father's death. Their relationship had always lacked communication. They tinkered together with some of the old cars in the back lot in years past, but as his dad's alcoholism got worse and worse, they saw each other less and less. Neither of them spent much time at home and rarely spoke when they were there. Pete never had any indication his father loved him or took pride in anything he did. He hadn't done anything for Pete to take pride in either, but Pete still felt a deep sadness he couldn't explain. His two younger brothers stayed out of their dad's way and really didn't know anything about him except that he lived there.

Now, more than a week since his father died, Pete sat beside his mom on the porch swing, looking at his new truck. "Ma, do you want me to do anything for you?" he asked. "Shouldn't we be doing a funeral or something?"

"Thanks, honey," she said, her smile looking more defeated than encouraging, "but it's just best left alone. He left us alone a long time ago. I'm sorry for all the years he wasted, and I'm sorry he wasn't a good father to you and your brothers. He wasn't even a husband. I'm not sorry for him; I'm sorry for us."

Pete put his big arms around her and hugged her like he did when he was a little boy. "Mom, I'm gonna make it up to you startin' right now. I'm gonna spend more time with the boys."

Pete had never paid much attention to his younger brothers, but now he realized how much they needed him. They were both in high school and by some miracle had not been in any major trouble.

"I'll see if I can get them to come to church with us," he suggested.

Irene looked surprised. "Us?"

"Yeah. I've learned a lot there, and you'll see how nice the folks are. You'll hear how much God loves you, and me, and even LeRoy. I've got a plan, but I ain't tellin' it yet. You'll see. It may take a while, but you'll see."

Irene sighed and gave Pete another hug. "You're a good boy, Peter."

Pete hadn't heard that from anyone in his life. He turned away with a lump in his throat and a big idea in his head.

SADIE HAD BEEN ESTRANGED from her parents since she left Utah two years earlier. They had thrown her out when she took up with a bad crowd and became pregnant. Their absence at the wedding had saddened her because she hoped that would break the ice between them. Being so far away from Grace, the Troudes and the friends she had made at church in Highland made her painfully aware of how much she missed her family. She looked forward to Blaine's internship coming to an end in three weeks. Homesickness had set in, and she determined that when they returned to California, she was going to Utah and visit her parents. It was time they met their son-in-law and their beautiful granddaughter. She would make a way to get back into their good graces. As she began thinking about going home, her plan became clearer and clearer. She poured it out in one of the many letters she wrote to Grace.

Dear Grace,

I am so excited about coming home. Blaine only has three weeks left in his internship, and he's ready to finish up. Angel is walking (or toddling) everywhere now. You're going to have so much fun with her. She can even say Mama and Dada, sort of.

We saw Glen the other day. He comes by the house and eats with us once in a while. I think he comes to see Angel the most, but we enjoy his company. He sure talks a lot about you and asks us all kinds of questions about you. Ha! I wonder why?

He told us about everything that had happened since you got home, and we were so sorry to hear it. Sounds like you had a terrible homecoming. I suppose you didn't want us to worry, and that's why you didn't tell us, but Glen updated us anyway. It must have been a terrible shock about Marilyn. Who would ever have thought her capable of such a thing? And we were so sad to hear about Nancy's death. We will all miss her so much.

I've decided when I get home I'm going to try to get together with my parents. They have to meet Blaine. He's such a good guy, and I'm sure they'll love him and be surprised at what a good pick I made. And Angel; they'll go nuts over her. I'm not sure just how to go about it yet, but I'll figure it out. They can't keep hardened hearts forever.

See you soon.

Love you,

Sadie

THE CHURCH SERVICE ended, and Pete, LeRoy and Irene exited.

"She smiled at me again, Pete." LeRoy punched Pete in the arm. "I'm telling ya."

"She pro'bly smiles at everybody." Pete teased LeRoy about everything, but in this case he hoped his friend was right.

Pete's mother joined in the conversation. "Why don't you smile back at her?"

"I can't smile back until I get my teeth fixed," LeRoy said, ducking his head. "And Pete says he'll go with me to the dentist. I'm a little scared." They all laughed.

Pete loved having his mom on his arm. She had been a little nervous about going to church, but he had assured her that her new jeans, blouse, and sweater he got for her were perfect, and nobody would judge her. He and LeRoy didn't even wear their Sunday-go-to-church suits, just to prove they didn't have to dress up to be there. Instead, they wore their new jeans and polo shirts with their names on them. People had accepted them either way, but they even left their new caps at home, because they remembered Grace telling them to keep them off in church.

"I guess I was afraid to go to church all these years. I never thought it would be so friendly and welcoming." Irene hugged Pete's arm as they walked to the Charger. "Next week, let's see if we can get your brothers to come."

"I'm gonna get my ma to come, too." LeRoy grinned. He had quit chewing tobacco, but he was still missing a couple of teeth near the front.

Irene spoke up. "Let me invite her. We haven't seen each other for years, and we used to be friends a long time ago. I'd love to see her again."

Pete dropped LeRoy at his house and as he shut the car door, Pete said, "Come over after you change your clothes. I need your help." He didn't say why, but he told him to wear his old work clothes.

When they arrived home, Irene slid out of the car and thanked Pete for taking her. "I want us all to go next week. I really liked it," she said.

Pete changed to his dirty clothes, grabbed a banana, and went outside. He knew his mom was wondering what he was up to because he usually came home and plopped down on the sofa to watch sports on TV all day. He smiled to himself. *Let her wonder. She'll find out soon enough.*

Pete started the tow truck just as LeRoy arrived. Together they hooked up one of the old junk cars that cluttered the one-acre lot and towed it away. After a while, they returned and loaded up the next useless car.

At the end of the day, after LeRoy left, Pete came into the house covered with dust. He knew he was smiling like a Cheshire cat, but he couldn't stop himself.

"So that's that!" Irene said, looking up at him, her eyes shining. Tears trickled down her cheeks. "I can't believe you did that. You've heard your dad and me argue about those old trashy cars your whole life. He promised a million times to get rid of them but never did. Now they're finally gone. You have no idea how happy you've made me."

"That's only the beginning, Ma. I promise I'm gonna make it up to you for all the sad years in your life. You just wait and see. Oh, and by the way, how about this here?" He pulled out a roll of bills. "I got at least two hundred dollars a car at the salvage yard, and for some a little more. There's three thousand dollars just for you!"

He knew his mother had never seen that much money in one bunch in her life. She clutched it to her chest, looked up toward heaven, and cried some more.

"Oh, Ma, don't do that," Pete said, feeling his cheeks burn. "You might get me ta cryin.'" They embraced and blubbered and laughed together.

Then they walked to the back door and looked out over the dirt expanse. There were still tools, parts, and equipment scattered here and there, but Pete had a plan for that, too. He thought of Grace and how neat she was. Someday he would bring her to the house to meet his ma, and it wouldn't look like the junk hole he had grown up in. He had made a change in his heart, and he planned to make a change in his family's life as well.

CHAPTER 31

Grace had slept in that morning, so when the phone rang she was still sitting at the kitchen table sipping coffee. She answered on the third ring.

"Hi, Grace. This is Sheldon. I just had the strangest call."

"What's up? Is everything okay?"

"Yeah, as much as it can be, I suppose. I've been able to visit Marilyn a couple of times since they sent her to Chino Women's Prison. It's very strange and uncomfortable, but at least it only takes about thirty minutes to get over there. She keeps telling me to forget about her because she's going to be incarcerated for at least twelve years. It's awful. I still can't believe she could've done something so terrible. It just goes to show you, sometimes you don't know the person you're married to."

Good time to change the subject, she told herself. "So what about the call you got?"

"It was a guy named Pete Jensen from Barstow. He wanted to know if I could help him sell his mom's house and buy a condo for her. He said he's a friend of yours, but he didn't sound too sharp."

Grace laughed out loud.

"Yes, that would be my dear friend Pete. I'm surprised he didn't call me first, but he knows Phil had a real estate business here. Hmm. That's interesting."

"He's quite a character. I'm not sure I want to go to Barstow to do this, but if he's your friend . . ."

"I'm going out there soon," said Grace. "He wants me to come and go to his church with his family. I'll talk to him about it then and explain he'd be better off using an agent in Barstow who works that area and knows it better. Do you have any friends out there you'd like to give the referral to?"

Sheldon paused a moment. "I'll return his call and tell him I'll have one of my real estate friends in Barstow call him. I don't want to be unappreciative, but that would work better."

"I think that's a good idea. I've never been to his house, but when I bailed him out of jail—and that's another story—he told me adamantly that he didn't want me to go to his place. I think he was embarrassed, so it may not be worth much. Assure him I'll help him with it when I get out there. In fact, I'll call him in a while. You go ahead and tell him the referral plan. I don't want to butt in too quickly. This may be a lark. Thanks, Sheldon."

"I wasn't going to return his call," he said, "but I'll do it for you."

IT WASN'T AN HOUR LATER when the phone rang again. Grace had just showered and dressed and was thinking of going out to the patio to water her plants. She picked up the phone in her room and answered.

"Hello, Grace," came the response. "It's Pete. I have a lot to tell you. Ma went to church with LeRoy and me."

She smiled. "That's great, Pete."

"I haven't mentioned my two younger brothers to you because we ain't spent a lot of time together since LeRoy and me started our business and hung out at the bar. I mean . . . we ain't hangin' out at Buford's anymore. Anyway, I'm gonna take my younger brothers to church pretty soon."

"That's wonderful," she said, pleased at the way Pete was reaching out to his family.

"But that ain't . . . *isn't* what I called about. I've been cleanin' up my Ma's place, and I wanta sell it and get her a better place to live. A nice place with grass outside."

"Well, that'll be wonderful. How can I help you?"

"So far, I'm doin' good. I hauled off all the junk cars, cleaned and sold all my dad's tools—and there was a lot of them – and I've made over five thousand dollars. I want to help my mom get out of this dirt patch. She deserves better."

"That's so good of you."

"Oh, and I forgot to tell you. My dad kicked the bucket."

Grace gasped, and her hand flew to her chest. "Oh, Pete, I'm so sorry. When did that happen?"

"About three weeks ago. It don't matter. He wasn't much of a dad. Drunk all the time and never did nothin' for us. Truth is I'm glad he's gone. Now I'm the man of the family." There was a pause. "I guess I always was, 'cept now I want to do somethin' really good. I want to make God happy with me."

Tears bit her eyes. "Pete, God loves you just the way you are. He's happy you accepted Jesus as your Savior. You don't have to do anything to earn His approval. But I love what you want to do for your mom. I'm so proud of you." She could almost see his cheeks turning red at the compliment.

"I called your husband's old partner and told him how I wanted to sell Ma's place and get her something nicer," he went on to explain, "but he told me to call someone here in Barstow or they'd call me. I might need your help to know what to do next. If I make an appointment, could you come out?"

Grace was not sure how involved she should be. But if Pete needed help, she would do what she could. After all, he helped her when she needed help.

"Listen, this is a crazy time," she explained. "Sadie and her family will be home next week, and I'm trying to get the house set up so they can have plenty of room here for a while. I don't think I told you, but I met a man in India that . . . well, we liked each other . . . a lot."

"An Indian?"

She swallowed a chuckle. "No, he's from Southern California. We're hoping to spend some time together and get better acquainted. He'd like for me to go back to the country of India with him."

"When?"

"Well, I don't know," she answered honestly. "We have a lot to learn about each other first. When he gets back to the states, we'll see how our relationship develops."

"Hmmm. Maybe me and LeRoy better look him over."

Grace stifled another laugh and went on, ignoring Pete's comment. "You make an appointment with a local real estate person and call me. But, Pete, don't let him come to the house until you've got it in shipshape order as best you can. Okay?"

"Ma and I are both workin' on it. My brothers even helped me with the tools and paintin' the inside of the house. They think we're just puttin' things in order, but it's gonna be better than that. And – are you ready for this? – I quit smokin'!"

GRACE WORKED HER WAY through Phil's closet. She had always taken his clothes to the cleaners, but now she sorted and folded in order to donate them to someone. She heard stories of widows who found solace in smelling their husband's clothes after they were gone. Grace sniffed some of Phil's things, but they all smelled like they were fresh from the cleaners. His pillow still smelled like him, so she hugged it up close every night when she went to bed.

Grace folded every shirt and tie perfectly in matched sets almost as if they came straight from a store. She kept the pants on hangers and put all the shoes in a large garbage bag. Sheldon wore about the same size as Phil, but she wasn't sure how he would feel about wearing Phil's clothes. She thought about giving them to Pastor Troude. If they fit, he would have a whole new wardrobe; if they did not he would know people in the church who would appreciate them. She called him to check it out.

"John, how would you feel about having some of Phil's clothes?"

His answer was immediate. "I'd love that. If they don't fit, we're always keeping clothes here in our Mercy Ministry room to give to the needy. Is that all right with you?"

"Sure. I'd offer them to Sheldon, but I'm afraid that would be too painful for him. I'd rather know you used them or passed them on to a good cause. All right, I'll get them to you soon."

When she was done for the day, she loaded the bags into her Lexus, stopped by John's office for a cup of coffee, dropped off the clothing, and returned home. It would take more bags and more trips to finish the job.

SADIE, BLAINE, AND Glen made plans to travel together and arrive at LAX as a group. Grace would pick them up, and she could hardly wait. As she drove to the airport, her anticipation grew. She couldn't decide what excited her most, seeing Sadie, Angel, or Glen. She loved Blaine too, of course, but he would have to be last on the list this time.

The drive proved challenging, though it was not quite as bad as she got closer to the airport. But every time the traffic came to a stop, her anxiety built.

When she finally arrived at baggage claim where they had arranged to meet, she could see her four travelers waiting on the sidewalk with their bags. Grace pulled up to the curb and parked. She popped the trunk and rushed around the car to the sidewalk. Who to hug first? They all came at her at once: Sadie, Glen, and Blaine with Angel in his arms. A big group hug caused other drivers to honk in frustration, so they quickly threw in one bag after another until the back end was packed full. Glen then claimed the passenger seat next to Grace, and the Markem family took the back after they installed the carseat and strapped Angel into it. Each person had to hold an extra bag that did not fit in the trunk. Grace pulled out of the terminal area and headed toward Pasadena.

"How was the flight?" Grace asked.

All three adults started to answer at once. They stopped and laughed.

Glen spoke first. "Grace, how about you? How was your drive to the airport?"

Once they got on the road, they all told their stories, one at a time, about the long trip home.

"We're just glad to be home safe and sound," Blaine concluded. "I think we're all rum-dumb from traveling so long. It'll probably take us a few days to get back to normal."

"I have your room all ready for you," Grace said. "The nursery freshened up and . . ." Her voice trailed off as she pushed away memories of Philisity. "Glen, if you don't have anyone waiting for you at home, you're welcome to stay at our house for a few days. I have another extra room for you."

"I think I'd better be dropped off at my house in Pasadena if that's okay," he answered. "I really need to get my land-legs back, get some sleep, read my mail, and catch up with myself. Then I'll be a human again. I'll call you tomorrow. Is that okay?"

Grace nodded. "I understand. You must be exhausted. If you promise you won't wait more than a day or two, I'll let you go." She gave him a coy smile.

Grace dropped Glen at his home in Pasadena, and Sadie moved up to the front seat. Grace thought Sadie would kick into her usual chatter, but she put the seat back and fell asleep in seconds. A quick peek over her shoulder confirmed that Blaine and Angel were both out cold as well. Grace had been looking forward to having her family home, but so far they weren't much company. She chuckled to herself.

LEROY, WHO SEEMED QUITE excited about getting new teeth, told Pete he hoped they would win more than a smile from the girl named Tammy who always sat a seat in front or behind him at church.

Pete wasn't so sure, but he willingly went with LeRoy to the dentist. While there, he made an appointment for himself. Neither of them had ever been to a dentist before, so they were surprised it wasn't worse than expected. Cleaning came first, a couple of cavities filled here and there, and a small bridge for LeRoy was all they needed.

The next time they attended church with their moms, LeRoy walked right up to Tammy as they exited and said, "Hey, Tammy."

Pete stood off a bit, watching and listening, trying not to grin. His mom and LeRoy's stood nearby, chatting up a storm.

The girl replied, "Hey, LeRoy." They both smiled, and LeRoy stepped away and joined Pete.

"Well, was that it?" Pete asked.

LeRoy didn't answer, but even his ears were red.

"I swear I saw stars circling your stupid head," Pete said, chuckling. "Why didn't you ask for her number or somethin'?" Pete realized he had just become the wingman in this scenario.

"I . . . I . . . I . . . couldn't get no other words out," LeRoy stammered.

"If yer conversations are gonna only be two words, it's gonna be a long time before you get a whole sentence out."

"Oh, shut up, Pete. I ain't talked to a real girl since high school. I'll do better next time."

"I thought you were really brave, LeRoy," Irene encouraged.

LeRoy's mom hugged him around the waist and kissed his cheek. "You did good, son."

Irene added, "And thank you so much for helping Pete clean up around our house. He's pushed me to clean up really good inside too. You'd think he was getting the house ready to sell."

"I thought you knew . . ." LeRoy blurted out.

Pete's heart skipped a beat. This was not the time or place to break the news to his mother. He knew he had to tell her – and soon – but he hadn't figured out when or how.

"Shut up, LeRoy. She's doing a great job. She knows I want to do for her what my dad never did, and we're all working on it together."

BLAINE AND SADIE HAD put Angel to bed and then apparently turned in themselves, as they did not come back out of their room.

When the phone rang, Grace, who still sat at the dining room table, sipping a last cup of tea, picked up the phone and was pleased to hear Pete's voice. "How's everything going?" she asked.

"Great. A real estate guy named Ken Hayes is comin' to look at the house tomorrow. Can you come out? You'll know more about the house business and what to do."

Grace thought for a moment before answering. "Yes, as a matter of fact, my family came home from India, but they're all so out of it, I know they'll probably sleep most of the day tomorrow. No need for me to be here."

"Oh, man, that's a relief! And if you can stay long enough, I'd like for you to go with me and Mom to look at condos in town."

"That would be fun. Sure. I'd be glad to." Grace was pleased to have something to occupy her time while her family got over jet lag.

"Ma doesn't know anything about this," Pete cautioned, "so I'll need your help."

Grace was stunned. "What? She doesn't know you're going to sell the house? Don't you think that's something you should run past her?"

"No, yes, well . . . maybe. I mean, I wanted to surprise her, but I'm not sure how she'll take it because she's lived in this old house ever since she got married. So I guess I've just been puttin' off tellin' her about it."

"Well, this should be interesting. I'll be out there by . . . what time is the guy coming?"

"Ten o'clock."

"I'll be there at nine-thirty to meet your mom. Maybe, if we have a little time to chat, she'll warm up to me and feel comfortable. I hope."

"Wow, Grace. That sounds perfect. I'll just tell her you're comin' out to meet her and nothin' else."

CHAPTER 32

Exhausted, Glen dragged himself into bed. He wanted to see Grace more than anything, but at this point he could not even think straight. He fell into a deep sleep in seconds.

He awoke and looked at the clock. The numbers looked blurred, and he blinked his eyes in order to focus. When he saw the time clearly, he nearly leapt out of bed. "Eleven-thirty! I slept sixteen hours!"

He went to the bathroom and took a shower. By the time he dressed, he almost felt human. A cup of coffee and a piece of toast satisfied him perfectly for the moment. The food gave him just enough energy to sit back down in his recliner and drift off again.

Awaking with a start, he reached for the phone and dialed Grace's number. He planned to drive to Highland and spend the afternoon and evening with her, but the phone rang and rang, and he got the recording machine.

"Hi, Grace. I hoped we could get together today," he said. "I slept all night and half the day, and now I'm fit as a fiddle. Call me when you get this." Then he fell back into a quiet nap.

All day he waited and wondered if he had been too forward with her. Maybe she had second thoughts. She did invite him to crash at her house, and she did not say anything about being gone. He called several times but didn't leave another message.

GRACE HAD ENJOYED GETTING up without an alarm clock for the past few months, but today the alarm sounded at six-thirty. Sadie and family were still sleeping. She quickly put on her makeup and slipped out of the house about seven-fifteen. McDonald's offered a breakfast sandwich with a cup of coffee, and she decided to take them up on the offer. Not her usual choice, but she needed to hit the road by seven-forty-five to get to Barstow, find Pete's house, and arrive by nine-thirty.

Driving provided a pleasant pastime as traffic was light going her way. She felt exhilarated with the prospect of helping Pete pull off this surprise. At least it wasn't something dangerous like towing someone's car or escaping with a bag of money. She chuckled to herself. In the past year, her life had taken some weird turns, worthy of a novel. As she drove, she began to pray.

Lord, thank you for all you've done in my life. I was a fool for leaving home last summer on the Turnaround bus. Taking up with a strange woman named Isabel and moving in with her and her demented son was reckless, yet you shielded me from harm. I worked at the casino, surrounded by sin and crime, but you sent me help through Sadie. When I was being chased by Jerry and Madeline who were determined to gun me down, you protected me. When Sadie's car broke down, you sent Pete and LeRoy and a law enforcement guy with skills to deliver Angel. When Sadie was thinking she'd be a single mother, you sent Blaine. You took Phil from me, but you gave me Nancy and John to comfort me. When I got lost in depression, you opened a door to a mission trip to India, and crossed my path with Glen's. Your ways are not our ways, but they are better. Thank you so much for my life and whatever you have planned for me in the future. I trust you.

As she left the freeway at Barstow, she felt fulfilled and ready for the next chapter of life. She knew she could do it with God's help.

IT WASN'T THE DRIVE or the limited hours, but Sheldon found it painful to visit Marilyn. Seeing her in prison clothes saddened him. As he pulled up in the parking lot, he breathed a prayer. *Jesus, let me be encouraging in some way.*

He realized if the tables were turned, she would probably bring him something sweet to eat, but that was not a guy thing. He came empty-handed. She had not told him anything she needed.

When he got to the visiting area, he sat down and waited for her to be ushered in to the other side of the glass. To his surprise, she smiled and looked fairly content. They both picked up the phones.

"Hi, Honey," he said. "How are you doing?"

"I'm fine. And thank you for coming, Sheldon."

Uncertain about how to start a conversation, he looked into her eyes and shruggled. "Do they treat you okay?"

"It's actually better than I expected. I know I've only been here a few weeks, but I'm learning a lot about myself, my past, my temper, my life, and God."

Phil smiled. "That's great. Pastor Troude is helping me along the way too."

"There's even a chance I'll get out of here when I still have some life to live *if* I behave myself. I've found out I can take some classes and . . . who knows? Maybe I'll come out as a college graduate. That's what I always wanted."

Sheldon was surprised, not only by her words but also by her positive tone. "I didn't know that, Marilyn. You never talked about it."

She shrugged. "I guess I never thought I'd be smart enough. And maybe I'm not, but I'm going to try."

"That's great. I'll cheer for you from outside, I promise."

The first few weeks after Marilyn's arrest had been dismal; then came the transfer to the prison after her case was settled. But now she seemed the happiest Sheldon had seen her since before the cruise. He hoped this euphoria would continue. He usually spent their visiting time listening to her complain about the food and some of the other inmates.

"How's business?" Marilyn asked, interrupting Sheldon's thoughts.

He smiled. "Business is great. Now I know why you wanted to travel for a couple of months. To get me out of working sixteen and eighteen hour days, right? Now I do it so I won't have to go home and be alone. It also made me realize I could hire good help at the office to keep things going when I need time off."

Marilyn smiled, reminding Sheldon of the beautiful woman he knew she was deep down. "Sounds like we're both learning," she said.

"Yes," Sheldon admitted. "I've found out I can take off one or two days a week, and our associates do just fine. They make sales just as well as I do. The money keeps coming in, and Grace gets her percentage as well." He immediately regretted what he'd said about Grace because that might still be a sore spot for Marilyn.

Marilyn seemed to ignore his mention of Grace. "It's not all bad here," she said. "I'm taking my punishment, but even that has its positive aspects. I'm going to start college . . . and listen to this. They have softball teams in each cellblock. I've already made the team, and they have intramural games all the time. I even heard that if we behave, at some point we may get to play in tournaments outside of here. Can you believe that?"

"Well, it beats picking up trash beside the freeway, for sure."

They managed a little laugh.

"It's gonna be okay," Marilyn said. "If you're still available when I get out, I know we can make it."

As the guard stepped up to alert them the visit was over, they stood and put their hands together on the glass. Marilyn threw a kiss, and Sheldon silently mouthed, "I love you."

Despite Marilyn's last words – *If you're still available* – ringing in his ears, Sheldon exited with new hope. Life had taken another turn, but he'd keep busy and look forward to a better future. He still had a hard time believing Marilyn could carry out such a heinous crime, but he had become even more in awe of a God who could forgive even murder if there was repentance. His newfound faith resided fresh and sincere in his heart, and he had Pastor Troude to thank for that. After golf, Sheldon would treat John to lunch and that's when John had shared his faith and the love of Christ. Sometimes bad things had to happen to help us realize our need for a Savior, Sheldon reminded himself. And it sounded like God was changing Marilyn as well. He had made provision for her to grow in her faith even while she was incarcerated.

GRACE WAS PLEASED SHE and Irene seemed to hit it off immediately. Pete's brothers were gone to ball practice, so the house was quiet.

"I'm just sorry it isn't a Sunday because I'd love to take you to our church," Irene said. "The people are so nice, and I've gotten so I'm looking forward to it each week. It's changed our lives."

Grace smiled. "I remember when Pete and LeRoy came to our church the first time. Did you know they stood up on stage when my granddaughter got dedicated? Well, she's not really my granddaughter . . . she's the daughter of my friend Sadie, and her name is Angel."

Irene nodded. "I knew they went out and bought some suits to go, but I didn't hear much about it. I think they took a liking to your whole family . . . *and* church."

Grace smiled again. "Pete told me a little about your church, but he invited me out here today, not only to meet you, but to give you a little surprise."

Pete had apparently been eavesdropping in the other room and, on cue, entered the kitchen. "I even had Ma make some cookies for you. Do ya want one?"

Grace noticed Pete's hand trembling slightly as he offered her a cookie from a plate, then set them on the table.

"A surprise?" Irene appeared puzzled as she looked from her son to her guest. "Having you here isn't a surprise, but I'm happy to meet you."

Grace smiled her reply and waited for Pete to take the lead.

"Okay, here's the deal, Ma. I've invited a guy over to look at our house." Pete wrung his hands as he waited.

Irene frowned. "A guy? Who? Why?"

"Well, ya know how we've been fixin' everything up, and it looks the best it has since I can remember."

"Yeah, so . . . ?"

"It wasn't just so we could invite Grace." He looked from his mother to their guest. "Sorry, Grace. I didn't mean it that way." He returned his attention to Irene. "Anyway, the guy is a real-estate guy, and he's gonna tell us what this place is worth so we can list it to sell and get you into a nicer place in town."

After a brief pause, Irene put her hands to her face, and a few tears sprang loose. "Really?" she managed to choke out. "How could that happen?"

"Between all the junk cars, Dad's tools and equipment, our old tow truck, the money Grace paid us, and the money LeRoy and I have made with the new truck, I've saved up over eighteen thousand dollars."

Irene grabbed the end of her apron and covered her eyes as sobs came from within. "I'm so thankful for everything you've done already," she cried as she glanced up at Grace and then at Pete. "When you started to clear the yard of old cars and junk, it made me wanna neaten up the house more than I ever had before. Even your brothers have pitched in and painted the inside." The sobs subsided and her gaze returned to Grace. "I've always been so busy takin' in ironing, I didn't have time to keep things nice. Somethin' has lit a fire under Pete, and we've all caught it. He's even helpin' me with the expenses."

The whole day was magical, and Grace felt blessed to be a part of it. Ken Hayes, the realtor, listed the property and took them to see several condominiums in town, which Irene loved. He promised a quick sale and encouraged them to fix what they could.

Irene could not stop thanking Grace for all she had done for Pete and their family. Grace felt she had not really done anything, but she was excited for Irene and her boys. In fact the two younger boys showed up just as Grace was leaving, and she was pleased to get a chance to meet them.

It was almost five o'clock by the time Grace left. She felt sorry for not leaving a note for Sadie to tell her where she had gone. Since being alone for six months, she was not used to answering to anyone. She hit the road and hoped to get home quickly.

———⚜———

"OH, MY GOODNESS," GLEN exclaimed as she walked in the door. "Where have you been?" He jumped to his feet to greet her.

"We've been worried sick about you," Sadie cried, hurrying to her side, followed quickly by Blaine and Angel. "Where have you been?"

Sadie, Blaine, and Glen stood around as if holding trial, with Grace as the defendant. She put down her purse and gave them a group hug while Angel clung to her legs.

"I'm sorry," she said, feeling terrible for not having left a note. "I guess I'm not used to answering to anybody. I thought you'd sleep all night and all day, so I went out to Barstow to help Pete and his mother."

Sadie lifted her eyebrows. "Really? What now?"

"Pete's father died recently," she explained, "and he's been trying to fix their place up so they can sell it and buy a nice condo for his family, somewhere with grass, neighbors, and newness of life."

Sadie seemed pleasantly surprised. "Wow, sounds like Pete has really changed."

Grace nodded as Angel tried to climb her leg and pull herself up. "He and LeRoy have gotten involved in a church, and now they have both their mothers attending as well. It's been a life-changer for all of them. In fact, they want me to come out again and go to church with them soon."

"I want to go, too," Sadie said and raised her hand.

"Well, if you're going, so are we." Blaine bent down and picked up Angel, then raised his hand with Angel's hand in it.

Glen raised his hand. "If Blaine and Angel are going, then I'm coming, too."

They all laughed as Grace said, "Okay, that's settled. We'll have to wait until they tell us when. Meanwhile let's get dinner started. I'm starved!"

Grace and Sadie made dinner and chattered non-stop the whole time. Blaine and Glen entertained Angel in the living room, and Blaine explained a little bit about Pete and LeRoy's part in Angel's life.

When dinner was served, Grace asked Glen to bless the meal before they all dug in. She felt the happiest she had in months. Her life had fallen apart a year ago, and now God was putting it back together in a completely unexpected way. He had given her a new family, new friends. . . and a new love.

THE NEXT MORNING, THE phone rang, and Grace was surprised to hear Sheldon's voice on the other end. She hoped there was not some sort of problem with the business or Marilyn.

Sheldon assured her that was not the case. "I just wanted to call and tell you how well Marilyn's doing. Those first few weeks were terrible, and I hated to go visit. I didn't even know what to take to her or how to manage the sadness."

"So how's she doing?" Grace asked. She had not yet figured out how to forgive Marilyn or even visit her. She was, after all, a murderer and had robbed Grace of her husband.

"To tell you the truth," Sheldon said, "it's been amazing. Her parents came to see her, and they hadn't spoken in years. Marilyn said her dad appeared to be sober, and that's something I've never seen before."

Grace nodded. "That's good."

"There's more. She's getting ready to enroll in some online college courses for one thing. I knew she always felt inferior to you and your college education. She's really excited about it."

Grace nodded. "I'm glad she's at a place where those things are available."

"That's not all of it. She's on a softball team. They have regular intramural games, and she hopes to play in local tournaments outside the prison. Can you believe that?"

"Wow!" Grace was surprised. "Next thing you know she'll be doing hair and makeup for the other prisoners." She chuckled.

"Oh, she's already got the corner on the market there. I swear, Grace, she's better off there than she's ever been. She even mentioned learning more about herself and God."

"God works in mysterious ways, doesn't He? And our job is to trust Him." Grace was pleased to hear the change in Sheldon. "God is able to take what was meant for bad and turn it into good."

"You're so right, Grace. Thank you for not hating us in all of this. I mean, she killed Phil even if she didn't mean to. Something neither you nor I would have thought possible. Will you ever be able to forgive her?"

It was a question Grace was not ready to answer, so she deflected. "Life's been so crazy for the last six months, Sheldon. I haven't had time to deal with that in my own heart yet."

"I understand," Sheldon said. "Speaking of forgiveness, John Troude contacted me, and we've been playing golf. With Nancy and Marilyn gone, it keeps us both entertained and distracted from our loneliness. He's been wonderful, and we've kind of held each other up. I had no idea I'd miss Marilyn so much or play golf with a preacher."

She smiled. "I'm happy you and John have become friends. He's a great guy and the kindest man I've ever known. And by the way, I have an idea of what you could take to Marilyn next time you go."

"Oh, really? What's that?"

"A new catcher's mitt." Grace surprised herself with the idea, and Sheldon seemed receptive.

CHAPTER 33

They had just finished dinner when the phone rang. "I'll get it," Sadie offered.

Grace smiled at Sadie's helpfulness. She so appreciated her and had come to love her as the child she never had.

Sadie answered the phone and then chuckled. "Hi, Pete. No, this isn't Grace. It's Sadie. I hear you got rid of the old delivery room."

Sadie laughed, and Grace imagined Pete did too.

"Hold on," Sadie said. "I'll get Grace."

Grace got on the line and quickly realized Pete must be excited about something because his words tumbled over each other.

"I want . . . I mean . . . could ya . . . what I called about . . . Wait, let me start over." She heard him take a deep breath. "We sold Ma's house and bought the perfect place for her and us boys. Me and LeRoy are doin' a great business, and we're thinkin' about getting' our own apartment maybe pretty soon. Can ya . . . would ya . . . we, I mean, me and Ma and LeRoy want you to come out and go to church with us and see Ma's new place. Would ya?"

Grace's smile reached across her face. She couldn't imagine anything she'd like to do more than accept Pete's invitation. "I'd love to. When would be a good time?"

"How about June fifteenth?"

Grace hesitated. "On June fifteenth last year I left home on the Turnaround Bus. So much has happened since then; it seems like an eternity."

"Hmm. That's the Sunday after next." Pete paused for a moment. "I think we'll have another surprise for you by then."

By now Grace was well aware that Pete loved surprises. She imagined there weren't many surprises in his young life. Now Grace had an idea. "Well, then, I think I'll have a surprise for you, too."

Pete told her what time to come and where, but he didn't tell anymore about his surprise, nor did she tell him about hers.

FOR THE NEXT TEN DAYS, Glen spent every available moment with Grace. Some days they sat out in the backyard swing and talked all day. First about background, school, families, and careers, but soon their conversations became deeper and more emotional.

Glen wanted to know everything about Grace, but he tried to keep his questions gentle. "It must be very difficult to deal with the loss you've suffered in the past year," he said. "Is there any way I can be a comfort to you?" He thought Phil's death and the loss of Philisity must still trouble her heart, but he wanted her to be able to talk about it openly with him . . . if that would help.

Grace took a breath and looked off into the clouds. "Yes, you can help me." She blinked her eyes as tears began to form.

Glen took her hands in his and waited patiently.

"Would you be willing to go with me to visit Philisity's grave and the columbarium where Phil's ashes are sequestered?"

"Of course, I would," he said. "I'd gladly go with you." He wanted to ask when but held back for fear of appearing pushy. As her tears spilled over onto her cheeks, he put his arms around her and drew her close, allowing her to weep openly. This was the first time he had seen her express such deep emotions, and he wondered how long she would wait to set a date for them to go.

"Let's go tomorrow, if that's okay," she said as she wiped the tears away. "I know I won't forget either of them, but I don't want them to be a mystery between us."

"I understand," he said. "When you feel sad, I want to comfort you, and when you feel glad, I want to share that joy." He hugged her close and said, "We can do this together."

GRACE WAS RELIEVED as she watched things unfold, resolving many of her concerns. Blaine started his Master's classes and his lawn business was thriving. The girls had not only kept up with his customers they added three new ones. He was auditioning for a roll in a play, so he agreed to keep the girls on as partners for as long as they were at the college. Sadie got busy registering for some junior college classes, and she found out Fran's daughter was pregnant, lived close, and was happy to babysit for Angel a few hours here and there. Everything seemed to be falling into place.

On June fifteenth, Glen brought his SUV, and Grace sat in the passenger seat, while Blaine, Sadie, and Angel filled the backseat. They would have invited John, but he had a congregation to preach to on Sundays.

They arrived in Barstow and found the church without any problem. Pete, Irene, and her younger sons were waiting on the sidewalk. Next to them stood LeRoy and two women.

When Grace and the family unloaded, she could see the surprise on Pete and LeRoy's faces. "I brought my whole family and my new friend, Glen," she announced.

After Pete introduced his mother and brothers to Sadie and her family, LeRoy stepped forward with a woman on each side.

"Grace, and you guys, this is my mom, Mamie." He lifted her hand with his right hand. Then he lifted the younger girl's hand in his left hand and said, "And this is my girlfriend, Tammy."

Grace was so happy for LeRoy and pleased that he had a new, improved smile and no telltale tobacco stains on his chin.

Everyone shook hands and hugged. Pete and LeRoy seemed surprised that Grace brought everyone with her, and Grace was still a bit surprised to see both of the men's families dressed up and waiting for them.

Pete led them all into the church where they filled up the two front rows. With all of them and Tammy's parents, who were already inside, there were fourteen of them. Once they were seated comfortably, Pete and LeRoy disappeared.

When the service started, Pete and LeRoy were still AWOL and their guests fidgeted nervously. Grace looked around for them, but they were nowhere in the sanctuary. *Where in the world did they go?*

The pastor came to the podium. After greeting the congregation, he said, "Today is a special day." He looked toward the side door. "Fellas, come out and join me on stage."

Pete and LeRoy peeked out but hesitated for a moment.

The pastor gestured for them to come on out before speaking. "Pete Jensen and LeRoy Ratcliff are being baptized today."

Grace's heart swelled with joy as she watched Pete and LeRoy enter the stage, wearing baggy shorts and T-shirts that said, "I HAVE DECIDED." They stood one on each side of the pastor, and both smiled at their families. Grace fully expected to see one or both of them wave to their moms like little kids do when they are on stage. But they didn't. Still, it was easy to read the excitement on their faces. They were both blushing as the pastor led them to the baptistery at the side of the stage.

"I'm going to ask them to give a bit of their testimony," the pastor said.

Pete stepped into the water first. "Ooh, that's cold."

Everyone laughed.

"I just wanna say thanks to our friends Grace and Sadie," Pete began. "They invited us to a church, and we learned about Jesus. I've decided to follow Jesus because He died for me, and I want to live for Him." He crossed his arms over his chest, and the pastor dunked him backward under the water, then pulled him out . . . with some effort. The congregation applauded and cheered. A volunteer helped Pete step out of the tank and wrapped a big towel around him.

It was LeRoy's turn. "The same fer me," LeRoy said and stepped into the water. Everyone laughed again, but they clapped and cheered when he came up out of the water grinning from ear to ear.

"WHAT A SURPRISE! WHAT a wonderful surprise," Grace said as they exited the church after the service. The day was far from over, and she already felt it was one of the best ones she had ever experienced. Two lives had been changed, and who knew how many others might be influenced by those two changed lives?

With hair still damp, Pete and LeRoy emerged, but they had changed into dry clothes. They beamed like two bright light bulbs.

Pete turned his attention to Grace. "Hey, did ya notice another surprise in the parking lot?" He pointed to the far corner.

Grace turned to look in the direction he pointed. "Oh, my. What a beauty!" she said when her eyes caught sight of their new tow truck with the words "Jensen and Ratcliff Towing Experts" painted on the door. After Sadie, Blaine, Glen, and Grace finished their oohing and aahing, Blaine scooped up Angel and they all loaded into the car and left the parking lot following the truck.

The whole group went to Irene's new condo where they had potluck lunch for everyone. Mamie brought a box of fried chicken and potato salad from the Truck Stop, and Irene had made sandwiches for everyone. Grace and Sadie added fruit salad and chocolate chip cookies. Tammy's parents supplied a variety of cold drinks and ice cream.

No family reunion could have been more fun. Laughter and good cheer filled the condo. Elbow-to-elbow, they exchanged stories about LeRoy and Pete and congratulated them on their baptism. When they finished eating, Pete's brothers excused themselves and went outside to play catch in the quad.

"Now for *my* surprise," Grace said in order to get everyone's attention as she stepped to the center of the room.

"Wait a second," LeRoy interrupted, scratching his head. "I thought your surprise was bringin' the whole family to Barstow."

Grace grinned and looked at Glen. "Why don't you tell them?" she asked.

Glen stepped to Grace's side, put his arm around her waist, and got straight to the point. "Grace and I are getting married in a month, and you're all invited."

There was a surprised gasp from everyone before the room erupted into a big cheer and the biggest group-hug that ever took place.

"Wait," Glen called out over the chatter. "That isn't all. Shortly after the wedding we'll be leaving to go back to India to teach English again. But we plan to come home every summer." This time there were no cheers but lots of congratulations and questions.

———⁓◯⁓———

PETE THOUGHT HE MIGHT tell Grace how he and LeRoy were the ones who pretended to be kidnappers and collect a five-hundred-thousand dollar ransom from her husband last summer when she ran away to Las Vegas. He even thought about telling her how they got her driver's license. But he decided to keep that secret. He didn't know the depth of her forgiveness, and it might not be a good idea to test it. She had become a friend forever in his book. This time he knew he and LeRoy had done a good thing . . . a very good thing.

―⁜―

ON THE RIDE HOME, GRACE asked Blaine and Sadie if they were willing to house-sit for the next ten months.

"Are you kidding? That would be wonderful. We were wondering how we could afford an apartment."

Blaine chimed in. "I got the part in a play, and my business is thriving. But with school, I won't have much time to work with Bernard and the girls."

"I want to take some junior college classes," Sadie said. "And Fran's daughter said she'd take care of Angel. God is so good! We accept your offer . . . right, Blaine?"

"Of course. Thank you so much, Grace, for all you've done for us. And letting us stay in your house is an added blessing we never expected."

―⁜―

GRACE HAD PUT IT OFF as long as she could, but she knew she had to visit Marilyn before leaving the states. She wasn't sure how it would go, but she had to do it. It was a loose end that needed to have a knot tied in it.

As she entered the prison waiting room, she thought about how far she had come from her safe fourth grade classroom. Never had she imagined she would visit a jail to bail out friends or a prison to visit another.

"Hi, Marilyn." Grace sat down on the visitor's side of the glass.

"Hello," Marilyn mumbled, hanging her head.

Grace had become accustomed to dressing for comfort since her retirement. She wore her Calvin Klein jeans and a loose T-shirt. No more St. Johns suits. She hoped it would help, at least a little, to make

Marilyn feel less intimidated. "I guess you didn't expect to see me here."

Marilyn, eyes still downward, shook her head. "No. You should hate me for what I did. I'm *so* sorry." She looked up as tears filled her eyes, then quickly spilled over and ran down her cheeks.

"I'm sorry, too," Grace said, remembering what Sheldon had told her about Marilyn's feelings toward her. "If I ever made you feel inferior or as if Sheldon worked as Phil's underling, I'm truly sorry. If I seemed uppity or arrogant, I'm so sorry."

She saw Marilyn swallow. The obviously repentant woman's voice cracked as she spoke. "I was hateful and jealous of both of you."

Grace nodded. "It's over. You're paying for your crime, and I came to tell you I forgive you. I hope you'll forgive me if I seemed snobby or superior."

Marilyn pressed a hand against the glass, the chain connecting to her other hand strained by the pull. "Oh, Grace, I'm so sorry. I wish I could undo what I've done. I wish I could blame it on the craziness of menopause or the abuse I endured when my dad was drunk. But it was my own anger that I let get out of control. I'll be sorry forever."

"It hasn't been easy for either of us," Grace said, "but the Bible clearly says Jesus forgave us, and we in turn are to forgive others. Our salvation depends on it." Hesitantly she reached up and placed the palm of her hand against Marilyn's palm, the two separated only by the glass.

After a moment, she lowered her hand and spoke, "I couldn't think of anything I could bring except maybe cookies, and I'm not much of a cookie baker, I'm afraid. Sadie made some for me to give you, and I brought them, but the guards confiscated them. It didn't occur to me they might think there was poison or a knife in them."

Marilyn cracked a half-smile. "Ha. They probably ate them."

Grace smiled back. "I also brought something I thought you might be able to use. The guards took it also, but I'm sure they'll give it to you after their inspection."

"If it's something good to eat, I'll probably never see it."

"No. It's a study Bible like the one Pastor Troude gave me when I first accepted Christ. I wish I could put it directly in your hands."

"That's okay. Don't worry about that. I'm sure they'll give it back to me soon. Thank you so much. Someone gave me a little one, but the print's so small I can hardly read it. I've been going to the Bible class several times a week. I think being here is going to make me a better person."

Grace smiled and nodded. "I wrote something in the front page. I hope you like it. The guard said you can't have it until they've inspected it carefully. I'm sorry about that, but I guess they do that to everything that's brought in. At least we know they can't eat it." They chuckled.

Marilyn smiled. "That's so nice of you."

"I heard you're going to take college classes and play softball, but I knew I couldn't bring you a bat." They both responded by rolling their eyes.

"I'm going to India to teach English," Grace continued, "but I'll be back in ten months, and I'll come and see how you're doing." She didn't mention her engagement to Glen.

"Thank you, Grace."

Grace left the prison feeling good inside. The burden of unforgiveness was lifted from her, and she felt like she'd done a good thing that was pleasing to God. A very good thing.

SEVERAL HOURS AFTER Grace left, the guards handed the Bible over to Marilyn. She opened the front page to see what Grace had written.

To Marilyn,

If we confess our sins to God, he will keep his promise and do what is right: he will forgive us our sins and purify us from all our wrongdoing. (1 John 1:9) KJV

If you forgive other people when they sin against you, your heavenly Father will also forgive you. (Matthew 6:14) NIV

Jesus loves you.

Grace

DISCUSSION QUESTIONS:

WHO WAS YOUR FAVORITE CHARACTER? WHY?

WHAT WAS YOUR FAVORITE PART OF THE STORY? WHY?

WHAT WOULD YOU LIKE TO CHANGE ABOUT THE STORY? WHY?

IS IT POSSIBLE FOR GUYS LIKE PETE AND LEROY TO CHANGE? HOW?

HAVE YOU KNOWN ANYONE WHOSE LIFE DRAMATICALLY CHANGED WHEN THEY BECAME A CHRISTIAN?

HOW DID YOUR LIFE CHANGE WHEN YOU BECAME A CHRISTIAN?

IF YOU WERE IN GRACE'S SHOES, WHAT WOULD IT TAKE FOR YOU TO FORGIVE MARILYN?

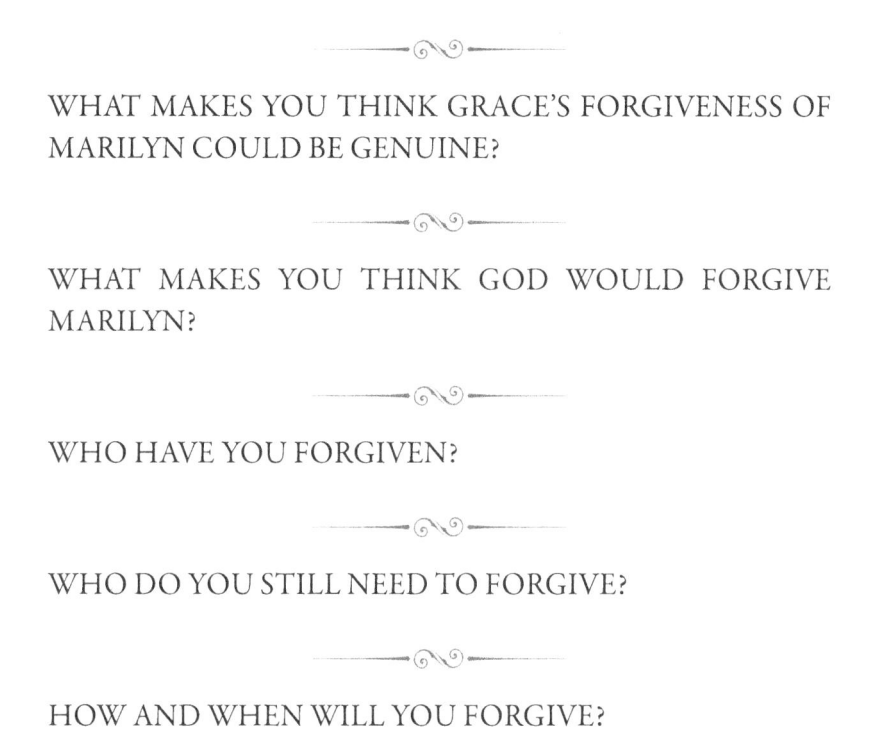

WHAT MAKES YOU THINK GRACE'S FORGIVENESS OF MARILYN COULD BE GENUINE?

WHAT MAKES YOU THINK GOD WOULD FORGIVE MARILYN?

WHO HAVE YOU FORGIVEN?

WHO DO YOU STILL NEED TO FORGIVE?

HOW AND WHEN WILL YOU FORGIVE?

FROM THE AUTHOR:

I HOPE YOU'VE ENJOYED *The Turnaround at Sea*. It's fiction, but as a Christian, I know the joy Pete, LeRoy, and all the rest found when they turned their lives over to Jesus. If that's something you'd like to experience, just pray and ask Jesus to forgive your sins, come into your heart, and direct your life. If you believe Jesus is the son of God and He loves you, you are born again. Reading the Bible and attending a good Bible-teaching church will help you on your journey.

John 3:16 For God so loved the world, that He gave His only begotten son, that whoever believes in Him should not perish, but have everlasting life. (NASB)

John 3:3 Except a man be born again, he cannot see the kingdom of God. (KJV)

If you commited your life to Christ through reading this book, or have more questions about salvation, feel free to contact me at www.SayItWithHumor.com[1]

---

1. http://www.SayItWithHumor.com

ABOUT THE AUTHOR

Karen Robertson lives in Wildomar, California with her husband Barry. She has retired from education, real estate, coaching, clowning and comedy. Her writing always includes humor and how God is working in her life or the life of her characters. *Turnaround At Sea* is the second in her Turnaround Series. Recently, she has published a humorous memoir titled *Pandemic Pandemonium* and an ebook about her special grandson, Les, a brain cancer survivor, and their relationship titled *More for Les*.

Contact her for speaking engagements or just to tell her how you enjoyed her writing: kanwrite@SayItWithHumor.com

You will also find some of her comedy videos on her website www.SayItWithHumor.com[1]

Check out her TEDx speech on the power of humor titled *Livin' Life Laughing* at https://www.youtube.com/watch?v=pc5bGXUQyT0

---

1. http://www.SayItWithHumor.com

ACKNOWLEDGEMENTS

Thank you to my friend April Miller and other beta readers Linda Dosier, Linda Spahr, and Eve Gaal.

The final product wouldn't have been possible without Kathi Macias, Editor and friend. She patiently makes my writing readable and smooths out the wrinkles.

A special mention goes to Michele Van Dusen who has been a real encouragement. She encourages me to write more because she's going for the Guinness World Record for being acknowledged in the most books. I don't know who keeps track of such things, but I know she does.

Don't miss out!

Visit the website below and you can sign up to receive emails whenever KAREN ROBERTSON publishes a new book. There's no charge and no obligation.

https://books2read.com/r/B-A-PCHM-HEANB

BOOKS 2 READ

Connecting independent readers to independent writers.

Did you love *Turnaround at Sea*? Then you should read *More for Les*[1] by KAREN ROBERTSON!

So, there I was, standing shoulder-to-shoulder with Mark Wahlberg. Most women would say, "A dream come true," but in my case, it was a prayer answered. He is adorable, but I'm over seventy, and I was on a mission.

Sure, I've dreamed of being a movie star, but on that day my title was "unpaid extra" in a movie I would never go to the theater to see . . . R-rated . . . but I had a reason for being there and only God could have orchestrated it. It was October 2014. Here's the story of how I appeared in the ComiCon scene with Mark Wahlberg in Ted 2. I'll start from the beginning.

---

1. https://books2read.com/u/3R8xAB

2. https://books2read.com/u/3R8xAB

In 2003, right after his fourth birthday, my grandson, Les Paul Fountain was diagnosed with medullablastoma, otherwise known as fast-growing pediatric brain cancer. As a result of the tumor, surgery, radiation, and chemotherapy, he would never be a "typical" kid again. He's Special.

This is my story about Les and me. I know I'm not your average grandparent. When Les was diagnosed, I was retired. I'd been a teacher, administrator, success coach, clown, real estate salesperson, freelance writer, tour guide, and motivational speaker. I wanted to use all those skills to help Les. . . and I lived close andI had time.

My motivation for telling this story is to encourage others whose lives are intertwined with a special person who needs your help. You might be a teacher, a doctor, a parent, a relative or a friend; this is for you.

CPSIA information can be obtained
at www.ICGtesting.com
Printed in the USA
BVHW042356270922
648047BV00002B/92

9 798201 139063